Rosemary Rowe is the maiden name of author Rosemary
Aitken, who was born in Corwall during the Second World
War. She is a highly qualified academic, and has written more
than a dozen bestselling textbooks on English language and
communication. She has written fiction for many years under
her married name. Rosemary is the mother of two adult
children and has two grandchildren living in New Zealand,
where she herself lived for twenty years. She now divides her
time between Gloucestershire and Cornwall.

Acclaim for Rosemary Rowe's Libertus series:

'Superb characterisation and evocation of Roman Britain. It
transports you back to those times. An etirely compelling
historical mystery'   Michael Jecks

'The story is agreeably written, gets on briskly with its plot, and
ends with a highly satisfactory double-take solution'
                                Gerald Kaufman, *Scotsman*

'In the crowded historical crime realm, Rowe is one of the most
adroit practitioners'   *Good Boook Guide*

'Rowe has had the clever idea of making her detective-figure a
mosaicist, and, therefore, an expert in puzzles and patterns.
Into the bargain, he is a freed Celtic slave . . . and a character
with whom the reader can sympathise'   *Independent*

'This engaging and sympathetic character once again has a date
with danger and double dealing . . . Rowe's pacy writing style
ensures that the action never flags'   *Western Morning News*

'Libertus is a thinking man's hero . . . a delightful whodunnit
which is fascinating in the detail of its research and the charm
of its detective team'   *Huddersfield Daily Examiner*

'Cunningly drawn and the very devil to fathom until the final
pages'   *Coventry Evening Telegraph*

Also by Rosemary Rowe

The Germanicus Mosaic
A Pattern of Blood
The Chariots of Calyx
The Legatus Mystery
The Ghosts of Glevum

Murder in the Forum

Rosemary Rowe

headline

First published in 2001
by HEADLINE BOOK PUBLISHING

This edition published in paperback in 2004
by HEADLINE BOOK PUBLISHING

10 9 8 7

ISBN 0 7472 6103 2

Printed and bound in Great Britain by
Clays Ltd, St Ives plc

Headline's policy is to use papers that are natural, renewable and
recyclable products and made from wood grown in sustainable forests.
The logging and manufacturing processes are expected to conform
to the environmental regulations of the country of origin.

HEADLINE BOOK PUBLISHING
A division of Hodder Headline
338 Euston Road
LONDON NW1 3BH

www.headline.co.uk
www.hodderheadline.com

For my daughter

Author's Foreword

Murder in the Forum is set in 187 AD, when most of Britain had been for almost two hundred years the northernmost province of the hugely successful Roman Empire: occupied by Roman legions, subject to Roman laws and taxes, criss-crossed by Roman military roads, peppered with military inns and staging-posts, and presided over by a provincial governor answerable directly to Rome. The revered Emperor Marcus Aurelius was dead, and the Empire in the hands of his increasingly unbalanced son Commodus, who was more inter-ested in excesses, debauchery and gladiatorial spectacles (in which he liked to take part) than in the business of government. This led to enormous power being left in the hands of the Prefects of Rome, including Tigidius Perennis – the notional kinsman of the fictional Perennis Felix who features in this book.

The political tension which underlies the story, therefore, is historically attested and so are many of the political events alluded to in it. The rebellion of the lance-bearers of Britain, the consequent fall of Perennis, the appointment of Helvius Pertinax as Governor of Britain, and Commodus's suspicion of everyone around him are all a matter of record. Indeed, Commodus may well have had cause to fear – his own sister had earlier attempted to have him assassinated, and some British legionaries did indeed favour Pertinax to take his place, although Pertinax – as suggested in the narrative – quelled the conspiracy firmly and denounced the ring-leaders.

Commodus was more than Emperor; he regarded himself as a living god, the reincarnation of Hercules, and as such received the tributes and sacrifices of the people. His word was absolute. Any man carrying an imperial warrant carried the Emperor's authority and therefore wielded considerable power. The wax seals which identified such documents were so important that they were often protected by ornate 'seal boxes' when in transit: failure to honour a duly-sealed warrant could carry the death penalty.

Of course, for most inhabitants of Britain, such power-struggles were remote events and they were content to live their lives in the relative obscurity of the provincial towns and villages. Celtic traditions, settlements and languages remained, especially in the countryside, but after two centuries most townspeople had adopted Roman habits. Latin was the language of the educated, and Roman citizenship – with its commercial, social and legal status – the ambition of all. Citizenship was not at this time automatic, even for freemen, but a privilege to be earned (for those not lucky enough to be born to it) by service to the army or the Emperor, although slaves of important citizens (like Libertus) could be bequeathed the coveted status, along with their freedom, on the death of their masters.

However, most ordinary people lacked that distinction: some were freemen or freed-men, scratching a precarious living from a trade or farm; thousands more were slaves, mere chattels of their masters, with no more status than any other domestic animal. Some slaves led pitiful lives, though others were highly regarded by their owners: indeed a well-fed slave in a kindly household might have a more enviable lot than many a freeman struggling to eke out an existence in a squalid hut.

Roman civic building was very fine, even to the modern eye, and private mansions often boasted splendid mosaic pavements, under-floor heating, upper floors and even latrines. Town dwellings and apartments, however, usually lacked kitchens, and most town-dwelling Romans simply bought their food at the take-away stalls and tavernas which abounded in all centres of habitation. Wealthy men, such as Gaius in the story, might have kitchens, often mere annexes to the main building (because of the risk of fire) and built on the downhill of the house next to the latrine – in order to utilise the running water, where that was available. The presence of such a kitchen might well influence the choice of appropriate accommodation for a visiting dignitary – Roman banquet cooking was legendary for its splendour. (Country houses, which wealthy citizens such as Marcus possessed in addition to their town dwellings, were always equipped with elaborate kitchen blocks and it seems that many Celts continued to try to cook in their houses over an open fire, although chimneys were not commonplace. Most towns had a form of fire brigade.)

There was, however, no civic rubbish collection – hence the pile of bones and waste outside of Gaius's house. Middens are attested in the back streets of several towns at this time, although it appears that enterprising farmers came (at night, when wheeled transport was permitted within the walls) to collect the stinking stuff to fertilise their fields, or it was slowly washed into the river by the rain.

Power, of course, was vested almost entirely in men: although individual women might wield considerable influence and even own and manage large estates, females were excluded from civic office, and indeed a woman (of any age) remained a child in law, under the tutelage first of her father, and then of any husband she might have. Marriage officially required her consent (indeed she was entitled to leave a marriage if it displeased her, and take her dowry with her), but in practice many girls became pawns in a kind of property game since of course there were very few other careers available for an educated and wealthy woman. So girls were married, or married off, for the sake of a large dowry or to cement political alliances. The daughters of rich families, particularly ugly girls (such as Felix's wife), were undoubtedly at a greater disadvantage in this regard than their poorer, and prettier sisters.

The Romano-British background in this book has been derived from a wide variety of (sometimes contradictory) written and pictorial sources. However, although I have done my best to create an accurate picture, this remains a work of fiction and there is no claim to total academic authenticity. Commodus, Pertinax and Prefect Perennis are historically attested, as are the existence and (basic) geography of Corinium (modern Cirencester), Glevum (modern Gloucester) and Letocetum (modern Wall in Staffordshire).

Relata refero. Ne Iupiter quidem omnibus placet. (I only tell you what I heard. Jove himself can't please everybody.)

ROMAN BRITAIN

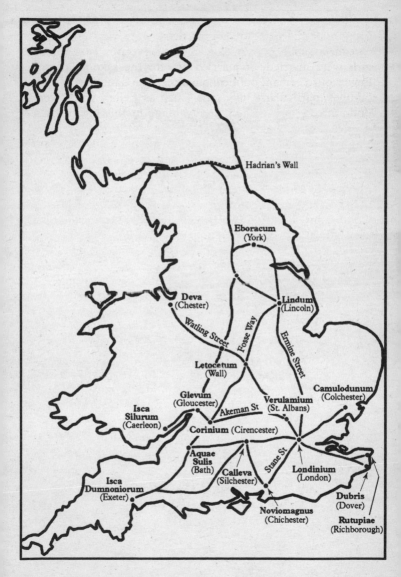

Chapter One

The man lying outside the basilica was dead. Messily dead, the way a person is apt to be when he has been dragged for miles at the wheels of an official Roman carriage. As this man had obviously been.

This was not a clever deduction on my part. The official Roman carriage in question was standing right in front of me, and the unfortunate victim was still attached to it, his hands bound to his sides, so that he could not protect his face, and the chains just long enough to protract the agony, allowing him to stumble after the cart until his heart was bursting, and then when he tripped – as he inevitably would – dragging him remorselessly headlong. The official Roman who must have given the instructions was still sitting smugly inside his conveyance.

I looked at the hapless corpse and blanched. Not at the battered head and bloodied limbs – I had seen men executed this way before – but at the remnants of uniform which still adhered to the body. That scarlet tunic and golden edging meant one thing only: the wearer was a servant of my patron, Marcus Septimus Aurelius, the regional governor's personal representative. In fact, I suspected that I knew the victim. It was hard to be sure, of course, after such a death, but I thought it was a rather pompous young envoy whom Marcus had once sent with me when I was investigating a crime: an arrogant, self-important youth, vain of his pretty looks.

1

Not any more.

I glanced at the smug Roman. Of course, he was a stranger (and carrying an official warrant to travel, or the carriage would not have been permitted within the gates during the hours of daylight), but one didn't have to hail from Glevum to see that the man he had executed was no ordinary slave. Anyone sporting that fancy uniform was clearly the cherished possession of a particularly wealthy and powerful man. So either the man in the carriage was a passing imbecile who had lost the will to live, or he was a very important personage indeed.

He saw me gawping. 'Well?' He threw open the door of his carriage. I realised that up until now he had been waiting for someone to do it for him, though his carriage-driver attendant was nowhere in evidence. He didn't get out. 'You! You are here to attend on Marcus Aurelius Septimus?'

I gulped. There was no simple answer to this. Yes, I was there on my patron's business, I had just been visiting his official rooms, but I was not exactly 'attending' him since he was twenty-odd miles away, doing a bit of 'attending' of his own. Marcus had recently lost his heart – or at least his inhibitions – to a wealthy widow in Corinium and he was there again, doubtless neglecting the affairs of state to pursue affairs of a more personal nature. I pondered my reply. The man in the carriage did not look as if he would have time for fine distinctions.

I was right.

'Well, are you or aren't you? I want an audience with your master.'

The tone alarmed me. It was deliberately insulting. Bad enough if I had been wearing my usual tunic and cloak, but (since I was visiting Marcus's rooms) I was wearing a toga, which only citizens can wear. That should have ensured me a little respect: I was a Roman citizen as much as he was, and he could see that perfectly well. Yet the man addressed me as if I were a slave.

I didn't protest. I had just glimpsed the toga he was wearing. A purple edging-stripe is a sign of high birth or high office – the broader the better – and the smug Roman had a deep purple stripe so wide it seemed to reach halfway round his body. I have never seen so much purple on a single garment. On his finger glittered the largest seal-ring I have ever seen: even at this distance I could make out the intricate design. And he spoke in the strange clipped tones of the Imperial City itself. Mere citizenship would not protect me from this Roman, toga or no toga.

I said, humbly, 'Marcus is not here, Excellence.'

'So I was told.' He glanced disdainfully over his shoulder, towards the shattered body on the flagstones.

I swallowed harder. This, presumably, was the news for which my poor vain, arrogant friend had paid with his life. I was talking to an old-style Roman then. Perhaps the man had imperial connections. The Emperor Commodus, too, was said regularly to execute messengers who brought unwelcome tidings. That kind of casual barbarity was rarer in Glevum, under my patron's comparatively benevolent eye – though Marcus was an Aurelian himself, and rumoured to have connections in the very highest places.

I, however, had none and that was worrying me. I was a mere freed-man, and although I had been awarded citizen status on the death of my ex-master, Marcus was my only protector.

A crowd was beginning to gather at the verandaed stalls on the other side of the forum, keeping a discreet distance, but pointing and whispering with undisguised curiosity. The Roman was beginning to look dangerous. Clearly he was not accustomed to being goggled at by a raggletailed crowd like this: slaves, thieves, shoppers, beggars, scribes and

3

stallholders, to say nothing of itinerant butchers, pie-sellers, cobblers, bead-merchants, turnip-sellers and old-clothes men. Equally clearly, he didn't like it. I wished I had my patron's protection now.

But at this moment, Marcus was a day's journey away, his envoy was dead, and I was about to bring this visitor even more unwelcome tidings. Marcus was not only absent, he was likely to be away for some days. I felt that the information might be injurious to my health.

I said carefully, 'I am sure, Excellence, my patron would wish to entertain you, if he were here . . .'

The eyes which met mine were stonier than those of the painted basalt Jupiter on the civic column behind me. Their owner was about as communicative as the statue, too. He said nothing. The silence was deafening.

'If only, most revered Excellence, I knew whom I had the honour of addressing . . .' I mumbled, keeping myself at a respectful distance, and ensuring that my bowing and shuffling meant that my head stayed decently lower than his. This wasn't easy, since he was still sitting in the carriage and I was standing on the flagstones outside, but I managed it. Marcus calls me an 'independent thinker', but I can grovel as abjectly as the next man when the moment demands. Even my best grovelling produced no flicker of a thaw in the Roman's manner, but it did provoke a response.

'My name is Lucius Tigidius Perennis Felix. Remember it.'

I was hardly likely to forget it. Some years ago a man called Tigidius Perennis had held the post of Prefect of Rome, and become the most feared and powerful man in the world after the Emperor Commodus himself. Of course, this was not the same Perennis. That particular Prefect had long since fallen from favour, and been handed to the mob for lynching. But that only made this man the more dangerous. Anyone who bore the Perennis name and survived was obviously someone to be reckoned with.

Most of the Prefect's family had been executed with him, so any relative – especially a namesake – must have enjoyed special protection to escape as this man had. I realised, with some dismay, that I was probably talking to a favourite of the Emperor himself. That would explain the nickname 'Felix' – the fortunate – and why the man was now driving around the Empire on an official warrant, with an imperial carriage at his command.

I said, fervently, 'I shall not forget it, Excellence. Your name is written on my very soul.'

That was no lie. Branded on my brain would have been nearer the truth. In fact the more I thought about it, the more alarmed I became. This man was an imperial favourite – and although Commodus called himself 'Britannicus' this was not his best-loved island. There had been several military plots here to overthrow him, and to install the governor, Pertinax, as Emperor in his place – that self-same Pertinax who was Marcus's particular friend and patron. Of course, the plots had been put down, by Pertinax himself, but Commodus still suspected conspiracy on every hand – and here was his emissary from Rome, looking for Marcus.

Yesterday the official augurers at the temple had warned of 'unexpected storms'. I liked the arrival of Perennis Felix less and less.

My feelings must have been showing in my face. Felix, for the first time, allowed himself to smile slightly. It was not an attractive smile and his voice was positively poisonous as he said, sweetly, 'A problem, citizen?'

I had, at least, acquired the courtesy of a title. I was debating whether 'yes' or 'no' was the less dangerous answer to his question when we were interrupted by the arrival of a swarthy soldier striding down the basilica steps at the head of a delegation of magistrates. That alone was enough to confirm his status – this was Felix's driver. No ordinary soldier would dare to force the civic dignitaries into second place. He did not so much as glance at me as he strode past me to the carriage and, assisting his passenger to the pavement (as if Felix was a delicate woman instead of a strong and very ugly man), engaged him at once in hushed and private conversation.

The magistrates hovered behind him, not daring to interrupt. Glevum is an important city, a republic in its own right within the Empire, and these men were its most eminent citizens. Yet they were cowed. From their wringing hands and apologetic smiles, I gathered that they felt as uneasy about this sudden visitor as I did.

I looked at the carriage-driver. He was handsome in a glowering sort of way, in a shorter-than-regulation leather skirt, revealing long tanned legs and muscles as hard and gleaming as his shirt-amour. He was bare-headed, without wreath or helmet, his dark hair flowing, like a barbarian's, his cloak fastened dramatically across his breast with an expensive pin. Not much like an average military carriage-driver, in fact, although from the way Felix was looking at him – like a wolf regarding a particularly succulent peacock in a pen – I guessed that the young man had been specially chosen, and singled out for additional duties.

I was wondering whether I dared now slip unobtrusively away when Felix suddenly looked towards me, raised a peremptory hand and summoned me to him.

'You! Whatever-your-name-is! Come here.'

'My name is Libertus, Excellence,' I burbled, hurrying towards him as fast as I could, bobbing all the way. This was not a moment, I felt, to stress that I was a citizen by giving my three full Latin names. I need not have concerned myself. Felix was not listening.

'You know where Marcus is?'

I nodded. In bed with his wealthy widowed lady, if he was lucky. I did not suggest this to Felix, however. 'He had pressing business in Corinium,' I offered humbly. That was true, after a fashion. I did not say what he was pressing.

Felix gave me his Jupiter stare again. 'That amuses you?'

If I had been guilty of the faintest amusement it vanished instantly. 'No, Excellence.'

'Very well. Then you will fetch him to me.' He must have seen my appalled look – Corinium was miles away.

I said hastily, 'It will take some time, Excellence. It is a day's walk.' And another back, I thought bitterly. Even supposing that I could impress on Marcus the urgency of my errand, and persuade him to come at once.

Felix looked at me with contempt. 'You will return with him tonight. Zetso shall take you in my carriage, as soon as I have settled in this house they promise me. It is doubtless a provincial hovel, though it belongs to one of the decurions, apparently.'

So the civic magistrates had been sufficiently awed to offer him one of their own town houses, instead of putting him in an official inn or finding him rented accommodation. It didn't altogether surprise me, although I felt a certain pity for the unfortunate owner. He would be turned out of his house (though that was probably a blessing, with Felix in residence) with no thanks, forced to beg a room from friends or relatives, and almost certainly grumbled at for it afterwards. I couldn't imagine a Glevum residence, however well appointed, being good enough for Felix – at least in his own estimation. There are moments when I am glad that I have only a workshop by the river with a tumbledown attic over it. At least I am not expected to vacate it for passing dignitaries from Rome.

One of the magistrates intervened nervously, almost

tripping over his toga-ends in his desire to please. 'If your most exalted Excellence will condescend . . .' He stepped forward and murmured something to Felix, who permitted himself a kind of smile.

'Better still,' the Roman said, addressing himself to me, 'they are proposing a civic banquet for me this evening. Marcus may attend me there. You may tell him so.'

'Yes, Excellence.' I tried to disguise my dismay, imagining Marcus's fury at such an invitation, which he could hardly refuse. That alone would have made me reluctant to go – not to mention the fact that I had a mosaic business to run, and customers of my own to see to.

I *didn't* mention it. Had I been remotely tempted to do so, the sight of that battered corpse on the cobbles would have taught me discretion.

Felix followed my glance. 'Yes,' he said. He turned to his driver. 'Zetso, once you have installed me in my house you had better take that' – he gestured towards the body – 'outside the walls and dispose of it. Stake it out somewhere, as the barbarians do – his master can find the body and bury it if he has a mind to. Always supposing that the crows have not found it first.'

I blanched. Leaving the body unburied! It was an appalling idea, even to a Celt. The Romans are usually far more superstitious in such matters, and will not even permit the burial of the decently dead within the walls of a city for fear that their spirits may return to haunt them. Felix, it seemed, feared nobody – not even the dead.

My revulsion seemed to please him, and for the first time he nodded almost affably. 'It will be a warning. Perennis Felix is not to be trifled with.' He smiled at the driver, a cold, unpleasant smile. 'Nor his servants either.'

The driver's swarthy, handsome face was a mask of carefully controlled passivity, but in spite of himself he flushed slightly, and I saw him flinch. So there was an additional reason, perhaps, for the calculated cruelty of that execution? One smile too many at the handsome Zetso, one glance too many in return? It seemed only too likely. How else would this ugly Roman keep his sexual favourite faithful?

If Zetso was to drive me to Corinium, alone, I would have to be very careful indeed.

Felix was helped back into his carriage. 'You know the way to this house?' he said to Zetso.

The man nodded.

'Then, drive on!'

Zetso raised his whip and the horse lurched into life, dragging the carriage smartly towards the narrow entrance to the forum, scattering the startled crowd and sending them stumbling in all directions. Dogs barked, pigs squealed, a woman dropped her turnips as she fled. A basket of live eels was overturned on the flagstones, and the fish fell wriggling under the wheels, the body of the dead envoy dragging grotesquely among them.

'Outside the East Gate, then, before the hour,' Zetso called to me, over his shoulder, and then they were gone, leaving market people and magistrates staring after them.

I had no water-clock or sundial, and no way of estimating time, so I could only shrug helplessly as I picked my way among the scattered turnips. I would simply have to get to the East Gate as promptly as I could.

Chapter Two

I calculated that I had time to return to my workshop first. Zetso still had that corpse to dispose of, and that would take him more than a few moments. A staked, unburied body would have to be carried a long way outside the gates. And first he had to take his master to his newly annexed abode.

All the same I did not wish to keep Felix's driver waiting.

So I hurried. Back though the town and out of the gates to where a makeshift suburb of humble shops and dwellings huddled together outside the walls, on the marshy land beside the river. No fine paved roads and handsome buildings here – only running gutters, crowded streets and the hammering, shouting, smoke and stench that always accompanies manual industry. I turned into a particularly noisome little alley, stepped over a pile of stone and marble chippings into a ramshackle front shop, poked my head around the frowsty curtain that separated customers from the kitchen-workshop behind and called, 'Anyone there?'

A curly-headed lad of fourteen or so, wearing a leather apron and a cheeky grin, rose to his feet from where he had been cutting tiles on the floor, screened from my sight behind the table. 'Master? You are back early.'

This was Junio, my servant and assistant, and as my eyes became accustomed to the light I could see what he had been working on, a series of tiny red tiles for one of the new 'pattern pieces' we were making for prospective customers. It was good work, and I was about to say so – I have been

11

teaching him my skills against the day when he gains his freedom. In the meantime I am glad of his assistance. I may be fit and youthful for my age, but I am an old man of almost fifty.

Before I could speak, however, Junio forestalled me. 'What is it, master? You look as if you have encountered a ghost.'

I thought about that battered, broken form in the forum and shuddered. 'The next best thing,' I said, and sinking down on my stool I told him all about it.

Junio fetched me a goblet of mead and heard me out in silence. When I had finished he shook his head. 'This Felix sounds a real brute. And casually summoning Marcus to him, like a slave. Your patron will not care for that.'

'He will care even less for my interrupting his love-life,' I said irritably. 'So if you have quite finished stating the obvious, perhaps you could find me my best cloak and a twist of bread and cheese for the journey, before Felix comes looking for me. I have no wish to travel in the same fashion as Marcus's poor herald.' That was an attempt at levity. Of course, I am a citizen and unlikely to be subject to quite such summary execution.

Junio shivered. 'Do not joke about such topics, master.' But he made particular haste to do my bidding. He scuttled up the stairs to the shabby sleeping-quarters above, calling as he did so, 'Shall I bring my own cloak also? Surely you want me with you?'

I did. Very much. Not only because having a slave in attendance would visibly enhance my status and increase my comfort, but also because I have been teaching Junio my other skills as well. He has a sharp mind and has often helped me with his powers of observation and deduction. I would appreciate his company at any time, and never more than now, dealing with Felix Perennis. Whether Marcus agreed to accompany me or not, I was much more likely to come out of this alive if I had an observant witness at my side.

And it was possible that Marcus would not consent to come – after all, he was an aristocrat in his own right, and rumoured to be related to the Emperor himself. In that case I shuddered to think what my fate might be. All the same, I called back after him, 'No, I think not.

'There will not be room in the carriage,' I said, when Junio reappeared. 'Even if Zetso did condescend to carry slaves, Marcus will have his own attendants with him and they would take precedence over you. I should have to leave you behind.' Even Junio could not argue with the logic of that, but he looked so crestfallen that I added encouragingly, 'Besides, someone has to look after the shop.'

There was a measure of truth in that too, since my workshop is made of wood and situated interestingly between a tannery and a candle-maker's, but Junio looked unimpressed. After all, he had accompanied me on many such expeditions before. However, he said nothing. He placed bread and cheese in my pouch and helped me into my cloak in silence, and – swiftly damping down the fire and putting up the shutter as if to wordlessly demonstrate how easy it would have been to shut up the premises – he accompanied me out of the house and back through the city to the East Gate.

Zetso was already there.

It was a fine arched gateway, with an imposing gatehouse over it, and set at the end of an impressive thoroughfare flanked with fine statues. It was intended to make visitors stop and stare, but nobody was looking at it today. All eyes were on the carriage, the imperial crest emblazoned on the doorway, the splendid golden horses and the even more splendid carriage-driver. Zetso was posing on the step, displaying his bronzed legs to advantage, to the obvious admiration of one of the soldiers manning the gate. I breathed a sigh of relief – my keeping Zetso waiting might otherwise have been dangerous.

All the same, I got in quickly; under the eyes of the crowd I felt like an actor in a spectacle. I tapped the side of the carriage to show that I was ready, and we were off.

I thought at first our cracking pace was for the benefit of the watching guard, but even after we had skirted the straggling northern suburbs and joined the main road over the escarpment where the town was far behind us, we still galloped towards Corinium as though our lives depended upon it.

As perhaps – considering the fate of Marcus's herald – they actually did.

I had half hoped to use the journey as a time to collect my thoughts and prepare a conciliatory approach to Marcus, but it was impossible. I needed all my concentration to hold myself on the seat. If Perennis Felix travelled like this, I thought, alternately bumping his head and his nether regions, no wonder he was bull-shouldered and short-tempered. But, although the jolting addled the brains and numbed the hindquarters, it did reduce the journey to little over two hours.

Even when we reached Corinium there was no time for contemplation. The town guard threw open the gates at the first glimpse of the imperial blazon, and almost before I had time to lean out and shout directions to Zetso, we were bouncing along the crowded streets, scattering ladders, donkeys, handcarts and pedestrians as we went. However, we reached the house without any actual fatalities; the imperial crest worked its immediate magic on the gatekeepers and we drove straight in like the Emperor himself.

I was familiar with the house from a previous visit on official business with Marcus, but even so I was impressed again. It was a magnificent mansion, with a walled garden and carriage drive, more like a country villa than a town dwelling, and a pair of matched slaves was already hurrying out to meet us. Marcus was a lucky man, I thought. He was already legal guardian to his lovely widow under the terms of her husband's will, but if he married her he would have the full usufruct of this estate in addition to his already considerable wealth. And here I was about to interrupt his courting. I was not looking forward to it a bit.

Other slaves came out to tend the horses and Zetso was led away, muttering, to the servants' quarters to be fed and watered in his turn. I was led ceremoniously into the atrium, where dates and watered wine awaited me. I cared for neither, but I took a little for form's sake – anything was welcome after that jolting in the carriage – stated my business and settled down to wait.

I did not wait long. After a very few minutes, in which I prepared and rejected a dozen little speeches, Marcus himself strode into the room. He was angry, tapping his baton against his leg in a way which would usually have had me cringing. He had evidently been disturbed at an unwelcome moment; his short fairish curls were tousled, his face was flushed and his fine purple-edged toga showed every sign of having been donned in a hurry – even the gold brooch at his shoulder was fastened askew.

But although he was scowling ferociously, by comparison to Perennis Felix he looked positively benevolent. My mind cleared, and I simply knelt before him, making a humble obeisance. 'Most revered Excellence, accept my abjectest apologies for this unwarranted intrusion on your esteemed presence.' Marcus, unlike Felix, was susceptible to flattery.

The scowl thawed a little.

I added for good measure, 'A thousand pardons to your lady, too, for this unwarrantable interruption.' With Marcus in this mood, I was careful to avoid naming her, for fear of sounding familiar. The widow was called Julia, in fact, but that was such a common name in the Empire – after the famous Emperor – that Marcus always referred to her as 'Delicta', or 'beloved', to distinguish her from the dozen other Julias that he knew. I hardly felt that I could do the same.

My circumspection seemed to have some effect. Marcus extended a ringed hand. 'Well?' He was still sounding stern. 'There had better be a good explanation.' He did not invite me to stand.

'I hope that you will think so, Excellence. Tigidius Perennis Felix is in Glevum, and has sent me in his carriage to fetch you. I am to tell you that there is a banquet for him this evening and he hopes – requests – that you will attend.'

I was expecting an outburst, but there was none. Indeed, there was such a protracted silence that after a while I raised my forehead from the level of his ankle-straps and glanced up at my patron. He was staring into space with a strange expression on his face, as if in the grip of some unaccustomed emotion. I knew what it was, however. I have experienced panic often enough to recognise it when I see it.

'Master?' I ventured.

Marcus seemed to come to himself, and he gestured to me impatiently. 'Oh, do get up, Libertus. I can't think properly with you grovelling about down there.' As I obeyed, gratefully (tiled floors are hard on ageing knees), he added, 'Immortal Jupiter! Felix Perennis. In Glevum! You know who he is, I suppose?'

'A relative of the former Prefect of Rome?' I was proud of my earlier deductions. 'And presumably, since he survived the executions, a particular favourite of the Emperor's.'

'Enjoys the imperial favour, certainly. A matter of money, I imagine. I doubt if even Commodus really likes the man.'

'You know this Felix, Excellence?' I am inclined to forget

that Marcus spent most of his life in the Imperial City.

'It would be difficult to avoid knowing him. He had a finger in every profitable pie in Rome – forests, vineyards, olive groves, shipping, sheep. No doubt, when his cousin fell, Felix could offer a sufficient sum to persuade Commodus of his own innocence.'

'A loan?'

Marcus laughed. 'A bribe. It will be called something else, of course, as these things always are. A donation to some public works, perhaps, but of course Felix won't expect to have it accounted for. Besides, he has always provided the Emperor with other valuable services as well – women, horses, wine. He also keeps a substantial private guard of the toughest swordsmen that money can buy, and was known to be savagely jealous of his kinsman the Prefect. Altogether, it was obviously enough to save his life.'

'So now he is enjoying his turn at influence? Travelling the Empire as an imperial envoy?'

Marcus sighed. 'If only that was all.'

'There is more?' I was surprised. What I already knew seemed alarming enough.

Marcus picked up a goblet from the serving tray which had been provided, and held it out absently to be filled. 'Do you know what happened to Prefect Perennis?'

'Not entirely. Surrendered to the crowd for justice, as I heard it,' I said carefully, darting Marcus a warning look. There were slaves present – one was even now filling his goblet – and Zetso was waiting in the servants' hall. No doubt he was, among other things, a spy, and Felix would have equipped him with adequate bribes. In the circumstances one could hardly be too careful. These were not even Marcus's own slaves.

Marcus ignored my signals. 'Thrown to the crowd,' he said. 'You know why?'

17

I did, of course, but I shook my head. 'It was some time ago.' I knew how to be cautious, if Marcus did not. I do not enjoy his privileges.

'Accused of misappropriating funds from the public purse,' Marcus said, swallowing his wine at a gulp and gesturing for more.

'Perhaps that was true,' I ventured. 'The Emperor in his wisdom . . .' Commodus is a fool and a lecher, but I wasn't about to question his judgement with the servants listening.

Marcus snorted. 'Of course it was true. It had been true for years. Commodus knew it, but he didn't care. He virtually allowed Prefect Perennis to run the Empire – it gave him more time for debauching women, dressing up as a gladiator, flirting with his coachman and generally making a public spectacle of himself.'

'Excellence!' I pleaded. This kind of talk could easily get one executed for merely listening to it. 'The servants.'

He looked surprised. Marcus, like many Romans, is so accustomed to slaves that he thinks of them as animated tools, no more capable of seeing and hearing than chairs or tables. I, on the other hand, was once a slave myself. I could imagine, only too easily, how readily a little gold could loosen household tongues. Every slave dreams of buying his own freedom.

Marcus followed my glance. 'Ah! The servants. I should dismiss them, do you think?'

I shook my head. 'With respect, Excellence, I think you should instruct them to wait here . . . outside the door.'

He thought about that for a moment, then nodded and gave the order. Then, with the servants safely out of earshot, he turned to me again. 'Very shrewd, old friend. I should have sent them straight into the arms of Felix's driver. I was saying . . .'

'You were telling me about Prefect Perennis,' I said, feeling so weak with relief that I would have welcomed a glass of wine myself. 'There was a march on Rome by some disaffected lance-bearers, threatening to storm the city because they hadn't been paid. Commodus was terrified of them, blamed it all on the Prefect, and had him thrown to the mob. That is, as I heard it.'

'So you did know.' Marcus sounded aggrieved. 'Do you also know where those rebellious lance-bearers came from?'

I genuinely didn't, and I told him so.

'Well, that is the most significant thing,' Marcus said, somewhat cheered to have part of the story left to tell. 'They came from these very islands – part of the Britannic legions. They were in revolt. And when Perennis fell, another man was recalled from disgrace and sent here to restore control. Someone whom Perennis had hated, who was so successful that the troops wanted to make him Emperor. His name was Pertinax. You remember Pertinax?'

I was about to say, 'Naturally I remember him, Excellence, since he is your patron and my Governor,' when the implications of this struck me.

'But surely,' I burst out, 'the Governor's loyalty is not in question? He was almost killed last year putting down that rebellion against Commodus.'

Marcus shook his head. 'Our revered Emperor distrusts everyone. Perhaps he is right. He had hardly succeeded to the purple before his own sister tried to assassinate him. And the legions did want to acclaim Pertinax as Emperor. Commodus will not forget that.'

'You think that is why Felix has come? To seek out similar plots?'

Marcus looked at me gloomily. 'You understand servants, my old friend, but you do not understand imperial politics. The Emperor would not send a conspicuous figure like Felix to discover a plot. He will already have a dozen spies in place.'

Remembering Marcus's previous indiscretions before the servants, I could only blanch at this revelation. 'Then why is he here?'

Marcus said gloomily, 'I imagine he feels that he has scores to settle. It took the rebellion to make Commodus sacrifice his former friend to the mob, but Pertinax had always advised the Emperor against him. And vice versa. It was Perennis who had Pertinax disgraced and exiled in the first place. So when the Prefect fell, Pertinax was recalled to Rome.'

Where, I thought, he would have helped to oversee the aftermath. Felix had seen his kinsmen executed, their estates seized, and their power removed. It had almost certainly cost him a huge sum to escape a similar fate himself. And now here he was in Glevum looking for Pertinax's closest friend and representative. I could see what Marcus meant. Matters were not looking good.

'Well,' Marcus said wearily, 'I suppose we shall find out very soon.'

'Then you will come with me, Excellence?' If I sounded disrespectfully relieved I couldn't help it. My chances of seeing tomorrow, at least outside a filthy jail, had just brightened considerably.

'I see no help for it. Though this Zetso of yours will have to wait a little longer. I have promised to attend the curial offices this afternoon to arbitrate in a legal dispute. I shall send and tell him so.'

I nodded, doubtfully. Felix would not like this, but Marcus was right. Even Felix must take second place to imperial business. I said, 'With respect, Excellence, I suggest you do not use the slave-boys outside to take your message. They may have been listening at the door. Allow me to summon one of the servants I saw in the courtyard.' In the light of what Marcus had said about spies it seemed an elementary precaution.

He smiled. 'An excellent idea. You have a shrewd mind, Libertus. I suppose you would not care to accompany me to the courthouse? I should be interested in your opinion on the case.'

He meant that he was interested in my support, I recognised. My opinion would be of little value. I know nothing of the intricacies of Roman law. Marcus, on the other hand, was necessarily an expert. As the governor's direct representative, he was constantly called upon to hear difficult cases. In the absence of Pertinax, he was the most senior judge in this part of the country, although of course any citizen might appeal over his head directly to the Emperor. But, as I say, I know little of the law.

'Zetso will not like it if we leave the house together.'

Marcus snorted. 'Zetso will do as I tell him. He is only a carriage-driver. Indeed, he can drive us to the *curia*. Now I have thought of it, I want to have you with me – it is an interesting case. An elderly citizen surprised his daughter in adultery, under her husband's roof. He killed her lover – as the law permits – but allowed his daughter to escape. Strictly, he should have killed them both, so the lover's family have seized him and brought a case against him for murder.' He smiled broadly. 'What does your shrewd brain tell you, Libertus? How would you find?'

This was not the time for discussing legal niceties. Zetso was still waiting. Besides, Marcus's smirk suggested that he had already decided on his verdict. 'I don't know, Excellence. I suppose the man is technically guilty?'

He beamed triumphantly. 'Undoubtedly. And yet, the grounds for accusation seem unjust, do you not think?'

He paused dramatically so I mastered my impatience and

said, as he clearly hoped I would, 'So, you have found a compromise?'

'I shall listen to the evidence, find for the family and sentence the old man to exile. Three days to leave the Empire, and then all of his possessions will be forfeited.' I must have looked surprised, because he laughed. 'Only, of course, I found a way of letting him know this yesterday. He has sold his house for gold, and his wife and remaining daughter are already halfway to Isca with the money and most of his goods. His mother was a Silurian, from beyond the western borders. It will not be difficult for him there.'

He was so pleased with himself that I was bold enough to venture, 'Then the case should not take long. Perhaps, Excellence, you should tell the carriage-driver of your plans? He could drive us directly to Glevum when you have finished.'

He flushed. 'Indeed. I will have the slaves pack my things and bring them after me. That way Zetso can wait for us at the court.' He strode to the door, summoned a slave from the courtyard (to the astonishment of the two outside the door) and gave his orders. Then he turned back to me. 'In the meantime, I will go and let Delicta know what is happening.' He frowned. 'I wish I knew what in Hades Felix was up to.'

I tried to find something comforting to say. 'Perhaps it is not as worrying as we suppose. Perhaps he does wish to see you on business.' I brightened. 'Maybe he brings a letter from your family in Rome. Your mother has been sending to you recently by every courier she can find.'

It was a feeble suggestion, but it was not impossible. Marcus's father had died long ago – making him a man in the eyes of the law – but his mother had recently remarried and her new husband had offered Marcus legal adoption to ensure the inheritance. Wealthy Romans are always doing that, largely because a contested will is likely to cause a costly legal wrangle, with most of the estate ending up in the imperial coffers. Perhaps that is why marriage and the foundation of a family is regarded as almost a civic duty.

Certainly Marcus's mother and his new stepfather seemed to think so. Every messenger from Rome seemed to bring a new missive from them, urging Marcus to take the plunge, and usually offering a list of suitable, well-connected young Roman virgins for him to select from.

Marcus, however, had never felt the need. As one of the wealthiest and most powerful men in the province he could naturally take his pick of any good-looking young woman in Glevum, and not infrequently did. Of course, marriage would not necessarily preclude such activity, but it was likely to curtail it severely, especially if the bride had powerful relatives. So Marcus had never shown the slightest inclination to marry. Until recently, that is. I had begun to wonder whether his beautiful Julia Delicta had won him over completely. Clearly she had matrimonial ambitions. Respectable widows do not entertain gentlemen in their homes in the middle of the afternoon unless they have definite expectations of a wedding.

If I hoped to comfort him with thoughts of matrimony, however, I had failed. Marcus was looking more agitated than ever.

'Great Olympus, Libertus, I hope not. Great Jupiter, lover of lovers, preserve me of all things from that!'

Chapter Three

I must have been looking astonished, because even Marcus –
who is not much given to noticing the reactions of his
audience – looked at my face and said hastily, 'You would
feel the same way in my place, Libertus. It is my mother's
interference I am afraid of. I got a letter from her only
yesterday – sent via a trader bringing olive oil to the market
– and she is full of schemes which she thinks are "for my
benefit". Of course, I wrote at once to dissuade her. I only
pray she hasn't carried out her ideas in the meantime. That
letter would have taken almost a month to get here.'

In spite of everything, I could scarcely repress a smile. It
was hard to imagine anyone as wealthy and important as
Marcus even possessing a mother, let alone a mother who
told him what to do. But one look at his face told me that this
was no smiling matter. 'And what was her idea, Excellence?'

'She has been threatening for some time to find me a
bride, if I do not choose one for myself,' Marcus explained.
'Now she is talking of speaking to the Emperor about it –
asking who might make a suitable wife for me. She doesn't
seem to see how serious that is. If he made a recommendation
I should be more or less obliged to marry the girl, whatever
I thought of her. I dare not offend Commodus.'

I could see the force of that. 'And you suspect a candidate,
Excellence?' It was not a difficult deduction. His face was the
picture of dejection.

'It occurs to me,' he said despondently, 'that Felix has a

25

daughter. I saw her once, in Rome, before I left. She was only a child then, but she was already unattractive – just like her mother, a face like a cavalry horse and a whine like a donkey. Oh, great Minerva giver of wisdom! You know, Libertus, that could be why he's here. Links with my family would give Felix some solid allies in Rome – at present he must be reliant on the Emperor alone, and that is never wise. Dear Jupiter! Forced into marriage with his hideous daughter – wouldn't Felix love to bring me a message like that!'

I hastened to backtrack. 'You don't know that, Excellence. It was only a suggestion on my part. It is more likely that he is here on a political errand.' Strange – only a moment or two before, that had seemed a much more threatening alternative.

Marcus shook his head. 'No, it would make sense. The Emperor would speak for Felix, and if she is ugly her father would be desperate to dispose of her. My mother would think it a wonderful match – all that property and wealth . . . Dear Jupiter! The girl must be twenty-one by now, so she must be a perfect fright, not to have found a husband at that age. And yet if the Emperor has suggested it, I can hardly refuse—' He broke off, interrupted by the return of the messenger he had sent to Zetso. 'Well?'

The boy was breathless with hurry. 'Most excellent master, I delivered your message to the driver, and he awaits you at the carriage. He merely urges that you fulfil your business at the *curia* as soon as possible. Lucius Tigidius Perennis Felix proposes a feast tonight and hopes that you will attend.' The slave was choosing his words with care, and I guessed that the message had been delivered in much more forceful terms.

Marcus cocked an eyebrow at me.

I nodded, although in fact this was not quite as I understood it. Surely Felix was guest of honour rather than host at this banquet? But this was no time for fine distinctions. 'I am at your service, Excellence.'

Marcus sighed and waved the slave away. 'Very well, go and prepare my possessions for departure.' The slave hurried off, and Marcus poured himself another glass of wine – unheard of indignity – before he turned to me. 'Why ever didn't I marry Delicta weeks ago? If I arrived back in Glevum a married man, it would have been too late. Felix would not even have a grievance.'

There was no answer to that. The widow was beautiful, intelligent, wealthy and eager to have him. In his position I would have wed her long since. I said nothing.

Suddenly he brightened. 'Great Mercury, Libertus, I wonder if I could marry her now?'

I stared at him. 'Now? This afternoon?'

'Why not?'

'You can hardly claim *usus* marriage,' I said. 'You have been sleeping with her under her roof rather than your own. And certainly not for an uninterrupted year.' That was rather a presumptuous remark and I regretted it instantly, but Marcus was too preoccupied to care.

'I cannot propose a *manus* marriage either – I cannot notionally "buy" her from myself. But I could do it another way – a formal statement in front of a magistrate and a family augurer, witnessed by seven citizens. After all, I am going to the *curia*. Delicta's *auspex* will be there and I happen to know a friendly magistrate. It is a little irregular, but he owes me a favour or two. I'm sure he would oblige us.' He grinned. 'What do you say, old friend?'

'The lady will consent?'

'Of course she will. She has been telling her brothers for weeks that we intend to marry. And she will see the sense in this. Of course, she needs her guardian's formal permission – but since I am her guardian,' he grinned, 'I will send for her at once.' He made towards the door.

I intervened. 'Allow me, Excellence. I know the house and

I will take her the message myself. That way no servant knows of it. If Zetso asks questions while you are gone, all he will learn is that you were going to the *curia*, which he knows anyway. I suggest that we go openly. I will have the lady send all her maidservants on errands to the front of the house, then put on a hooded cloak and follow us discreetly on foot out of the back gate. Zetso will pay little attention to her movements. Let us hope your magistrate is amenable and the *auspex* finds the auguries favourable.'

'I found for him last month in a tax case,' Marcus said wryly. 'That should help to tip the entrails in my favour. And only yesterday I put the magistrate in the way of buying the house in this law case we are about to attend. The accused man was pleased to part with it at a very low price. I imagine the magistrate will be amenable.'

'Then all you need is seven citizens to witness your declaration.'

He glanced at my Roman toga, more than usually frowsty after our headlong journey to Corinium. 'Six,' he said.

So I was to be party to this escapade. Well, I had some sympathy with it, and in any case I could hardly refuse. I contented myself with saying wryly, 'You realise, Excellence, that we have no proof that Felix brings any letter of the kind? You may find that you have married your "Delicta" for nothing.' If the lady was to be married to my patron, I thought, I might risk the familiar name.

I expected a rebuke for my insolence, but Marcus merely grinned. 'All things considered, Libertus, I think that is a risk I am prepared to take. And if my family do not care for my marrying a provincial, they have only themselves to blame. Now, I will go and prepare myself for the *curia*. You can speak to Delicta, if you will.'

I had no preparations to make, so I took the two slave-boys with me and went out into the back courtyard where the private quarters lay, each bedroom opening separately off the covered walkway which bordered the inner gardens on three sides. I knew the layout of the house from my previous visit and I was able to lead the way to the widow's apartments, a pair of interconnecting chambers: a small outer dressing room and sleeping quarters within.

At my signal one of the slaves tapped on the door. A handmaiden opened it. I could see Julia Delicta herself, seated in a gilded chair in the inner room, attended by a group of female slaves. One knelt before her with a mirror, another held a collection of oils and combs, while a third adjusted the exquisite blond tresses to her mistress's satisfaction. It was a striking picture, made more striking because Delicta's hair was of precisely the same remarkable golden-blond as that of the maidservant who answered the door. Of course – as I realised a moment afterwards – this was hardly surprising, since it was the same hair: the slave's tresses had clearly been shorn off at some time and fashioned into an elaborate wig. Presumably Delicta liked it and was having a second one grown, or the girl would have been sold on again. Many fashionable women bought slaves for exactly the same purpose.

It was not a pleasing thought. My own wife, Gwellia, had been snatched from me and sold into slavery when I was. She too had beautiful hair: a waterfall of raven locks which had haunted my dreams ever since. I had no idea where she was – beyond a rumour that a Celtic slave of the same name had been sold to Eboracum – though I had searched for her tirelessly ever since I gained my freedom. The thought that she might be used in this way, as a kind of human sheep to be shorn for her mistress, was not an agreeable one.

Then Delicta saw me, and smiled a greeting. All disapproval evaporated. I recognised, not for the first time, what an exceedingly attractive woman she was. 'Libertus!' She motioned away her slaves, rose gracefully to her feet, and came towards me, extending a perfumed hand. 'Excuse me that I was not present to greet you. I heard that there were visitors in the house and I was preparing myself to meet them. I did not guess that it was you. What a pleasure to see you again!'

She had a way, a gift almost, of making every man she spoke to feel like an emperor. I was not immune to it myself. Fortunately I have been a slave, and slaves learn early how to suppress desire, even of the most involuntary kind. I pulled myself together. 'Lady, there are matters I must discuss with you.' I nodded towards the maidservants. 'In private, if I may. It concerns your guardian.'

She understood at once, and came out unattended into one of the arbours. I stationed the slave-boys out of earshot, and, sitting down beside her, told her of the plan.

At first she was doubtful. 'But, Libertus, there are arrangements to make. There should be a feast, sacrifices, gifts to the servants. I do not even have anything suitable to wear.'

As this would be her third wedding she would hardly need the ochre veils and floral trimmings of a new bride, but I suppose all women are the same. Gwellia would have had the same impulse. I said gently, 'With respect, lady, I suggest you wear your normal clothes. Fine robes would only create interest among your slaves – and who knows whom Zetso may already have bribed to bring him information?'

She was still hesitating. 'But the festivities . . .'

'They can be arranged later. If you do not marry him today, you may lose him for ever.' I saw her face and produced my trump card. 'Of course, he might be prepared to go to Rome, wed this girl and then divorce her – there would be no shame in that once he had done his duty by her.' Made her pregnant, I meant, though Celtic delicacy prevented my saying so to a lady.

Romans, however, have fewer inhibitions. 'Get her with child? I won't have that. Besides, Marcus is such a soft-hearted fool, he would lose his heart to the infant and I should never win him back. No, I'll do it. What exactly does he want me to do?'

I outlined the instructions we had agreed, and she listened attentively. 'Very well,' she said, 'I will do as you suggest. But with your agreement, I shall bring two of my servants with me. Have Marcus send me the boys who were attending him. That way they cannot report to Zetso, and it cannot be claimed that I was abducted. If Felix is the kind of man you describe, he would seize on such an excuse to declare the contract illegal.'

I nodded, appreciating her intelligence. I added one or two suggestions of my own. Then I accompanied her back to her door. 'I am sorry, lady, to drag my patron from you,' I said, loudly enough for the waiting handmaidens to hear. 'But Perennis Felix awaits him. I am sure you understand.'

She was quick-witted as well as beautiful. 'I suppose it cannot be helped,' she replied, her voice a model of disappointed affront. 'Make my farewells to Marcus. He need not bother to seek me – I am going out, to choose some new cloth for a *stola*. A poor widow must have some amusements in life.'

I went back to Marcus with this news, and he chuckled proudly. 'A remarkable woman, Libertus. Now, are you ready? Zetso is waiting.'

Which is how I came to be a witness at the wedding. In fact it was all very simple. Marcus tried his case, and by the time it was finished Delicta had arrived, with her attendants, and the six additional witnesses had been found. She took off her hooded cape, and stood demurely, looking stunning in a simple long-sleeved sleeved tunic and a *stola* in shades of amethyst. It was hard to know what wedding outfit could have been more becoming. The magistrate and the *auspex* did what was asked of them, we witnesses added our seals to the contract, and Marcus and Julia Delicta formally made their vows. '*Ubi tu Gaius, ego Gaia*' – 'Where you are Gaius, I am Gaia.' They even exchanged rings as tokens, hurriedly blessed on the imperial altar.

Then we returned to Zetso. Delicta would follow us to Glevum in a few days, where Marcus had promised her all the formal feasts and celebrations she could wish. Zetso was bad-tempered at having been kept waiting, but was obviously entirely unsuspicious. Marcus and I sat in the carriage, bouncing home, and smiled at each other triumphantly.

If we had known what lay ahead we might not have been so delighted.

Chapter Four

It was getting dark by the time we got back to Glevum and the gates were closing but Zetso scarcely seemed to slacken pace. He was justified: at the first glimpse of the imperial carriage the huge studded gates were opened again with such alacrity that I am sure the poor guard responsible must have reported afterwards to the military *medicus* with a rupture.

Once back within the city, however, our progress was much slower. The edict which restricts wheeled vehicles within the walls during the hours of daylight may keep the roads clear for military and imperial transport by day, but it has a contrary effect after the gates are closed. At twilight the *colonia* becomes a heaving, torchlit jostling mass of horses, donkeys, oxen, carts and waggons as every tradesman and freed-man tries to move his goods around the city before total darkness overtakes him.

Zetso was doubtless chafing, and I was no less impatient. As soon as I had delivered Marcus, I hoped to hurry back to the comparative safety of my workshop, where any threat of vivicombustion was likely to be of an accidental kind. Besides, I wanted to tell Junio about the fair-headed slave: unless I was much mistaken this was the same maidservant with whom he had – quite improperly – struck up a certain friendship the last time we had visited the house, although at that time she had just been shorn and had no hair at all. Naturally he did not suppose that I knew anything about it. I was rather looking forward to teasing him on the subject.

Marcus, however, had other plans for me.

'We will alight here,' he said, tapping the side of the carriage to alert Zetso, as we stopped for the twentieth time to let a laden handcart extricate itself from the wheel-ruts in the paving. 'We are only a javelin throw from my apartment. I can at least rinse my head and feet and change into fresh robes. There is no opportunity to visit the bath house before attending this banquet, but I prefer not to put myself at a disadvantage by arriving to meet Felix looking completely crumpled and travel-stained.'

'But, Excellence!' I protested, feebly. The thought of encountering Felix again was already an unpleasant one; the idea of finding him impatient and furious was even less appealing.

Marcus silenced me with a glance.

'It will not take us long. My slaves will be waiting, and if the carriage makes this kind of progress it will hardly have moved more than a block or two before we return. No doubt we will not be the last arrivals. The commencement of a feast is always a haphazard affair.'

He was right, of course. The Romans are known for their obsession with punctuality and order, dividing the day carefully into hours and always consulting their water-clocks and hour-candles. But since the length of an hour varies at different seasons according to the quantity of daylight, in fact clocks and candles are only an approximation and it is almost impossible for any private citizen to calculate the time with any accuracy. Even the public sundial in the forum, consecrated to Jove and imported into Glevum at great expense, was constructed for Roman sunshine and seems strangely to be effectively useless for ours, even supposing our sun happens to be shining. Most men, summoned to a private dinner, will simply aim to arrive there before sunset, while at an evening banquet, like this one, there are certain to be stragglers. Felix had not even specified a time.

All the same, I was anxious. 'Perhaps, Excellence, I should stay with the carriage?' I ventured, as Zetso, reluctantly, abandoned the reins and came round to open the door.

Marcus paused in the act of alighting. 'And leave me to walk the street unaccompanied? Besides, surely you wish to make your own ablutions? My slaves can bring you water and oils, at least.'

'I thank you, Excellence, but that is hardly necessary. When I get home . . .'

Marcus frowned. 'But, Libertus, old friend, you are not returning home. At least, not yet. I wish you to accompany me to this banquet. The driver can go on ahead and tell them we are coming – you and I will send out for litters.' He allowed Zetso to help him from the carriage and strode purposefully away.

Zetso looked at me, and smirked. I got down unaided and he drove off with a flourish. I seized a link from a passing torch-bearer, who glanced at my patron and yielded it without a murmur. Marcus still counted for something in this town.

I padded after him. 'But, Excellence,' I pleaded, holding the light aloft and trotting along by his side, 'I was not invited. Besides, you are concerned about your toga. Look at mine.' I gestured helplessly. I had hardly looked crisp and pristine in Corinium, and I was far more crumpled and dishevelled now.

Marcus waved my excuses aside. 'This is a civic banquet, Libertus, given by the dignitaries of the city. I believe I would qualify among their number?' That was an understatement. Marcus was one of the most influential men in the whole province. 'I shall therefore feel free to invite anyone I choose. In any case, you have business there. I have decided to ask you to design a small commemorative pavement, in honour of this visit.'

I sighed inwardly. Marcus was likely to feel that the honour of such a commission was of more value than mere *denarii*, so the task was likely to bring me a great deal of prestige, but not a great deal in the way of bread and candles.

He misinterpreted my dismay. 'As for your appearance, Felix will have to endure it. He was the person who summoned us in such haste, and in any case I think it hardly matters. You are not, after all, an important person.' He smiled. 'Except, of course, to me.'

There was no intended insult in this. Marcus was simply stating a fact. I *was* unimportant, sufficiently so to be paraded before Felix as a kind of living protest at the peremptory nature of his summons. It was not a role that I looked forward to.

Nevertheless, it was useless to protest further so I accompanied Marcus the rest of the way in silence. I was in any case slightly breathless from keeping pace with him; Marcus is much younger than I am and he was striding along very purposefully. Had he been a lesser man, I might almost have thought he was hurrying.

His town apartment was a fine one, the whole of the first floor over a wine shop near the forum, and we soon arrived at it. Marcus was right about the time it took to change. With a dozen servants to strip him, wash him, robe him and groom him he was cleansed, perfumed, bejewelled and immaculate in a sparkling new toga almost before I had finished rinsing the dust of the journey from my extremities in a bowl of rainwater.

My patron, however, was not a happy man. The death of his herald (whose identity I had tactfully omitted to mention in my own account of the day) was already the talk of the household, and he had learned of it from his scandalised servants while he was being dressed. As we made our way to the street – accompanied this time by a bevy of slaves whose spotless tunics were a rebuke to me – he was clearly fuming, not so much at the loss of the slave as at the affront to his own dignity. This, of course, was why I had not told him. Marcus in this mood was a very dangerous man.

Fortunately, it did not occur to him that my omission was deliberate. Identifying a dragged corpse is not easy, and he simply supposed that I had not recognised it. I was happy to allow him his illusions.

'Imagine it!' he muttered, as we went out to join the litters which had been summoned for us. 'My herald, dragged to death in the road like a common traitor. Felix shall pay for this, Libertus, mark my words.'

I said nothing. I am not accustomed to litters, and the business of balancing aboard the narrow couch as it was first hoisted from the ground by its handles by two unevenly matched slaves, and then carried at a smart trot down uneven streets, was taking all my concentration. I was almost glad when we had to make a lengthy pause to let a funeral procession pass – a long straggling line of pipers, dancers, weepers and wailers. In Roman cities funerals – except those of really important people – are always held at night.

Marcus was still fuming when we arrived at our destination.

'Here we are,' he said, dismounting and dismissing the litters. 'You know the house.'

I did. It belonged to one of the most senior of the town magistrates, Gaius Flavius Flaminius. I should have guessed as much – if I were looking for a man to donate his house to Felix for a fortnight, I could not have found a better candidate. Gaius was a wealthy man and had once been influential, but since the death of his young wife he had become an ineffectual old shadow with no interests in life beyond his pair of brindled dogs, one of whom could even now be heard howling fruitlessly somewhere in the interior. Whoever had offered Gaius a bed had clearly drawn the line at his dogs.

'Ugly brute,' Marcus said, referring to the dog. 'I wonder someone does not stop its whining.'

If Gaius had whined with protest about being obliged to give up his house, I thought, he had no doubt been similarly ignored.

Marcus frowned. 'I suppose Felix decided that the banquet should take place here, rather than in any public building, although of course *we*' he meant the town dignitaries – 'were still called on to provide the food, cooks, servants and entertainment. I gather that I have provided wine.' He sighed. 'A trick that Felix learned from Commodus, I imagine. He sometimes does the same when he pays a visit outside the capital. It may create difficulties for everyone else, but it is highly convenient for the guest of honour. If anyone is to make their way home through the dim streets of an unfamiliar city in the cold of dawn, it will not be him. Well, there is no point in standing here. Shall we go in?'

The house was ready for company. Lighted torches flanked the entry and the sound of music and voices was already emerging from the open doorway, where a burly doorkeeper was standing, armed with a stout stave and a threatening frown, and already regarding me with suspicion.

Fortunately, my patron was clearly an important man, even to those who did not know him, with his wide purple stripe and his six panting slaves accompanying the litter. At a word from him the doorman stepped back reluctantly to let me pass, and turned his attention to another guest drawing up at the door. However, I felt him monitoring me. It was the same throughout the evening. Every time I raised my head

I was conscious of some servant watching me, with dis-approving eyes.

Nonetheless, we made our way inside and were announced by the usher. Formalities were beginning. The two reception rooms and the *triclinium* – the dining area – beyond them had been turned into a sort of three-part room by opening the screen doors in between. Low tables were set out with dining couches around them, in groups of three as fashion dictated, and strictly graduated in terms of grandeur and comfort, so that nine people could sit around the top table, nine at the next and so on.

I calculated that there must be at least fifty-four people expected – most of whom seemed to be here already – and the houses of all the magistrates in Glevum must have been pillaged for the furniture. Even so there was a cluster of lowly stools around a rickety trestle right at the back against the wall. I had no doubt whatever where my seat would be.

The rooms were alive with activity. All Glevum seemed to be there, important men most of whom I knew by sight and – like any sensible tradesman – spent much of my time avoiding: aediles, questors, magistrates, priests, augurers and senior commanders from the garrison. Slaves were moving among the guests distributing banqueting wreaths, knives, spoons and napkins. A trio of nervous-looking musicians were tuning up in a corner, and a nubile young dancing girl was adjusting her costume so that it showed off her assets as flatteringly as possible.

Poor child! If she hoped to impress the guest of honour, she was wasting her time. Felix, splendid in purple edgings, was reclining at the high table, a goblet in his hand, patently ignoring the earnest conversation of the ageing magistrate beside him, and gazing with speculative interest at the dusky young male acrobat limbering up in an abbreviated loincloth at the other end of the *triclinium*.

When he saw Marcus, however, he got to his feet and stood, waiting to greet us. Marcus walked deliberately towards him, and then – a little more than sword-reach distant – just as deliberately stopped.

Somehow there was a tension which communicated itself to the entire company. Conversation ceased, the musicians stilled their strings. There was a little rustle of anticipation, and then the whole room fell silent, motionless, as the two men confronted one another.

Like stags, I thought suddenly.

And the herd was watching now, waiting for the heads to lower, the imaginary antlers to lock.

It was Marcus who moved first. 'Tigidius Perennis Felix,' he said, his voice poisonous with charm, 'we meet again. An unexpected . . . honour.' There was a deliberate pause before the final word.

Felix smiled. If this was a sample, I thought, on the whole I preferred the scowl. 'Marcus Aurelius Septimus. It is good of you to travel so far. Greetings on behalf of the Emperor, and of your esteemed mother.' I saw Marcus stiffen. 'I trust I have not curtailed your . . . ah . . . business in Corinium too much.'

He said it with a leering smile. Obviously Felix must know by now what the 'business' had been. But Marcus was equal to it.

'On the contrary, Perennis Felix, my business in Corinium has reached a most satisfactory conclusion.'

Felix gave a lecherous laugh. 'Splendid.' He stepped forward and clapped my patron on the shoulder. 'Come then, let us take our places. The chief priest is waiting to make the sacrifices.'

Almost as though it were a signal, there was a little movement among the watching company, a visible lessening of tension. The murmur of conversation began again, and the slaves recommenced their progress with the serving baskets.

But the noise was still subdued. Over the hubbub, Felix's voice could be distinctly heard. 'I have reserved a place for you beside me. There are important matters that I wish to discuss with you.'

I saw the flush rise to my patron's face. I could see why. Marcus reclined at the top table by right, and usually – unless he was dining with the governor – in pride of place. The suggestion that he owed his place to Felix's patronage was deliberately insulting. But he held his tongue. The first skirmish, it seemed, had gone to Felix.

But Felix had not finished. He placed his hand familiarly on Marcus's elbow, and murmured something into his ear. I saw Marcus pull away angrily.

'On no account!' He spoke so loudly that people turned towards him, and there were one or two raised eyebrows and titters, hastily suppressed. I wondered what unsavoury proposition Felix had made. Whatever it was, my patron was having none of it.

Felix had turned the same colour as his edges, but he said smoothly, 'No matter. We will talk of this again. For now, let us begin the feast. Besides, there is someone I wish you to meet. A bit of a barbarian, certainly, but a very influential man. He comes from the wildlands on the south-western margins of this island, but he runs the biggest tin and copper operation in the province. He produces some of the finest bronze in the whole Empire. Everything from weapons to jewellery. I have dealt with him before, through a bronze-trader, but the prices are extortionate.' Felix gave his disagreeable smile. 'So I will see what kind of bargain *I* can strike. That is one of the chief reasons why I have come to this benighted country.'

He gestured towards a man whom somehow I had not

41

noticed before, perhaps because he was half hidden from my sight by a partition. He was conspicuous enough, in all conscience, here in this roomful of togaed officials – red-headed, flamboyant in Celtic plaid and a long Celtic moustache – yet somehow I had not seen him there, leaning quietly against a pillar with his back towards us, watching the musicians.

Felix led Marcus towards him, saying loudly, 'He will join us at my table. Unattractive, perhaps, while one is dining. The fellow speaks barbarous Latin, and insists on diluting his wine so much that it is scarcely wine at all, but one has to humour these people. I have had to send for extra water for him. His name is Egobarbus.'

As he spoke I craned forward to catch a better glimpse of the man that he had indicated. And gasped aloud. 'Dear gods.'

It was unfortunate, perhaps. Few people, seeing a scruffy Roman citizen in Glevum, would remember that I was once a freeborn prince among my own people, and that the wealthiest men of my homelands were at one time well known to me.

But it was so. I had met Egobarbus, or Andregoranabalus as he was properly called. His father then was the fabled owner of those mines of pure tin and copper on which the armourers of Rome depended for their bronze – a striking man, tall, red-headed, unpredictable, with a quick temper, a sharp mind, a foul mouth and a stout heart. I rather liked him, though he would make a ruthless enemy, and I had often dined at his table.

The son I had loathed on sight. He was the only child, and so petted and pampered by the womenfolk that he had come to think of himself as a kind of human Rome – the centre of the known universe. He had inherited his father's ginger hair and quick temper, but allied to it a temperament so casually

cruel and self-absorbed that even the trading Romans –
despairing of ever pronouncing his Celtic name – had
nicknamed him 'Egobarbus', 'I the beard', in honour of his
spectacular facial hair. He had long since shaved off the
youthful beard and adopted the long drooping moustache of
the Celtic nobleman, but the name had stuck.

The last time I saw him he was whipping a helpless puppy
for daring to bark in his presence. He was bigger than I was
in those days, but all the same I had distinguished myself by
seizing the lash from his hand and turning it on himself. It
had caused a rift between our households, and it was twenty
years since we had met, but I would have recognised him
anywhere. As doubtless he would know me.

That was what had caused my exclamation. For this was
not the man.

Chapter Five

I had no time, however, to warn Marcus. Felix and his party were already taking their places at the top table, and submitting to having their feet washed by the servants (a custom which has always perplexed me – I suppose it keeps the dining couches clean, but we Celts prefer to rinse our face and fingers before we dine). The rest of the company naturally followed suit.

I was allocated, as I expected, a stool near the rear wall, together with a stout citizen trader, who looked from me to Marcus, sighed, and carefully ignored me for the rest of the evening. We were joined at last by a sallow young man who arrived, breathless and panting, just as the chief priest from the Temple of Jupiter – a skinny old goat with a wavering voice which could scarcely be heard from where we were – was muttering his way through the ritual oblations and we all, finally, sat down to dine.

It was, of course, impossible to communicate with Marcus, or to hear any part of what was being said at his table. Not that there seemed to be much to overhear. Marcus was clearly still startled and affronted after his outburst earlier, and was listening with exaggerated interest to the aged magistrate on his right. Since this was Gaius Flavius, the dispossessed owner of the house we were dining in, I lost interest. I guessed that Marcus was enduring a prolonged lamentation on the topic of dogs and how they had been banished from the dining room.

After a while, Felix turned away with a dismissive gesture, and began a muted discussion with the supposed Egobarbus, who did not seem particularly delighted at the attention. In fact he was looking decidedly ill at ease, shifting awkwardly on the couch and looking doubtfully at the Latin delicacies placed before him.

I looked again at Egobarbus and wondered idly who his barber was. I had once had a moustache like that – though not half so luxurious – so I knew how much it cost in wax and constant trimming to keep it in that flamboyant state. Egobarbus seemed aware of it. He kept dabbing his moustache nervously with his napkin, and glancing doubtfully at Felix. I wondered if Felix was propositioning *him*.

However, there was nothing to be learned at this distance, and I turned my attention to the meal. It was more than welcome after a long day spent jolting in carriages, with only bread, apples and honeyed dates to sustain me. The food, even such of it as reached the stool-sitters, was excellent – ducks' eggs and partridge breast, stuffed pork and lovage – while the gilded birds, roast stuffed piglets and exotic cakes which were carried to the main tables were triumphant proof of what the finest cooks in Glevum could produce, without warning, in a day. As Marcus had told me, each magistrate had contributed some delicacy from his own kitchen.

Even so Felix seemed dissatisfied. He spurned the pork, the hare, the swans, and merely picked discontentedly at the more expensive imported delicacies, like olives, dormice and rabbit, though these dishes he mostly commandeered for himself. Gaius was looking grieved – doubtless these costly luxuries had been appropriated from his larder.

Personally, I made a splendid meal, unspoiled by fermented fish entrails since – being at the lowliest table – I could refuse that revolting Roman sauce with impunity. Marcus, from what I could see of him, also ate heartily.

From time to time, as usual on these occasions, the courses were interspersed with speeches as we rinsed our fingers in the bowls of water brought by the slaves. Then after the honeyed apricots and pepper – which were delicious – a local poet rose to his feet and recited, at excruciating length, an ode of welcome which he had written in Felix's honour – a piece of such unutterable banality that one felt the author must have expended more time in the final performance than he ever spent on the composition.

At last, however, he paused to draw breath, and the rest of his recitation was instantly drowned out by such sustained and deafening applause that he finally withdrew – no doubt holding a very good opinion of himself and his talents. The way was thus opened for the other entertainments and the wine, which the servants were already pouring through filters and mixing with water ready to serve into drinking cups. I caught the eye of the sallow young man opposite, and we exchanged grins of sympathy.

More than sympathy, when I came to look at him closely. It was nearer empathy. The boy looked as out of place here as I was, his hair thinning prematurely, his hands as work-roughened as my own and his toga no better quality than mine, either. And yet he was clearly a proper Roman, not just a Roman citizen, but a man from Rome: not only was his face unfamiliar, but when he spoke to the servants he used the clipped accents and stilted Latin characteristic of the Imperial City.

His name was Silvanus Flavius Octavius, he told me, and he was a tile-maker. That explained the toga – in Rome, tradesmen are often citizens, since any freeman born within the city walls has automatic right to that coveted status. But what had brought him here?

He seemed alarmed by the question, and the sallow face flushed. 'Oh, business, business,' he said vaguely. 'Making contact with your tile factory in Glevum.' He turned the conversation to mosaics, in which he had – or feigned – a professional interest.

Visiting the local factory? That was of course possible; Glevum is famous for its tiles. I was asking myself with some interest what, in that case, he was doing at Felix's banquet, when there was a sudden unscheduled change in proceedings, and I forgot my curiosity for a while.

There was a stir at the top table and Marcus rose to his feet. That was unexpected but not unprecedented. Rhetoric is highly prized among Romans, and an impromptu speech by some would-be orator is a possible hazard at any official function. But I had never seen Marcus do it.

He held up his hand for silence, and the diners – who had been looking forward, finally, to the appearance of the musicians and dancing girls – unwillingly settled back to listen.

Marcus was brief. 'Citizens, welcome on this auspicious occasion. I will not keep you long.' (Muted cheers and a little laughter.) 'I speak only to tell you that tonight there is a double cause for celebration. Not only is Perennis Felix with us, but my business in Corinium is finally completed.' (A little puzzled laughter.) 'Yes, gentlemen, I recently concluded a contract with Julia Delicta, in due form before a magistrate, and I am delighted to report that I am now a married man.'

At this there was such an outburst of cheering that – like the poet – he was for a moment unable to continue. Only two men present did not join the applause. One was Perennis Felix, whose cheeks had turned first scarlet and then white, as though someone had slapped him. The other was the sallow youth.

He stared at me for a moment, then said, as if I might understand, 'Phyllidia! Then everything is not lost.'

He set down his goblet, and before I could stop him he

had bolted from the room. The other diners carefully paid no attention, either to him or to me. Perhaps they thought it beneath their dignity: Octavius and I had already flouted convention by vulgarly discussing trade at the table. More likely they were simply being meticulously polite. It is not uncommon in fashionable circles for a man to desert his couch at dinner, usually to tickle his throat with a feather and thus make room for more. Indeed, in Rome *vomitoria* are often provided for the purpose. It is not, however, considered well mannered to notice this, and other guests merely go on talking about philosophy until the missing man returns.

Octavius, however, did not return.

I was curious, so curious that I might almost have followed him, but Marcus was looking in my direction. Felix, I noted, had managed to recollect himself and was joining in the enthusiastic tumult occasioned by Marcus's announcing, as he sat down, that he was sending out for an additional celebratory amphora of wine to be served at every table.

Now it was Felix who rose to speak.

'Citizens of Glevum,' he said, speaking the words as if they tasted of bad fish, 'I thank you for your welcome. I am, I confess, a little disappointed by the news. I had hoped to arrange a match between Marcus Septimus and my own daughter. Indeed, she is at this moment travelling to the Insula Britannia on that very account. However, since my dearest dream is now impossible, I can only ask you to raise your drinking vessels and hope the young man is as happy in his choice as he deserves to be.'

It sounded more threat than congratulation, but the assembled company was very willing to drink, especially at someone else's expense. Only Marcus did not charge his drinking cup, but raised it in acknowledgement. Felix sat down to scattered applause, and then the entertainment really began. Starting with the acrobat, naturally.

He was good, so good that Felix had him come back again after the dancing girls and give a second performance. And again after the musicians. Marcus's wine had arrived by this time, so much of it that it had to be carried in by servants of every kind – I even noticed Zetso among them, murmuring to his master – and the mood of the party was becoming hilarious.

The acrobat, having exhausted his repertoire, was resorting to tricks amongst the tables, balancing a goblet of wine on his forehead and curving himself slowly backwards until he rested on his hands and feet like a spider, and raising himself again without spilling a single drop. The whole audience laughed and cheered, Felix most of all. The acrobat flung himself into the air, somersaulted twice, and, landing lightly on his hands, walked upside down between the tables.

One of the guests seized a bowl of nuts and dates from the slave who was carrying them, and balanced it upon the upturned feet. The acrobat, still on his hands, danced over to the high table and, bending his elbows and knees, effectively presented the bowl to Felix to select from.

Felix was visibly enraptured. His swarthy face was flushed, his breathing fast, his tongue flicking out to lick his fleshy lips. He stood up, leaned forward and selected a nut, and slipped it into his mouth. He moved to take another, but the acrobat sinuously twisted his body and moved the bowl out of reach. There was a roar of approval.

Felix, flattered but sensing that he was being mocked, pushed aside the table and lunged after him, snatching a handful of nuts and holding them triumphantly. There were more cheers, and then the acrobat straightened his limbs and danced provocatively away, to tumultuous applause. In the centre of the room he flicked the bowl upwards with his feet, twisted himself upright and caught the bowl again, all in one fluid movement. The audience went wild with frenzy.

The acrobat turned back, to bow towards the top table . . . and stopped. Something was happening to Felix. He appeared to be choking. He was leaning on the end of the dining couch clutching his throat, coughing, gasping, spluttering, his face scarlet and his eyes bulging. Presumably he had swallowed one of the nuts. With all eyes on the performance no one had noticed his predicament.

Even now there was a moment of horrified inaction, and then, suddenly, everything was happening at once. Egobarbus, or whoever he was, strode over and began to thump Felix helpfully on the back. Slaves rushed forward with goblets of water and wine, someone else tried to force a piece of dry bread into his mouth. Even old Gaius reached into the recesses of his toga and offered a phial of a dubious-looking substance which he insisted was a specific against all ills, and had once saved his best bitch in similar circumstances. Only Marcus did not move. He stayed, reclining where he was, watching with a kind of horrified fascination while all around him surged forward with a dozen suggested remedies.

Felix, waving his hands helplessly, at first attempted to fight them off, but he was still spluttering and coughing and in the end, eyes streaming, he submitted to their attentions.

In vain. A crisis seemed to grip him. Gagging, gurgling, he clawed at the air a moment and then, with a terrible gasping groan, he pitched head forward onto the table, scattering everything to the floor. Meat, wine, water, dates and fragments of shattered bowls and pitchers joined the gnawed bones and debris already littering the tiles.

There was a terrified pause and then a dozen slaves rushed forward to lift the inert body to the dining couch. Someone suggested fetching their private physician, or the military doctor from the barracks. But we hardly needed the doctor to tell us what everyone in the room was aware of.

Perennis Felix was dead.

Chapter Six

Everyone reacted in different ways, as people do in a crisis.

Serving slaves froze where they stood, waiting for instructions. Guests withdrew into corners and whispered, or jostled forward to stare. No one doubted what had happened. The memory of that herald's shattered body in the forum was uppermost in everybody's mind and on everyone's lips. The souls of the unburied dead are notoriously vindictive.

Of course, that did not make this event seem any the less disturbing. Rather more so, if anything. The idea of an unseen vengeful spirit in our midst was decidedly discomfiting.

Some men, particularly those with little influence but a lively instinct for safety, attempted to put as much distance as possible between themselves and possible reprisals – human or supernatural – by loudly offering to go for help and dashing to the door. I might have attempted an exit myself, but I knew that it was hopeless. I had come with Marcus and there was no possible chance of pretending that I had been somewhere else all evening, and bribing a dozen witnesses to prove it, as some of the others would surely do. In any case the door-keeper, alerted by the sudden panicky exodus, realised that something unfortunate had happened and turned most of them back.

The remaining dignitaries eyed each other doubtfully. Fortunately all the senior civil and judicial authorities of the town were present, so there was no possibility of one group being less politically implicated than another. And there *were* political implications. The death of the guest of honour at a banquet is always an embarrassment, but even supernatural visitations were downright unwise when they caused an accident like this to a visiting favourite of the Emperor's, especially at a civil banquet in a province already suspected of being rebellious. Little knots of magistrates huddled together, muttering in low voices. Some gulped at their wine dazedly. One could see why.

A dozen muted arguments broke out, but as tempers frayed with anxiety voices became shrill and raised. The topics seemed to be the same – what to do next, who should do it, and exactly which kind of funeral rites would be appropriate. Clearly no one wished to take responsibility (since, if the Emperor ever made enquiries, a wrong decision was likely to be much more dangerous than no decision at all) but everyone had an opinion. Some urged caution and delay, or even sending to the governor for advice, as though time would somehow soften the enormity of the event. Others seemed to feel the need for immediate action and were loudly demanding sacred herbs from the garden, calling for blankets from their litters, or sending bemused servants in all directions with contradictory messages.

The poor acrobat, obviously terrified at the outcome of his performance, had edged the nut bowl surreptitiously onto a table, and tried to slide unnoticed back into the corner with the rest of the entertainers. The nubile dancing girl burst into tears and the musicians began whispering together, patting her on the arm and nodding knowingly towards Gaius as owner of the house.

Gaius saw them. The danger of the situation was not lost upon him. He buried his head in his hands and let out a howl that would not have disgraced one of his dogs. Not surprisingly. The accident had occurred in his house. At the very least he would be personally responsible for the costly and time-consuming rituals of purification and mourning. At worst . . . well, choking on a nut might be an accident, or vengeance from the dead, but Commodus was not noted for either his leniency or his logic.

As if summoned by the howl, two slaves came out of the kitchens with a salver of sugared fruits. News had evidently not spread to the neither regions, but when they saw what was happening they bolted back again, leaving the door open. Gaius's dogs, taking advantage of the moment, bounded in and added to the confusion by rushing around the room yapping and barking, leaping up on their master and lapping up the food under the tables. One of them, horrifyingly, began sniffing at the corpse.

It was at that point that Marcus finally took command. Whatever else, such indignity could not be tolerated. He strode over to the couch and pulled the dog away. At the same time he signalled to the musicians. The drums sounded and the lute-players touched their strings. Instantly the hubbub ceased and everyone looked towards Marcus. There was an almost visible ripple of relief. He was the most influential man present, and by stepping forward he had relieved others of the responsibility.

'Citizens! This is a most unfortunate accident. Naturally, you are disturbed. But at all costs let us preserve decorum. Gaius, call your dogs to heel.'

The old man gave a feeble whistle. The dogs ignored him but a pair of his slaves, obviously accustomed to the duty, seized the dogs by the iron collars round their necks and dragged them downstairs towards the cellars and kitchens.

Marcus watched this performance in silence. Then he spoke again. 'The body, I think, should be moved into a bedchamber. You, you, you and you,' he indicated a line of waiting slaves, 'go outside. Fetch a litter to place him on. The funeral arrangers will have one. Order the best they have, and bring the undertaker here. See that the *libitinarius* brings his anointers and pall-bearers and anything else that he needs.'

The lads scuttled to obey.

Marcus turned to the rest of us. 'We have all been in the presence of sudden death, and therefore we all need rites of purification. Fortunately, we have the high priest of Jupiter among us. He will tell us what it is necessary to do.'

That was a happy stroke. Even the Emperor himself was in awe of the gods. The old priest dithered out to the household altar, fussed importantly with his robes and said, in a cracked and faded voice, 'I shall need water, wine and oil. And a flame, from the Vestal altar in the atrium.'

Marcus gave a nod, and two slaves sidled away to fetch these necessities.

'And then there are the candles and herbs to set at the bedside.' More slaves departed.

There was a pause, while the requisite fire and liquids were fetched. Then the priest lit the lamp before the votive statues and began a long and complicated invocation of the gods in general, and Jupiter in particular, not forgetting the Emperor – in his role as divine being – and the household deities. He ritually washed his hands of death, and poured out conciliatory sacrifice, sprinkling herbs and some crumbs from the feast upon the sacred flame.

'Prayers too for the herald,' someone called, and the old man repeated the process with a morsel of bread and watered wine, dropping his voice to an incantatory murmur. The gods, being divine, were doubtless able to hear it. More mortal ears, like mine, were unable to distinguish a word. No doubt that was intentional. Commodus assuredly had his spies amongst us and would hear every detail of this ceremony. The priestly balance of duties between gods and

Emperor cannot always be an easy one.

Nevertheless, the effect was impressive. When he had finished he blessed the ceremonial vessels, and the slaves moved among us, offering each person present first the bowl of cool water and then a dish of ashes from the altar. One by one we took the garlands from our heads, dipped our hands and rinsed our faces in ritual cleansing, and solemnly placed a fingerful of ashes as a mourning sign upon our foreheads. Not one of us, I think, would genuinely have shed a tear for the lifeless figure lying on the couch, but there was something reassuring about fulfilling the rites. Even I, who am not a believer in the Roman pantheon, felt vaguely comforted, particularly when the old priest at the end of the ceremony picked up a bronze salver and struck it ringingly – striking bronze is a well-known Roman specific against malevolent spirits.

The slaves had by now returned with the funeral arranger, the most prestigious in the city, and he and his workers were loitering in the passageway waiting for the priest to offer the remains of the feast before the sacrificial altar. (Gaius's slaves would be delighted by that, I thought, since there was a good deal left over and the servants are, by tradition, permitted in the morning to eat the remnants which the gods have not consumed. I am not a sceptical man but it has been my impression that the gods are rarely very hungry on these occasions.)

At last the formalities were over and the *libitinarius* and his party were able to enter with the funeral litter, an elaborate couch affair on a bier, with gilded handles and an embroidered canopy. It was almost too wide for the entrance, but they brought it in at last, and set it down.

Two of the attendants came forward and laid the body tenderly on it. 'Keep the feet to the door,' the undertaker said, 'in case the spirit should wish to escape.' I saw Gaius flinch, no doubt wishing we had thought of this elementary precaution earlier.

The attendants hoisted the litter, and the mortal remains of Felix were borne away upstairs to be washed, anointed, dressed in the finest toga in his possession, and – since he had been a person of some importance – arranged on the funerary couch and brought back to the atrium for a few days of lying in state. Matters were in the hands of the professionals. There was an audible murmur of relief as the litter jolted out of the room and up the narrow stairway. The spectacle was over. By common consent the remaining guests ignored the elaborate social ritual of compliment and counter-compliment which precedes departure from a feast, and prepared to leave without further ado. Social precedence, however, was not so easily flouted, and many people held back doubtfully. Marcus, as the highest-ranking individual, should properly leave the banquet first.

My patron caught my eye and signalled me to him. At last, I thought. The vision of my humble bed floated invitingly before my eyes. And Junio would doubtless be awaiting me with a beaker of honest mead. It had been a long day.

Suddenly, however, one of the funeral attendants reappeared in the inner doorway. 'A thousand pardons, Excellence,' he said, addressing himself with practised courtesy to Marcus and ignoring me entirely, 'but who should close the eyes? And, being a gentleman from Rome, should someone observe the Roman convention?'

Kissing the lips of the deceased, he meant. It was a custom often practised in Rome, supposed to speed the departing soul. Marcus was looking at me. I shook my head. My duties to my patron encompass many things, but kissing the dead Felix was not one of them. The prospect was only marginally less horrible than the notion of kissing the living one.

That train of thought, however, gave me an idea. 'With

respect, Excellence, surely you should call on Zetso for this? In the absence of his daughter, who is still on her way, Zetso must know Felix better than any of us.'

Marcus frowned. 'Zetso? But he is a mere carriage-driver. It is not seemly for him to perform the rites for such an important man.'

I permitted myself a smile. 'In that case, Excellence, the duty should fall on the most senior and influential man present.'

'Then . . .' Marcus began, and then realised who that would be. 'Yes, perhaps you are right, Libertus. Zetso should close the eyes at least, and perhaps tell us also what grave-goods and funerary meats we should provide. Where is Zetso? I saw him earlier.'

But Zetso was not to be found, in the passageway or in the servants' ante-room. The undertaker's boy was still looking at us enquiringly.

'Libertus,' Marcus said darkly, 'you shall have the commission for the commemorative pavement. But think of something. Someone has got to do this.'

For a blind moment I thought it would have to be me, but then inspiration struck. 'Surely, Excellence, the owner of the house? He is, officially, the host.'

Marcus rewarded me with a beam. 'Of course.' Gaius was sitting miserably on a stool in the corner, and Marcus gestured to him, saying smoothly, 'Gaius Flavius Flaminius, you have been chosen for a singular honour . . .' and the poor old fellow was led away into his own bedchamber to perform his grisly task. We could hear him, a little later, piping up a feeble lament and periodically calling Felix's name as tradition demanded.

Marcus turned towards me, smiling. 'Well, I believe we have done all we can. The council will meet tomorrow to arrange the funeral. A public ceremony, naturally, with a pause in the forum for the body to be displayed and someone to proclaim a eulogy. So I must be sure to find that herald and bury him decently before then. We want no more unfortunate accidents. Where is Zetso? He will know where the body was left, and he can lead us to it.'

I shook my head. 'I do not know, Excellence. I have searched all the public rooms. Perhaps he has hidden downstairs, in the cellar or one of the storerooms. If he sees the hand of the dead in this, he must fear for his own safety. It was Zetso who staked out the corpse.'

Marcus gave a short, mirthless laugh. 'Perhaps. See if you can find him, Libertus. He can take us out tomorrow to find the herald in that comfortable carriage of his.'

'Us', I noticed. It seemed my customers would have to wait another day. 'Yes, Excellence,' I said humbly, and seizing a smoky taper in a holder I set off to look for Zetso.

The house was built on a slight rise, so there was an area below the rooms where we had been dining. It seemed the appropriate place to start.

Zetso was not in the kitchens, nor in the cellars, nor in the servants' room under the stairs. He was not in the latrine, although I surprised one of the erstwhile guests, a florid trader who was enthroned there, suspended over the drain with his sponge-stick in his hand. Zetso was not in the narrow store cupboards leading off the passage and filled with candles, wood and grain. In the last cupboard I opened, however, I did find something. One of Gaius's dogs.

It was lying quietly on the floor on a sort of rug, and it did not even lift its head as I approached. I might have shut the door and tiptoed away, but something made me lift my taper nearer.

No, I was not mistaken. It was not a rug, it was a plaid cloak, of the kind that the pretended Egobarbus had been wearing earlier. In fact, I was prepared to wager it was the same cloak. When I came to consider it, I had not seen Egobarbus since the dramatic end of the entertainments. I bent closer for a moment and then shut the cupboard door and ran as quickly as I could up the dim and unlit stairs.

I went to the lobby and exchanged a few words with the doorman, and then I returned to Marcus.

'Excellence?'

Marcus was talking to one of the *aediles*, the market police, but he turned impatiently at my approach. 'Libertus?' He did not care to be interrupted.

I took a deep breath. 'Forgive me, Excellence, but I think you must come quickly. I have not found Zetso, but there is something downstairs in a cupboard which I think you should see.'

Chapter Seven

'I hope,' Marcus said sternly as he followed me reluctantly down the short staircase, 'that this is as important as you say.' He was not dependent on my poor smoky taper, a slave with a fine oil-lamp was lighting his way, but he walked gingerly and with distaste, as though subterranean perambulations through the lower regions were not at all to his taste.

He had a point. The latrine in a town dwelling is never especially sweet-smelling, despite being over running water, but the odour from this one seemed to permeate the whole area. A man like Marcus, I realised, would probably not even demean himself by visiting the ablutions in a house like this: if he were staying here he would expect to be provided with servants, washing water and chamber pots.

'See for yourself, Excellence,' I said, opening the store cupboard with a flourish. In the better illumination the contents were clearer than before.

Marcus, who is not a lover of bouncy dogs, backed away hastily and motioned for the door to be shut before the dog awoke. All the same he had noticed the blanket. 'That cloak! It is the one which that Egobarbus fellow was wearing. Or one very like it. What is it doing here in the store cupboard?'

'I suppose it is just possible, Excellence, that either Gaius or Felix bought a length of the same cloth. Unfortunately we can hardly ask either of them since Felix is dead and Gaius is occupied in mourning him. Although perhaps the house-slaves would know.'

Marcus turned to the slave who was carrying the lamp. 'Well? You work in this house, don't you? Did Gaius, or Felix, purchase such a thing?'

The lad gulped and shook his head. When he spoke his voice was trembling with nervousness. 'Not that I know of, Excellence. I cannot imagine that my master would want such a piece of coarse Celtic plaid, His Excellence Tigidius Perennis Felix even less so.'

Marcus was looking impatient, and I stepped in hastily. 'I agree, Excellence. A most unlikely purchase for either of them. In which case I can only suppose that it is the cloak, and the man himself put it here. It occurs to me that I did not notice him again after Felix died. The doorman did not see him leave, either. I made a point of asking him.'

Marcus's frown deepened. 'Yet Egobarbus would not be easy to miss. Those whiskers and that cloak . . . By Jupiter, greatest and best! Libertus, I see what you are thinking. Somehow he came here and abandoned his cloak in order to escape without being noticed. Though he would have needed something to disguise those whiskers. A hooded cape, perhaps?'

I nodded, doubtfully. Roman citizens are not as universally clean-shaven as they used to be. Indeed, there has been quite a little fashion for beards since the Emperor Hadrian sported one, and naturally, since Commodus himself is bearded, much of polite society in high places follows the Emperor. But it is not usual in Glevum. Even I have to submit to the expensive horrors of a barber's shop occasionally – with its dreadful sharpened blades and its spiders-web-and-ashes dressing for nicks and cuts – though I generally prefer the ministrations of Junio with a pair of iron scissors. Most of the guests, and slaves, at the banquet tonight had been as smooth-faced as Vestal virgins, so Egobarbus was as conspicuous as a lighted torch. Even a hooded cape would scarcely have disguised that exuberant moustache.

'There is—' I began, but Marcus brushed me aside and was scowling down the narrow corridor.

'What is behind those other doors?'

I hastened to inform him. 'More store cupboards, Excellence, and the big entrance on the right is to the kitchens. Egobarbus is not there. I searched them not a minute ago when I was looking for Zetso.'

'Nevertheless,' Marcus said, 'we will search again.' He gestured the lamp-bearer forward and suited the action to the words. In vain. There was nothing in the other cupboards but grain and candles and nothing in the smoky candlelit kitchen but a group of startled slaves, who – drawn as they were from different households – were squabbling noisily about what scraps were whose, and who should be expected to clean the greasy salvers and rub the dirty knives with red earth and ashes. My visit earlier had caused consternation enough, but at the sight of a purple-striper in the kitchen they stopped their bickering at once, and dropping their various brooms and implements stood staring at us in mystified terror.

Marcus made a pretence of looking under the tables, but there was clearly nothing to see and he withdrew, muttering, 'Very well, get on with your work.' The slaves' hands resumed their tasks obediently, but their eyes never left us until we were once more back in the gloom of the corridor.

'Excellence,' I began again, but Marcus was not listening. His gaze had fallen on the glimmer of light beyond the skimpy curtain which screened the latrine.

'There he is!' Marcus strode forward and thrust the curtain aside.

The florid citizen-trader whom I had surprised earlier was standing there, his candle guttering on a shelf while he readjusted his toga. He stared at us for a moment in affronted astonishment, and then he and Marcus spoke as one man.

'You!'

Marcus recovered first. 'Tommonius Lunaris! What brings you to this house?'

The man he had called 'Tommonius' smiled faintly. 'The same occasion as brings you here yourself, Excellence. I was bidden to the feast by Perennis Felix. I had business with him earlier in the town. I was astonished to see you at the banquet – I thought you in Corinium. Was not the lawsuit scheduled for today?'

'Indeed it was. I presided at it before I came here.'

'And how did you find my old goat of a father-in-law? Innocent, no doubt, since he has wealthy friends on the council.'

'I found him guilty,' Marcus said. 'And sentenced him to exile.'

Tommonius smiled grimly. 'Where he will die in comfort in his bed. Well, I bear him no malice. He did me a favour, killing the scoundrel who dishonoured my bed. No, I reserve my anger for the courts – saving your presence, Excellence – and for this fellow's family, who brought this disgraceful case in the first place. What purpose did it serve except to bring me into disrepute and turn me into a laughing stock in every market place in the province? You know that there were itinerant pedlars calling after me in Glevum today? "Better hurry home, Tommonius, before your wife starts missing you and your father-in-law is charged with another murder." It prevented me from concluding at least one serious bargain.'

Marcus said placatingly, 'Yes, I understand it must be distressing. To learn that your wife—'

'My wife!' Tommonius exclaimed. 'That is not important. So, the woman had a lover – she was discreet enough, and it was no great loss. She brought no significant dowry with her when we married – her father's wealth is all in his home and business – and she had begun to bore me long ago. And I her. But I provided for her, she was decorative and her father's estate would have come into my hands when he died. It was an arrangement which suited us both.'

I stared at him. This was a peculiarly Roman view of marriage, I thought. But Tommonius had not finished.

'Now I shall have to divorce her,' he continued, 'and have her exiled to some tiresome island. I shall keep the measly marriage portion, of course, since she was caught *in flagrante delicto*, but thanks to this lawsuit I have lost all hope of the real money. The estate will have gone to that wretched lover's family as recompense for a trumped-up murder charge – such of it as the old man didn't manage to smuggle away with him. Thanks to the vagaries of the law.' He picked up his candle. 'By the by, I congratulate you on your own marriage, Excellence. May the lady bring you more good fortune than mine did.'

He made as if to leave but Marcus blocked his path. 'You saw what happened upstairs?' my patron asked.

'To Felix?' Tommonius nodded. 'Indeed I did. A pity, I had hoped to strike a bargain with him. I hear he was a great importer of goods. But Gaius says it is a judgement of the gods. I trust that is more just than the judgements of men.' He smiled. 'Excuse me, Excellence, but I have no great respect for the law – even if you are the one to wield it. Good evening, gentlemen.'

Marcus, who had listened to this in silence, inclined his head and stood back to allow the trader to pass. Tommonius retreated with as much dignity as a man can after he has been surprised in the latrine.

Marcus watched him go. 'You know who that is, Libertus? The husband of the woman in that murder case this afternoon.'

'Yes, Excellence,' I said respectfully. 'I had rather gathered that.'

'I heard that he had come to Glevum. I wonder why Felix invited him to the feast?'

I had no real answer to that. 'For the same reason that he invited Egobarbus, perhaps?' I suggested. 'Because he was hoping to strike some bargain with him and wanted to offer him entertainment at no cost to himself?' From what I had heard of Felix that seemed likely enough.

'Yes,' Marcus said. 'Egobarbus. We are no nearer to finding him.'

'Nor Zetso either,' I reminded him. 'And the man you call Egobarbus is—'

Marcus shook his head impatiently. 'Terrified out of their wits, most like, the pair of them, after what happened to Felix.' He motioned for the lamp and began to stride back down the corridor, rather to my relief. I suspect the speed of his step was not unrelated to the overpowering odour of the latrine.

I trotted after him.

Marcus was still talking. 'Zetso was bodyguard to his master and Egobarbus was the only Celt present. They must both have felt that if any questions were asked, they were likely to fall on *them*. The public torturers are not always scrupulous in their examination of non-citizens who find themselves under suspicion.' We were at the top of the staircase by now, and he waved away the lamp-bearer. Most of the other guests had taken advantage of our disappearance and made good their own, and slaves were already moving to clear the tables and sweep the floors with their bunches of broom. Marcus turned to smile at me. 'Well, it is too late now. I suppose it is unimportant. Fortunately, on this occasion there is nothing to be suspicious about. Felix died in full view of everyone, and there can be no doubt that it was an accident.'

I took a deep breath. 'With respect, Excellence . . .'

'What is it, Libertus? You find something in what I have said to disagree with?'

There was nothing for it now. I bowed my head. 'Three things, Excellence. In the first place, there was more than one Celt present. I am a Celt myself, from the same part of the island. That is how I come to know the second thing. That man is not Egobarbus, nor ever was.' I told him what I knew.

Marcus was dismissive. 'My dear old friend, it is twenty years since you met the fellow. A man may change a great deal in that time.'

'Indeed he may, Excellence, but there are some things he cannot alter. The Egobarbus that I knew was a taller man than I am, though I was a grown adult and he was still a boy. This fellow is the same height as me. He cannot have shrunk. And did you see his hands?'

'There was nothing the matter with his hands.'

'Exactly. But Egobarbus has a damaged little finger. I know, because I damaged it, with a whip.'

Marcus was staring at me now. 'Then who . . .'

I shook my head. 'As to that, Excellence, I have no more idea than you have.'

'Then he must be found. It may have nothing to do with this evening's accident, but the fellow cannot arrive here impersonating someone else.'

'Yes, Excellence, he must be found, and with more urgency than you think. I told you there was a third matter. There is also the question of the dog.'

'Ah, yes, I have been thinking of the dog. Too quiet, even for an old animal half asleep. And why was it in a cupboard?' He gave me a triumphant smile. 'I know what you are going to tell me. Gaius was boasting to me of the creature's tricks. Someone had fed it on ale. The old beast loves it. The drink makes it playful and then puts it into a drunken sleep for hours. Somebody learned of this, and gave the dog ale so that he could make his escape. This Egobarbus, probably. Confess, that was what you were going to tell me.'

I moved closer so that nobody should overhear me. 'No, Excellence,' I murmured. 'Worse than that. I'm very much afraid the dog was dead.'

Marcus looked startled. 'You think he strangled it with its collar? Or perhaps it was that slave who dragged it away?'

I shook my head. 'I looked, Excellence. There is no sign of damage to the neck – as there assuredly would be in that case. But there is evidence of vomit and foaming at the mouth. Now, it occurs to me that the animals were lapping up the food under the table. And in that case there has to be a possibility that whatever it was that killed the dog also killed Perennis Felix. Despite appearances, Excellence, I fear we may be looking at a murder.'

Marcus, unquestionably the most powerful man in Glevum, glanced around as guiltily as any schoolboy. 'I think,' he said carefully, 'that this theory of yours may be better kept to ourselves. Even if you are right – and there is no evidence at all that you are – as Tommonius said about his own affairs, what is to be gained by making it public? We shall merely have Commodus baying for blood, and all of us will be under suspicion.'

Himself especially, I thought, since he had been sitting nearest to Felix and had occasion enough to detest and fear the man. And he had brought in the extra wine. But I said nothing beyond, 'Indeed, Excellence, although it might be wise to prevent the servants eating the remnants from the high table. Another corpse might prove exceedingly embarrassing.'

He thought about that for a moment. 'That might be difficult. The slaves will expect to be allowed the scraps.

Anything else might attract speculation and gossip.'

'Unless you ordered them to be burnt at the Vestal flame?'

He flushed. 'Of course. A propitiation to the household gods. I was about to suggest it myself.'

I did not dignify that with a response. I merely said, 'So Felix will have his public funeral and that will be the end of that?'

'That is the safest option, do you not think?'

'I am sure it is.' I bowed. I wanted to go home. 'So you will not be requiring my services further? Except in the matter of the commemorative pavement?'

He gazed at me as though Diana had touched my wits. 'But of course I shall require your services. If there is any truth in your suspicions, naturally I wish to find the culprit. If you can prove to me who did it, of course we will bring a case against him. It is merely that, without clear proof of someone else's guilt, suspicion will assuredly fall on me. Much better if people do not guess that there might ever have been a case at all. I want you to come here and consult about the pavement, and while you are about it you can ask a few questions in the household, find out who put that dog in the cupboard, and what happened to Egobarbus. And Zetso too. They cannot have got far tonight; the city gates will be closed. You can report to me here first thing in the morning.'

'Excellence,' I pleaded wearily, 'it is already first thing in the morning. By the time I have walked home from here the bakers will be abroad in the streets.'

I must have sounded as weary as I felt. Marcus took pity on me, and sent me home in a litter.

71

Chapter Eight

In the morning I awoke to find the sun well risen in the sky, and the sounds of the day's business issuing noisily from the shops and streets nearby. Junio (who had waited up anxiously for my return) had already risen and gone downstairs from where the delicious smell of hot oatcakes fresh from the street vendor, the intermittent sound of stone on chisel, and a murmur of urgent voices wafted up to me.

It seemed I had a customer.

I struggled up from my comfortable bed of rags and reeds, splashed a little water on my face and hands from the bowl which Junio had set for me, straightened my tunic, donned my belt and sandals and made my way down the rickety ladder to the back kitchen-cum-workroom of my humble shop.

The oatcakes were there, visibly cooling on a wooden platter beside the hearth, where a cheerful fire was already burning. I looked at them longingly, but Junio's voice from the front shop beyond the flimsy partition drove any immediate thoughts of breakfast from my head.

'I tell you he is sleeping, and must not be disturbed.'

Not a customer, then. Junio knew better than to turn away business. Nor a message from Marcus either – that would have brought Junio pounding up the stairs to fetch me, whatever the hour. I was puzzled. A man in my situation rarely receives social calls.

'And *I* tell you I must speak with Libertus. There is some

chance that he might vouch for me.'

I frowned. I recognised the voice. Those clipped Italian accents were unmistakable – my visitor was the sallow youth I had met the night before. And he wished me to 'vouch' for him. That sounded ominous.

I stepped around the partition, the sudden daylight almost dazzling my eyes. 'Greetings, Octavius. You have found me, as you see. In what way did you hope that I could help you?'

The thin face looked hollower than ever, but the youth smiled and the work-roughened hands reached out to grasp mine urgently. 'Libertus. Have you heard the news? Of course you have. You were there, you must have seen it. Perennis Felix is dead. Poisoned. The whole city is talking of it. I did not know what to do, and then I thought of you. I found out where you lived, and came to find you at once, before they came to arrest me. You can at least bear witness that when I left the banquet he was still alive.'

I disentangled myself from his grasp. So, attempts at hiding the possible poisoning had failed. Poor Marcus, he would be first in line for questioning. Some of the magistrates would enjoy that. A great man gains many enemies in the course of his duties. And of course, if my patron were questioned, I would certainly be next. He had spent the day with me. I closed my eyes momentarily.

When I opened them, Octavius was staring at me anxiously. 'You had not heard?'

'I had not heard that he was poisoned,' I said, choosing my words carefully. 'Who told you as much?'

'A servant at the hiring stables this morning,' the young man said hotly. 'I called to see if . . . I called there early on private business, and was told that Perennis Felix was already dead. Something he ate at the feast. I knew what conclusions everyone would draw. And, of course, I had made myself conspicuous by talking that stupid old dodderer with the dogs into letting me attend the banquet.'

So he was there as Gaius's guest. That explained one mystery at least. But at the moment I had other concerns. 'And the stable-hand said poisoned? You are sure? It appeared to most of us that Felix had simply choked on a nut.'

'Clutching his throat and vomiting, he said. He gave a lively description.' His face cleared. 'Although, when I come to consider it, he did not actually mention poison. I simply supposed . . .' Octavius gave an embarrassed shrug. 'He even called after me, but I did not stop to listen. I thought the authorities would already be looking for me. Zetso saw me at the banquet last night, and he knew—' He stopped. 'But of course, if Felix merely choked . . . Libertus, I am sorry to have troubled you. I have been foolish, I think.'

I glanced at Junio, who had given up all pretence of cutting the piece of marble he was holding, and was listening with interest. I caught his eye and he raised an eyebrow questioningly. I nodded, and he disappeared inside to clear a place in the workroom and set out a pair of folding stools. I smiled approvingly. Like me, Junio had found the young man's words singularly intriguing.

I took my visitor gently by the elbow. 'From what you say about your early start, Octavius, I imagine you have not breakfasted? I do not suppose you returned to your lodgings?'

'It is of no consequence. I rarely eat in the morning. A beaker of water and a piece of fruit perhaps.'

'Then you will stay and breakfast with me? I have more robust Celtic appetites, and there are some fresh oatcakes which are not yet entirely cold.'

He shook his head with a kind of frantic haste. 'No, thank you, no. You are very kind, but there are things that I must do urgently.'

My grip on his elbow tightened. 'Octavius,' I said, 'I am sure you want to speak to your accomplice, whoever it is,' I had the satisfaction of seeing his face pale, but I went on inexorably, 'but first you will talk to me. It seems to me you have something to explain. First you appear at a banquet where it seems you have little business to be, and you disappear again with scarcely a word. Next you go skulking around the hiring stables at daybreak and rush away in a panic when you hear that Felix is dead. If I were a magistrate I would find this very suspicious. And then you lay a trail to my door by asking half of Glevum where I live. You owe me an explanation, at least.'

Octavius looked at his sandal-straps and shook his head.

'Then,' I said brightly, giving his elbow a warning squeeze, 'perhaps I should send Junio for the *aediles*? No doubt they will be interested in your doings. Your early morning visit to the stables, for instance.'

Octavius pulled his arm away. 'But there is nothing to explain. It seems that Felix was not poisoned after all. Besides, who would pay any attention to me? I am a humble tile-maker – not a powerful tyrant protected by imperial favour like Felix.'

I glanced at him sharply. An interesting choice of words, I thought. I said, slowly and firmly, 'Octavius, I understand that you come from Rome. That it is a big city, and no doubt they do things differently there. But this is Glevum. Here, everyone of importance knows everybody else, and every-thing unusual is a wonder. Your arrival – as a visitor from Rome – will have been noted, and commented upon, by every pie-seller, amulet-maker and horse-dealer in the city. Just take a look around you.'

Octavius glanced nervously up and down the street, where at this very moment a dozen urchins were ogling us, while a fat peasant woman with a basket of turnips on her back was whispering to a man with a loaded donkey, openly nudging him and nodding in our direction.

'So,' I said. 'Shall I send for the *aediles,* or will you settle for the oatcakes? Before they are completely cold?'

Octavius looked at me sorrowfully. 'It seems,' he said, 'that I have little choice.' He allowed me to steer him round the partition and into the inner workroom, and looked round him in dismay at the tile chips and the half-finished mosaic 'pattern piece' which covered half the table. I do not normally receive visitors in those dusty recesses – in fact I do not normally receive visitors at all – but these were special circumstances. Octavius, as I now knew, had a careless tongue and I wanted to get him inside the shop before he got us both arrested.

'Now then,' I said, when he was comfortably settled and furnished with a cold oatcake. 'Perhaps you can tell me what it was that really brought you to Glevum? And don't tell me that it was merely to visit the tile factories. You followed Perennis Felix, did you not?'

The youth turned as scarlet as his complexion allowed. 'In a manner of speaking.'

I sighed. Evidently extracting information was going to be hard work. I wished, fleetingly, that I had Marcus with me. One look at those wide purple stripes and aristocratic features, and people are falling over their sandal-straps to furnish information, before he calls on unpleasant official means of whetting their memories for them. It is a system that has worked well for us in the past. Today, however, I was on my own.

Or almost. Junio stepped forward with a beaker of water for me and our best drinking cup full of watered wine for the Roman. As he handed me mine, he murmured deferentially, 'Forgive me, master, that there are no honey-cakes for you this morning.'

I looked at him in astonishment. I rarely buy honey-cakes, though the oatcake-baker sells them.

Junio shot me a warning glance, and continued smoothly, 'The vendor told me she had sold them all. A Roman lady arrived last night, after the city gates were shut. She was obliged to stay at a lodging house just outside the walls.'

I nodded. There are a number of these, some official, some private and none of them very salubrious, making a living from unfortunate travellers who find themselves benighted outside the walls. 'And?' I enquired.

'The establishment does not offer food, but the owner recommended these honey-cakes and the lady sent out this morning and bought half a score of them. By the time I got there, there were none left. I am afraid you lost your honey-cakes to the daughter of Perennis Felix.'

Old gods of tree and stone, rain blessings on the boy! He had found a way to alert me to his news without transgressing the social code which forbids a slave to interrupt his master. It was significant news, too. One glance at Octavius's face was enough to tell me that. He had turned pinker than a skinned swan on a skillet. A little taper lighted in my brain.

'This would be Phyllidia, I presume?'

The skinned swan turned pinker than ever.

'So she was the reason you fled from the banquet – no, don't deny it, you muttered her name as you left.'

Octavius flushed deeper yet, but his answer was spirited enough. 'What matter if I did? I was breaking no law. Phyllidia hoped to arrive yesterday, but she was so late that I had given her up. As it seems that Felix had done too: he said at the banquet that she was on her way.'

I remembered Marcus's description of the girl. 'A face like a cavalry horse and a whine like a donkey.' Yet something in the way in which Octavius spoke her name gave me the distinct impression that he had a much more flattering picture of her.

I made a stab at the truth. 'So you had arranged to meet

Phyllidia?' He did not deny it, so I pressed my advantage. 'Did her father know?'

'Her father? By Hercules . . .' It was as if I had lifted the boards from a sluice-gate. Octavius had previously said little, but now the words poured out in such a torrent that I found myself leaning backwards. He swore by all the gods of heaven and earth – and a few from the underworld as well – that her father was a tyrant, a monster in human form, heartless, unfeeling, merciless. 'If he is dead, so be it,' he finished angrily. 'It was no more than he deserved.' He bit savagely into his oatcake.

In general I received the feeling that young Octavius did not altogether care for Perennis Felix. 'I think, citizen,' I said slowly, 'that you had better tell me this story from the beginning. How did you come to meet Phyllidia?' It was a reasonable question. The daughters of Roman dignitaries do not normally consort with plebeian tile-makers.

Octavius shrugged. 'There was work to be done on the roof of one of Felix's villas. It is a few miles from Rome, not far from where I have my factory. I brought some tiles. Felix was not there, though I had devoted half a day to travelling at his request, but his daughter was. She received me kindly – very kindly. I think that she was glad to talk to someone. Do you know, citizen, the poor girl was almost a prisoner in that house. Felix dragged her away from the city, where she had at least acquaintances and diversions.'

'After the fall of her relative the Prefect?'

If he was surprised at my deduction he did not betray it. 'So he claimed. But I do not think Felix was ever in danger. He is too much a private favourite with the Emperor, and more interested in money than politics. Commodus would not willingly have lost him. He supplied too many boys and wines, and trinkets for that concubine of his.'

I nodded. Marcus had said the same. Felix would have

enjoyed finding the boys, I thought. 'Phyllidia did not like the country?'

Octavius's face darkened. 'If she had a life like any other young woman, she might have liked it well enough. But her father prevented it. After her mother died she had no companions, no diversions, not even proper attendants, only an old crone of a handmaiden who reported her every move. Felix would not even permit her an amanuensis to write letters to her friends, and she could not do it herself. She never had an education – though the old monster could well have afforded it, even for a daughter.'

'So, you and she became friends?'

'Much more than friends. If she had been a commoner, or a slave, I would have married her. I almost had hopes that Felix would countenance a match. He has tried for years to find a husband for her, without success, and she is no longer young. Even a marriage to me would have been something. I made an approach to him.'

'But he would not agree?'

'Agree? He beat her when he heard of it, threw me out and used his influence almost to ruin me. And yet I could not see what more he hoped for. Phyllidia is a good-natured girl, but she is no beauty and she lacks the sparkle and education necessary for patrician society. Thanks to her father, she cannot even play an instrument or recite the poets. She might have married once, when she was younger, but the suitor wanted a huge dowry, and her father was too miserly to meet it. I would have taken her with none.'

He said it with such simplicity that I was touched. I too, had once loved a woman in that way, although my Gwellia had been skilled, and such a beauty that a dozen men would have offered for her hand, whether she brought them land or horses or not. Besides, I reminded myself, this interest was not wholly selfless. Dowry or no dowry, Phyllidia would presumably inherit a sizeable fortune one day.

In fact, she was probably about to do so. I looked at Octavius with interest, but he was still grumbling about Felix.

'Some *auspex* had told him that Phyllidia would one day be wealthy and wed, and for once her father decided to believe the auguries. He tried to make a match for her with a dozen men, all rich and in their dotage – all seeking favour with the Perennis family, of course. But Phyllidia learned to be so stupid and sullen that even they refused her in the end. It was the only way she could protect herself. And then there was this plot to marry her to Marcus. The Emperor had approved it himself, Phyllidia said, and though she wept and pleaded, Felix was implacable.'

This was a new view of Phyllidia. Marcus would hardly be flattered either, I thought.

'Felix arranged a coach and a chaperon and paid an armed *custos* to accompany them. There was nothing Phyllidia could do. She was just another consignment of goods, she said, being delivered to the buyer. Felix was to go ahead to Britain – he had some private business in Eboracum – and she was to follow and meet up with him in Glevum.'

At the mention of the northern *colonia* my spine prickled. I had learned, not long ago, of a Celtic slave called Gwellia living in Eboracum. I said, 'So you followed her on horseback?' I could understand the impulse. Given the faintest opportunity, I would make the long and dangerous journey to Eboracum – and I could not even be sure that this Gwellia was my wife.

Octavius nodded. 'We were to make one more appeal to Felix, and if that failed, we had agreed . . . we threatened . . . But it is of no importance now. Her father is dead. And nobody poisoned him. So I must find Phyllidia and tell her the news. She has probably jumped to conclusions and is worrying about me.'

'Octavius,' I said, 'you are a freeman and a citizen, and I cannot detain you. But I will give you a warning. Be careful that tongue of yours does not betray you. There are sharp minds in Glevum, and Commodus will not be happy at this death. The authorities would gladly find a culprit. I do not know how you planned to poison Felix, though I can well see why. I sincerely hope for your sake that you did not succeed.'

Octavius stared at me. 'But . . . you said that Felix had merely choked.'

'I said that he appeared to choke, and for the moment I am prepared to let the public believe it. But there are some indications, citizen, that it may not be true.'

His stare widened 'You mean, he may have been poisoned after all? Dear gods!' Octavius put down his drinking vessel, and before either of us could stop him he had bolted for a second time out of the door.

Junio made to go after him, but I restrained him. 'Let him go, Junio. He has caused enough speculation in the street by calling here already. He will not get far.'

Junio picked up the drinking cup. 'You think he murdered Felix?'

I sipped at my water. 'I do not know. I think he fears he may have done. Either that, or he thinks he knows who did. But it is fruitless to call him back. He will tell us no more for the moment, and anyway, this way I can finish his oatcake and' – I gestured towards the drinking cup – 'you may drink the rest of that if you wish.'

Junio was raised as a slave in a Roman household, and he actually likes watered wine in the morning.

Chapter Nine

'Master,' Junio ventured, putting down the drinking vessel, 'it is not for me to suggest it, but Marcus . . .'

I got to my feet. 'I had not forgotten,' I said. 'I am to attend on him this morning. If you had awakened me earlier I would have done so by now. And then the arrival of Octavius delayed me further. So you can fetch me my toga, and help me to get ready. Marcus will be impatient as it is.'

It was unfair, of course. It was hardly Junio's fault that I had slept long after sun-up, and I regretted my rebuke. But he was grinning cheerfully as he brought in my toga and began to shake it vigorously to expel the dust. 'I have done my best with this, master, brushed it and hung it from the window to freshen it in the air, but I fear this toga really needs a visit to the fuller's.'

I stood up and he began the laborious business of folding me into it.

'Will you go directly to Marcus, or will you try to find Phyllidia first?'

He was reading my mind. I had been asking myself the same question. 'I must wait upon my patron. Though, since his orders are to meet him at Gaius's house, I suppose it is possible that I may do both things at the same time. It would be natural for her to come to the house where her father is.'

'Even,' Junio said impudently, 'when he is "already" dead. That was an interesting remark, did you not think?' He grinned at me. This was a game we sometimes played in my

83

efforts to train Junio in other skills than mosaic-making.

I adjusted my clasp. 'You noticed that?'

'I noticed that you noticed. And that you were suspicious of his early morning visit to the stables. And that made me think. He didn't go to hire a horse, or he would have had one now. So he must have had some other reason for going there. To meet someone, perhaps, or to find out what horses had been liveried there overnight. He did not go to interfere with the animals – he spoke to the stable-boy.'

I nodded my approval.

'Then I remembered what the cake-seller had said, and it seemed to make sense. He was expecting Phyllidia and went to see if her horses had arrived. He may even have arranged to meet her there, though I do not suppose he would confess as much to us.' Junio had been straightening my toga as he spoke, and now tucked the folded ends neatly into my belt. 'There, now I think you will pass muster with your patron. Unless you wish me to trim your chin? Your beard is reappearing.'

'There is not time this morning, I am late already. Fetch me my cloak.'

This time when he brought both cloaks I did not dissuade him, and when I set off a few moments later, scurrying as fast as my toga would allow, Junio was with me, following at my heels.

The town was already abuzz with the news. The words 'banquet', 'Perennis' and 'dead' seemed to issue from every street stall and soup kitchen. Huddles of citizens whispered together in doorways, while an enterprising street vendor was doing a brisk trade in selling long strips of dark cloth which could be tacked around the toga as mourning bands. Even a skinny peasant, touting his pathetic bundles of firewood, who had probably never seen a banquet nor heard of the late Prefect of Rome, offered to tell us 'the latest tidings' in the hope of earning a *quadrans*.

I tossed him a coin, but he had nothing new to add, except that an announcement of the death had been publicly read in the forum. That was interesting: it meant that the undertakers had finished their grisly task and what was left of Felix was now lying in state for three days in Gaius's atrium. Presumably even now the first high-minded citizens were calling to pay their respects to the Emperor's favourite.

Indeed, as we neared the house, we were joined by a customer of mine, one of the town magistrates for whom I had once built a pavement. He was wearing a proper mourning toga, with ashes on his head, and was carrying a gift. He looked askance at my toga and my empty hands. 'Greetings, citizen.' He sounded surprised. 'I did not expect to find my pavement-maker here. Are you going to attend the lying-in-state?'

I explained that I was going to meet my patron.

'Ah yes,' he said, 'poor Marcus. An unfortunate thing to happen in his jurisdiction. The Emperor will not be pleased. I believe they have already despatched a messenger to tell him – and one to the governor also. It is bad luck for Gaius, too. It cannot be comfortable having an old acquaintance drop dead under your roof.'

'Gaius knew Felix?' It was the first I'd heard of it.

My customer shook his head. 'Met him once years ago in Rome, or so the story goes. Jove knows if there is any truth in it – the city is full of rumour. It makes me uneasy. I shall attend the lying-in-state, one dare not show disrespect, but then I shall go straight to my country house and stay there till the repercussions are over. This death may have been an accident, but somebody, somewhere, will have to pay for it.'

We rounded a corner, to find a little spectacle awaiting us. The narrow street outside Gaius's door was all but impassable: a small crowd had gathered, all bearing small funerary gifts – no doubt each bearing the donor's name – and arguing fiercely about who should be admitted first. Even in death, I thought, Felix exerted influence. Most important men had opted to come themselves, instead of merely sending their slaves to represent them, and the question of precedence was a lively one.

I was surprised how many had come. Citizens had three whole days to pay their respects. Perhaps, like my customer, these men planned to leave the city as soon as they had done their duty. Three days was in any case an interesting choice of time, I thought. I know that in Rome public figures sometimes lie in state for twice as long as that, but around Glevum old beliefs die hard. Local superstition says that the spirit comes back from the afterworld after the third day if the body remains unburied. Whoever was arranging the funeral was obviously taking no chances with Felix.

I jostled my way through the throng. At first I made little progress, but Junio wriggled ahead of me, crying, 'Make way, in the name of Marcus Aurelius Septimus,' and the crowd parted like magic. Junio winked at me and I stepped smartly into the gap. Marcus's name still counted for something in the city.

People must have been rather surprised to see the humble citizen they had made way for, and even more surprised when the doorkeeper gave me a reluctant nod of recognition, and opened the door a fraction to let me in.

'His Excellence is in the *triclinium*,' he murmured. 'He asked that I send you to him. That slave will show you the way.' He gave me another withering glance, and turned back to the business of admitting the waiting mourners in some kind of appropriate order without scuffles breaking out in the process.

In the corridor I turned to Junio. 'Take this,' I said, unfastening my leather money-pouch from my belt. 'Go down into the forum and see what you can discover. Any news of Zetso or the red-whiskered Celt, make sure you bring it to me. Meet me here again when the sun is over the top of the basilica.'

Junio nodded. Doubtless the soldiers had already been through the town asking questions, but sometimes a slave can find out more by looking and listening than a centurion learns from wielding his baton. A good many *humiliores* have discovered that the safest way to deal with the military is to remember nothing, even if events have taken place before your eyes.

Junio went out again, to the astonishment of the door-keeper, while I followed the other slave into the depths of the house. It was an eerie experience. The plastered walls and tiled floors seemed to echo with unearthly wailing.

As we skirted the atrium, we could see the professional mourners gathered around the bed, some wailing on their instruments while others moaned and beat their chests in truly professional style. Their keening ululation hung in the air, heavy as the smoke and smell from the herbs and candles around the bier.

Two senior magistrates, looking embarrassed and furtive, had already made their required homage and were sneaking away. Felix, uglier than ever on his funeral couch, stared grimly into space, paying no attention to any of it. His expression was so baleful, even at this distance, that I was glad to reach the *triclinium*.

The dining room had been swept and cleansed. The additional tables had been spirited away, the painted screen partition doors were closed again, and only the customary three couches (from which the room gets its name) remained. The whole impression was of space and elegance. Only the burnt offerings still lying on the altar gave any reminder of the night before.

Marcus was lounging on one of the couches, talking to Gaius who was sitting despondently beside him. There was a small bowl of fruit before them – a sure sign that Marcus, too, had now done his share of ritual lamenting. Until he had fulfilled that rite it would not have been proper to eat. Both men looked up when I came in.

'Libertus,' Marcus said sharply, extending a ringed hand in my direction. 'I expected you earlier.'

I bent low over the ring. 'Your pardon, Excellence. I was visited this morning by a young man from Rome. I met him here last night. He tells me Gaius invited him.'

If I hoped to startle the old man I was disappointed. Gaius shook his head mournfully. 'That young tradesman with the hairy hands? Yes, I invited him. He arrived here yesterday demanding to speak to Felix – part of the party from Rome, he said. I would have turned him away but he showed me a letter with the Perennis seal. I hardly knew what to do with him, so I asked him to the feast. Thought he could squat on a stool at the lowest table. He came, did he? I did not notice him. Nor hear him announced.'

When I came to think of it, neither had I. Octavius's late arrival had coincided with the religious sacrifices, so the name had not been announced. And he had sat opposite to me, with his back towards the top table. Had that been deliberate, or a happy accident? 'The young man left the feast early.'

Gaius got to his feet. 'Like the driver and that Celtic fellow with the whiskers,' he said heavily. 'Sensible men. I wish I'd had the courage to do the same. I might have saved him.' He shook his head hopelessly. 'Dead. So suddenly. And under my own roof. I cannot believe it. This has been a shock to me, you know. A terrible shock.'

It had. Manifestly so. Gaius was looking pale and hollow-cheeked, his face stricken, and his old eyes filled with genuine pain. This was no public ritual of mourning, this grief was sincere. I remembered what my customer had said. Perhaps, when Gaius knew him in Rome, Felix had possessed some redeeming qualities. I murmured, 'I am sorry. I did not realise. He was . . . a good friend?'

'More than a friend,' Gaius said. 'More like . . . a brother. A son almost.'

I tried to imagine what had endeared the swarthy Felix to the heart of this gentle old man, and failed. 'Citizen—' I began, but he interrupted me.

'I hear that there is talk of commissioning a mosaic from you in the public square.'

That sounded hopeful. 'I believe so.' I glanced at Marcus but he was peeling fruit impassively with the heavy knife from his belt. 'A small memorial pavement, perhaps, on the rostrum to mark the spot where the body lay?'

It was the obvious place. In big civic funerals the litter is always rested on a public platform during the last procession, so that the common people can gawp at it while an orator makes an uplifting funeral address. A small circular mosaic there would show respect without impinging on the landscape. Yet as soon as I made the suggestion I regretted it. I had forgotten how close that mosaic would be to the spot where the fractured corpse of Marcus's herald had been.

But Gaius was thinking of other things. 'Well,' he said urgently, 'when you have finished that mosaic, you can build another one for me. Here, in the *triclinium*, where he lay. Take up the geometric border at this end and replace it with something appropriate. Something to remind me of him. You will give me a price?'

I was astonished. I had hardly come here expecting to be offered commissions. But I knew a good offer when I heard one. 'I should be delighted to accept your commission, citizen. But I shall need advice. You speak of designing "something appropriate". What motif would you think suitable for a memorial to Perennis Felix?'

Gaius looked at me as though the gods had addled my wits. 'Perennis Felix? The man was a tyrant and a bully and death is too good for him. He was a curse in Rome and he has brought a curse to my house again. He can rot forgotten in the afterworld, or be fed to Cerberus for anything I care. I do not want a memorial to Felix, I want a memorial pavement for my dog.'

And, shaking his head sadly, as though to rid himself of the wailing and drumming which reached us from the atrium, he bowed his head to Marcus and walked slowly from the room.

Chapter Ten

After the aged magistrate had gone, there was a silence. Marcus continued cutting his apple with his knife and spearing little pieces of it into his mouth. I said nothing. I recognised from the furrowed brow that my patron was thinking.

At last Marcus spoke. 'I fear for that man, Libertus. He is crazed with grief. Cursing at Felix in that vicious way when this catastrophe has occurred beneath his roof.'

I nodded. 'It seems unwise of him,' I said carefully. 'The Emperor will have paid ears and eyes everywhere.'

'Precisely.' Marcus stabbed the last morsel of fruit and swallowed it. 'I am surprised. Gaius may be ineffectual, but he has always had a peculiarly shrewd instinct for keeping out of trouble. That's why he was so successful in business. Now, though, he seems to have lost all care for his own safety. He is concerned only about his dog.'

I did not know Gaius well enough to comment, but it seemed the old man had been behaving uncharacteristically throughout this whole affair. And, I recollected suddenly, he had given Felix some kind of concoction the night before, claiming it was a remedy. I did not, however, remind Marcus of this. He would have insisted on taking the old man under guard immediately, with two effects: rumours of murder would be all over Glevum by nightfall and I would never get a chance to question Gaius myself.

I changed the subject. 'I assume Zetso and Egobarbus have not been found, Excellence?'

'Not *yet* been found,' Marcus corrected me. 'It can only be a matter of time. We have alerted the soldiers at the town gate since daybreak and no one answering to either description has been seen trying to leave the city. They are both distinctive enough, and last night the gates were shut. They must still be somewhere in Glevum. We shall find them.' He looked at me sharply. 'You think they are together?'

It was not an idea that had occurred to me. It should have done. 'I suppose, Excellence . . .' I began, but Marcus was ahead of me.

'You are very shrewd, Libertus. We should not have overlooked that possibility. If we are looking for a flamboyant dark-haired soldier and a red-headed Celt, we might overlook two drab dark-haired civilians in tunics – although that red moustache would be memorable enough in any context.'

'Perhaps it is too memorable, Excellence,' I said. 'A moustache is not like a beard – an expert can remove it with two strokes of the blade. Yet it draws the eye. Without his plaid cloak and his moustache, can you recall what this so-called Egobarbus looked like?'

Marcus looked contemptuous for a moment. 'Of course. He was . . . he was . . . he was red-headed and a little more than my height,' he finished lamely. 'Yes, my old friend, I do see what you mean. That description could fit a dozen strangers who come and go in the city every day. There are a lot of red-headed Silurians on the western borders.' He gestured to the elderly attendant who had been hovering at the door awaiting instructions. 'You! Find me a messenger. Someone fleet of foot. I want to send new orders to the gates.'

The slave vanished at once in search of an errand boy, and Marcus turned back to me. 'And you, Libertus, what do you propose? I should like, if I can, to get to the bottom of this affair before news reaches the Emperor. I do not trust

Perennis Felix, and we may be in murky waters.' He wiped his knife-blade on the linen napkin and sheathed it again at his belt. 'You have my permission to question anyone. Discreetly, of course, but if there is trouble you may refer them to me. I shall stay here, in case the guards manage to arrest Zetso, or that confounded Celt for that matter.'

'Arrest them, Excellence? On what charge? With great respect, I must remind you that there is no public suggestion of a crime. Better, I think, to be seeking Zetso urgently simply to tell him of his master's death; and the Celt too. Felix had important business with him, I heard him say so. More than one person left the feast early and we do not want to suggest that there is anything suspicious about the death. Rumour would reach the Emperor.'

Marcus had been looking rather sullen but that remark roused him, as I hoped it would. 'Dear Jupiter, greatest and best! We cannot allow that. Yes, you are right. My words were ill-considered. Of course they will not be arrested – merely brought here to be informed of the news, and to perform appropriate mourning.' He got to his feet. 'Now, where will you begin? In the forum perhaps, to see what can be learned?'

I was being dismissed. I said, carefully, 'I think, Excellence, I would prefer to begin in the house. I have already sent Junio to ask questions in the town.'

Marcus waved a vague hand. 'Whatever you wish. Although I doubt that you will learn anything. Gaius and I have already spoken to the servants. Zetso went out during the entertainments saying his master had sent him, and nobody saw Egobarbus after the death. However, you are welcome to try. Once I have sent that message to the gates, I am going to the *librarium*, where Gaius has promised to furnish me with a slave and writing materials. I have letters to write.'

It was none of my business, but I asked, 'To Pertinax?'

'Of course.' Marcus smiled. 'And to my mother, too. Telling

her that I have done her bidding at last, and found myself a wife.'

'Speaking of that, Excellence,' I said, 'did you know that Felix's daughter was in Glevum? Apparently she arrived too late to be admitted last night, and spent the night in a rooming house outside the walls.'

Marcus looked at me without interest. 'More than that, she is here in this house. She arrived while I was lamenting by the body. She had not heard of her father's death, and had to be given a glass of strong wine and helped upstairs to lie down. When she is recovered, she will change into mourning clothes and come to make her own lament.'

So, I thought, Octavius had not managed to find her. 'Then you have not spoken to her yourself?'

Marcus shook his head irritably. 'No. I believe Gaius received her. Of course, it will be a double blow to her – finding she has lost her prospective husband as well as her father.'

I thought of what Octavius had said. It was possible that Phyllidia would be consolable – on both counts. It would have been tactless, however, to say that to Marcus. Instead I took a deep breath and said simply, 'Under whose jurisdiction will she be, Excellence, now that Felix is dead?'

It was daring. Marcus was clearly anxious to be gone. But it was a reasonable question. A woman, like a child, is not legally responsible for her own affairs: many women are wealthy and some effectively manage large estates, but they are still officially under the guardianship of a father or a husband or some other legally appointed male who can represent them in the courts. Marcus, for instance, was named Delicta's guardian in her husband's will.

I added, humbly, 'I wondered if Felix had appointed someone for Phyllidia. You, perhaps, since he wished you to be her husband.'

Marcus gave me a startled look. 'I have no idea. His will is presumably in Rome, so it will be some time before it can be read.'

I pressed my advantage. 'In the meantime, who is to act for her? Both her parents are dead, and all her relatives were executed when the Prefect fell.'

He frowned. 'I suppose, since she must have a guardian, we will have to ask the *praetor* to appoint one. It will have to be a senior magistrate in Glevum. Gaius perhaps, since this is his mansion – otherwise, I suppose, the duty would fall on me. Great Mars, Libertus, you do raise the most appalling ideas! Have you seen the girl? She is as plain as a sheep – and now, I suppose, it will be my duty to find her a husband.'

I thought of Octavius and smiled. 'It is possible, Excellence, that I can help you there. The young man who visited me this morning is very anxious to wed her, plain as a sheep or not. He is not a rich man, but with her father's death she does have a large dowry.' Which her guardian would have temporary administration of, although I did not voice that.

Marcus gazed at me thoughtfully. 'Perhaps you are right, Libertus. It is my duty to act for her in this way. And if there is a suitor, so much the better. Of course, she cannot marry him at once – it would not be seemly, her father being so newly dead.'

So the management of those estates appealed to him. I tried not to grin. 'Of course,' I said gravely, 'once the will is read . . .'

He saw the force of that. If there was a *querela* lodged – quoting the will and contesting what the guardian had done – it might well be a very costly business. Such lawsuits often result in the whole inheritance ending up in the imperial pockets. Much better to pass the girl – and her presumed estates – on to a husband as soon as possible.

Marcus nodded irritably. 'Yes, yes. Well, time enough to think of that when the funeral is over. Come in!' This to the elderly slave, who by now had returned to the doorway with a young page, and was fidgeting there, unwilling to interrupt. Behind them, tiptoeing towards us past the atrium, I could see Junio, back from his mission in the forum.

He was looking upset.

I excused myself from Marcus and went to meet my slave. He gestured me towards an alcove in the corridor and we stood there for a moment while the page scampered past us and out into the street, where some kind of commotion was taking place.

'You have news?' I said, rather unnecessarily. Junio's face was the colour of my toga – a sort of muddy white.

He nodded, gulping, and I saw to my distress that there were tears in his eyes.

'Junio,' I said urgently, 'what is it? What are they saying in the forum? Are they accusing me? Or Marcus?' Either of those things might put me in danger, I thought, and that would distress the boy.

Junio shook his head. 'No, master,' he said, and his voice was trembling. 'There is not much news of the men you were seeking. Plenty of rumour, but nothing one can trust – only that Egobarbus's carriage arrived at the North Gate and not from the south, as one might have expected. Zetso has not been seen, except in your company, since he was flirting with the soldiers at the town gate yesterday. Oh, and the herald's body has been staked out near the forest, out on the Isca road.'

Like all slaves everywhere, he was doing his duty, reporting to me the matters I had asked him to investigate. The real news, which he was bursting to tell me, had to wait until he had discharged that obligation.

'Well done, Junio,' I said, putting him out of his misery.

'And what is the other information which is breaking your heart?'

He looked at me sorrowfully. 'It concerns Julia Delicta, your patron's wife.' He sighed. 'You remember the bald-headed slave, the girl who was bought for her hair and then shaven?'

'I do.' I had been about to add 'and with whom you had a forbidden flirtation' but a look at Junio's face persuaded me that this was no time for teasing banter. 'Go on.'

'She went out this morning, early,' Junio said, 'to choose some new material for a *stola* . . . Delicta, that is, not the slave. She was in a state of high excitement – anxious to come to Glevum, and wanting everything new for her new role. She took her handmaidens with her – or rather they followed her litter – to shop and fetch and carry and take her purchases home. And that was how it happened. She was so long returning that they sent a slave to look for her. They found the body lying in an alley, beside the litter, and one of the litter-bearers lying with her in a pool of blood. They had both been stabbed and all the purchases were stolen.'

I was gazing at him in horror. 'Delicta is dead?'

He swallowed. 'Not Delicta, master. She is here. She left everything, at once, and came directly to Glevum. I saw the hired carriage outside Marcus's apartment. That was how I learned of this – one of the servants told me.'

'Then who . . .' I said, but I did not need to ask.

'It was Rosita, master,' and now he made no attempt to hide the tears. 'The bald-headed slave. Stabbed in the back and left to bleed to death. When they found her, the dogs were sniffing at her . . . Oh, master!'

It is not accepted behaviour in the best of circles, but I could not help it. I put out my arm and held the lad to me. 'We will find him, Junio, whoever it was who did it. As soon as I have finished this investigation here, I promise you we will go and find him.'

I spoke with such intensity that a smartly uniformed slave, coming in with a gift of fresh candles for the death-room, turned to stare at me in amazement.

Junio pulled himself together with an effort. 'Perhaps you will. Delicta has come to Glevum on purpose to petition Marcus to find him.'

I released him. 'Delicta is upset?'

'She is very angry. The slave was her property, she says, and cost a lot of money. The hair was almost ready to cut, and now the girl is worthless. To say nothing of the purchases that were taken. Some were worth even more than the slave. The thief must be found, Delicta says, and made to pay the fine.'

He said it bitterly, as if he resented that his lady friend was of less value than a length of material.

I said, 'It will not be easy to find him. I presume it was a man? A pity no one caught a glimpse of him.'

'But that is just it, master. Perhaps someone did. A man called at the back gate of Delicta's house this morning, asking for the lady of the house. He was told that she was absent, in the town. He was hooded and cloaked, and disappeared before the gatekeeper could question him, but he got a glimpse of the face. Delicta has brought the gatekeeper with her, to tell his story to Marcus.'

'Do you know what he says?'

'That the caller was young and dark with an apologetic manner. He left a length of silk for Delicta. He said it was a marriage gift.'

'A marriage gift? Who knew of the marriage?'

Junio shrugged. 'I asked the same thing, master, but it seems the story is all over the town. The witnesses at the ceremony . . .'

I nodded. News travels quickly in the provinces. 'A local man, then?'

'Perhaps not, master. The gatekeeper had never seen him before. And he spoke with an unfamiliar accent. Of course, the two events may not be connected. The man who made the attack may not be the same man who came to the back gate. But it is coincidental, don't you think?'

'First Marcus is present at a death in Glevum,' I said slowly, 'and the next morning someone makes an attack upon his wife – or someone who resembles his wife most strikingly from the rear. You haven't seen your bald-headed slave recently, Junio. The colour of her hair is most unusual – and Delicta wears a wig of it. It seems to me to be too much of a coincidence – two deaths so close to Marcus within so short a time.'

Even so, I had failed to notice one most important thing. And I was wrong about the deaths. There were not two of them, but three. I had forgotten the death of the litter-bearer.

I felt badly about that later, when I realised it. But it was easy to do. After all, he was only a slave.

In the meantime, I turned to my own servant. 'Junio, I must begin my enquiries. I shall go and see Gaius, on the pretext of talking about pavements. He has gone to his study. You will find me there. But first you should go and warn Marcus that his wife is waiting for him.'

I left him to it, and found a slave to take me to the *librarium*.

Chapter Eleven

I followed the servant up the stairs to where Gaius had his study. It was unusual not to have the *librarium* downstairs among the public rooms, but the design of this house, with its three large interconnecting reception rooms downstairs, presumably didn't leave room for that. Today, too, this arrangement had particular advantages: it put a staircase and a narrow corridor between the study and the dreadful wailing issuing from the atrium.

The slave tapped on the door, and I entered at Gaius's 'Come in.'

The old man was standing by a fine stone-topped table on which a series of wax tablets and *stili*, and even a length of costly fine scraped bark (of the kind used for legal documents), had been set out. He was clearly supervising the activities of a pair of slaves, one of whom appeared to be mixing octopus ink with ashes in a glass dish, while the other prepared a series of reed and feather pens. Obviously only the best and costliest equipment was to be provided for Marcus and his letters.

When he saw me, Gaius looked surprised. 'Your pardon, citizen. I was expecting your patron.'

I nodded. 'He will be here shortly. He has been delayed. It seems his wife has arrived from Corinium.'

I decided not to mention the dead slaves, but changed the subject. I nodded towards the table. 'When he does come I know he will appreciate your generosity. No one could ask for finer writing materials.'

Gaius looked pleased. 'I could hardly do less,' he said gallantly. 'For *Marcus*, nothing is a trouble.'

There was something about the way in which he emphasised the name which made the two slaves exchange glances.

'Most revered and senior citizen,' I said, according him the full dignity of his magisterial office, 'I wonder . . . a word with you in private?' He looked about to demur, and I added quickly, 'Marcus has given his approval.'

Gaius frowned, but he waved his hand in dismissal and the two slaves hurried off. 'Well?'

'It has been suggested, Reverence,' I began hesitantly, 'that . . . Felix . . . It is clear that you do not share the Emperor's extreme regard for him.' I was choosing my words with the greatest care. If I upset Gaius now, the results could be very uncomfortable – especially if I seemed to criticise anyone.

I need not have worried. Gaius heaved a deep sigh. 'That brute!' he said. 'No, I have no opinion of him at all. He was a cheat and a bully, and I cannot pretend that I am sorry he is dead.'

I tried again. 'Are you quite wise, your Honour, to make your feelings so clear? The Emperor will certainly have spies in the town, and people will talk, accident or not.'

For a moment the old man bridled. 'Do you dare to tell me . . .' and then thought better of it. 'No,' he said, 'perhaps you are right. I should guard my tongue. I should never have dared to be so outspoken when he was alive. I should have seen that he was just as dangerous dead.'

'You know something of Perennis Felix?' I suggested hesitantly. 'More than the rest of us, that is?'

Gaius looked at me. 'Beyond that he was a thieving, brutal rogue who would do anything for money? What else is there to know?'

'But you lent him your house?'

Gaius grimaced. 'What choice did I have? My house is often borrowed when a dignitary comes. It would have been too pointed to refuse this time. Felix would have learned of it, and then I should have suffered. Felix was an expert at revenge.' He smiled ruefully. 'Although I did try. I put a piece of rotting fish in the latrine and suggested the drains were offensive. It did me no good. My objections were simply overruled. I had to send one of the servants down this morning to get it out again.'

I had to smile at this inventive ruse. No wonder that area of the cellar had smelled so unwholesome. I was so encouraged by the confidence that I ventured a little further. 'It was suggested that you might have met Felix once before, in Rome.'

At once every vestige of friendliness vanished. It was as if someone had pinched out a wick. He said coldly, 'I do not know who told you that, or on what authority. I assure you, pavement-maker, I never set eyes upon the man before in my life. Nor wished to either. Now, if there is nothing more I can do to help you . . .?'

'I wished to speak to you about this pavement, your Honour,' I babbled, but it was too late. Not even discussion of his beloved dog could thaw the chill in his manner, and he was so dismissive that I began to fear that I had talked myself out of a lucrative commission.

In the end I abandoned it. 'Perhaps we can speak of this later, citizen,' I suggested, acknowledging defeat.

'Perhaps,' he said, stonily, and I was left to bow myself miserably out, while the slaves waiting outside looked at me knowingly and smirked. I was not even accorded the dignity of an escort down the stairs. Gaius summoned them again, and they went back into the study.

My discomfited retreat, however, was not without

advantage. As I made my way towards the staircase, the door opposite was opened from within by an aged maidservant, and a moment later I found myself face to face with the woman she had opened it for – a small, round woman of such strikingly unprepossessing appearance that it could only be the famous Phyllidia.

She was, as Marcus had so succinctly put it, as plain as a sheep. I could see why that expression had occurred to him. The woman had a wide, flat, determined face with small eyes, a long nose, a foolish chin and a generally ewe-like expression of amiable truculence. Not unlike a sheep's, either, were the short locks of coarse and hennaed hair escaping from under the unfashionable band and curling in defiant tufts around her forehead.

She was dressed for mourning in a dark dun-coloured robe which did nothing to enhance her radiance, and she carried a black mourning veil in her hand, ready to cover her face and head. An unkind man might think that an advantage – the ashes on her forehead only emphasised the sallowness of her complexion, and all the white-lead powder upon her face could not disguise a certain redness about the eyes.

She was accompanied by the aged handmaiden bearing an oil-lamp, and I recognised – from her manner and sour expression – that this must be the female jailer and family spy that Octavius had described. The hand of Felix still extended here. Yet, plain as she was, there was nothing of her father about Phyllidia: none of the malice, self-regard and cruelty which had declared itself in his every movement. For that reason, if no other, I gave her an encouraging smile.

'You are Phyllidia Tigidia?'

She looked at me blankly. 'I am.' She did not even ask me who I was. I guessed that she was accustomed to being questioned at every step. 'I am going to take my turn at the vigil.'

I did not move aside to let her pass, as she evidently expected. Instead I said, 'This must have been a dreadful shock for you.'

'Of course.' It was said without emotion, and there was no flicker of feeling on her face. Yet, surely, this woman had been taken faint at the news, and had to be half carried upstairs to lie down?

I made another attempt. 'You cared deeply for your father?'

This time there was the suspicion of a flush on the wide cheeks, and a fleeting shadow of a bitter smile. 'Is there not always feeling between father and child? Thank you for your sympathy, pavement-maker.'

So she did know who I was. I said, 'You know who I am?'

'I heard that a pavement-maker was expected. I was mistaken for you, briefly, at the door. When I saw you coming out of Gaius's study, in a plain toga and with calloused hands, the rest was not hard to deduce.' It was intended to put me in my place. 'Now, if you will excuse me, citizen.' She stepped forward, and I was obliged to fall back and let her pass, together with her triumphant handmaiden.

But I had one spear left in my armoury. The girl was more intelligent than I thought, and she did not altogether despise tradesmen, as I knew. As she set foot upon the staircase, I murmured, so that only she could hear, 'I have seen Octavius.'

She stopped. There was no mistaking the emotion now. Her whole face came alive, as though someone had lighted a candle in her eyes. She did not turn her head, but simply said firmly, 'Marida, you may leave us. Give me the lamp.'

The maidservant hesitated.

'You heard me,' Phyllidia said. 'Give me the lamp and go. Wait for me in the bedchamber. I have business with this citizen. Do it now. And do not lick your lips in that fashion. My father is dead – he will not pay you for your tales now.'

Marida sighed deeply but obeyed.

When the slave was out of earshot, Phyllidia turned to me. 'You have seen Octavius?'

'He was here last night,' I said. 'Looking for you, I think.'

She met my eyes, not the shy, sideways glance of the well-brought-up Roman virgin, but a frank enquiring stare. Yet there was something in the brown eyes which gave me hope for Octavius. If this was a sheep, it was at least a clever sheep. 'He is alive? And well?'

It seemed a strange question. 'He was, no more than an hour ago. Although he was strangely uneasy. He seemed to have been looking for you in the hiring stables. Then he learned where you had stayed last night and went rushing away to search for you.'

She closed her eyes. 'Great goddess Minerva, thanks be to your name!' She raised her voice. 'Marida!'

The old woman came out, so swiftly that I guessed she had been listening at the door. Phyllidia unclasped a jewel from her belt and handed it to the maid.

'Take this. Go into the town and find a temple of Minerva. Speak to the priest and see that he places this on the altar as a thank-offering.'

The crone stared at it doubtfully. It was a fine gem.

'Do it now,' Phyllidia said. 'I vowed it to the goddess if she heard my prayer. And be sure that I shall learn of it if you don't. I shall be speaking to the priests later, about the funeral. You know the punishment for theft – especially from the temple. You understand?'

Marida nodded sullenly.

'Then,' Phyllidia continued, 'when you have done that, you will go and find Octavius for me. Yes, Octavius. If this citizen is correct, he will be searching the inn for me. And no excuses that you could not find him. Do not return without him, or I will have you flogged. Do not suppose that I would not. I am the mistress now. Ask him to come here. I will meet him when I have done my duty by the corpse. And tell him . . . tell him all is well. Whatever he has done.'

She took the oil-lamp from the startled maid, and disappeared downstairs in the direction of the atrium. The servant shot me a venomous look, then shrugged her shoulders and trotted reluctantly after her mistress.

I watched them go. I did not follow them at once, but stood for a moment thinking about the events of the last twenty-four hours: the deaths, the disappearances, the marriage and the would-be-marriages. Yet Phyllidia appeared to have arrived here not with bridal dresses but with garments suitable for a funeral. How, I wondered, had she contrived that? It did not seem to make sense.

As I groped my own way down the stairs a moment later I heard Phyllidia's voice, strong and untroubled, raised in the lament.

Chapter Twelve

I returned to the entrance corridor, expecting to find Junio, but there was no sign of him.

The doorkeeper came out of his alcove, with its spy-hole looking out into the street, and scowled at me sourly. 'If you are looking for that skinny young slave of yours, he's gone. Sent out by Marcus Aurelius Septimus with a message to his wife.'

I cursed inwardly. Marcus had slaves of his own, and there were servants of Gaius, too, whom he might have sent on trivial errands. I had only the one slave, and my patron chose to send him – simply because he had been the message-bearer, no doubt. That was my fault; I should not have let Junio carry the news of Julia's arrival himself.

'Well,' the doorkeeper demanded. 'Are you going out or not? I'm opening and closing this door like a bridegroom's toga as it is.'

'I think,' I said slowly, 'that there is little else I can do here, for the moment.'

His hand went to the heavy lock.

'Unless there is anything you can tell me? About the disappearance of Zetso and the Celt last night?'

He sighed. 'I have told your patron all this. And my master, too. Felix's driver went rushing in and out several times, on missions for his master. The last time he didn't come back.'

'Several times?' I queried. 'How often was that. Twice? Three times?'

The doorkeeper glared at me as though he were a trident-holder in the arena, and I was the netman sent to trap him. 'Great Jupiter, citizen, I can't tell you exactly. I was letting people in and out of this door all night. How can I be expected to remember the movements of a single slave? About the Celtic gentleman, though, I am quite certain. He and his party came in through that door, like everyone else, but he didn't go out of it again. I would have remembered him.'

'His party?' I had not considered that. Of course, Egobarbus – or whoever he was – since he was a wealthy man, would presumably have arrived with slaves, 'like everyone else' as the doorman said. 'He had servants with him?'

'Oh yes. Two – or was it three – big strapping fellows in tunics. Three, I am almost sure.'

This was interesting news. One man may disappear. A group of three of four men is more difficult to hide. 'The servants must have left again, too?'

His scowl deepened. 'Do you think I am Janus, citizen, to remember the comings and goings of every slave? I don't know.'

I reached into the money-pouch at my belt, took out a coin and began fingering it ostentatiously. It is amazing how the prospect of an *as* or two can sometimes improve the memory.

He did his best. 'They probably went out afterwards, when there was a general rush for litters. I rather think they did.' He eyed the coin hopefully, but I made no move. 'I am almost sure.'

This was no use. The man would swear to anything for a reward. I tossed him the coin. 'If you think of anything, tell Marcus,' I said. 'I am going out now, but I will return.'

The man opened the door and I went out into the street. The air was cool and fresh after the heavy smoke of the funeral herbs and candles, but the crowd awaiting their turn at the lying-in-state had increased. Several of the magistrates, I noted, had left their slaves to do their waiting for them and gone away to do other things, but my former customer was still there. I avoided his reproachful gaze and sidled away down a side street.

I had thought, vaguely, of presenting myself at Marcus's apartment, but I thought better of it. My patron would expect me to have made some progress before I reported to him again. Then I remembered what Junio had told me and, avoiding the unwanted attentions of the fortune-tellers, money-lenders and beggars who always lurk in the less frequented streets, I made my way across the town to the North Gate.

Somebody there had obviously remembered Egobarbus's arrival, since Junio had heard about it.

I looked around for a suitable informant. There was no shortage of candidates. Tinkers, hawkers and doubtful medicine peddlers spread their wares at the foot of every pillar, and the usual grimy scoundrel with his pretended viper was performing his tricks to the astonishment of the innocent.

However, compared to my servant, I was at a disadvantage. Everyone expects a slave to indulge in gossip – who has come to the town, and who has left – since his livelihood may well depend upon tips and disbursements given in exchange for information. For a citizen – even an elderly citizen in a scruffy toga – to begin asking questions about a visitor is to invite immediate interest. Already the guards at the gate were looking at me suspiciously.

Outside the gates, in the straggle of buildings close to the walls, there was a *thermopolium*, a hot-food stall, selling hot drinks and questionable stew. I went through the archway and made my way towards that. These places are always hives of rumour. At the price of a bowl of greasy soup – in which goat's hooves and something else's eyeballs appeared to be important ingredients – I might find the information I was looking for.

'Ooh, yes,' the girl behind the counter said, pocketing the proffered coin with a grimy hand, 'I see everything from here, citizen.' She tossed her head, so that her long unwashed braids of hair swung treacherously close to the serving ladle, and favoured me with what she probably imagined was an inviting smile. It would have been more alluring, had she possessed a few more teeth.

'You saw the red-haired Celt arrive here yesterday?' I prompted.

'Fellow with red hair and long whiskers? Of course I did. You could hardly miss him. There was such a fuss about the carriage. It almost came to blows. The driver said he hadn't been paid, although he had been promised I don't know how much to drive halfway from Letocetum, collect them from an inn and bring them here.'

'Letocetum?' I was surprised. I had never been to Letocetum, but I had heard of it. An important staging post for the imperial army, a day's ride north-west on the road to Eboracum. Interesting, I thought. Eboracum was the town which Felix had been visiting on business.

'That's where the driver came from. I heard him tell them so, when they were arguing about the price.' She twined her greasy hair with a greasier hand.

'Them?' I said, seizing on a word. 'How many of them were there?'

The girl smiled again, showing her blackened gums. Unmarriageable, I guessed, and eking out a meagre living providing hot food for unsuspecting travellers and probably other services for any soldiers who had gambled too much of their pay and were no longer very particular.

'Only the man and his two servants,' she said. 'Funny that you should mention that. The carriage-driver kept insisting that he should have been paid for four. He threatened to fetch the *aediles*, but the Celt gave him a few *denarii* and he calmed down in the end.'

'He did?' I was surprised.

'Oh yes. The Celt changed his tune very quickly when he was threatened with the law. He couldn't hand over the money fast enough. And he promised to bring him the rest this evening. Apparently he was owed a lot of money by that Roman notable who died at the feast.' She grinned gummily and settled her tattered garment across her skinny hips. 'I don't suppose either of them will see their money now. A man must live while he can, don't you think, citizen?'

The conversation was taking an uncomfortable turn. I did not like the way she was nodding towards the squalid curtained recess at the rear of the shop. I abandoned all thoughts of learning any more, and put down my bowl hastily. 'Thank you,' I said, 'that was helpful.' And I hurried away.

'But, citizen,' she called out after me, 'you have not tasted your soup.'

'Another time,' I lied, and hastened back through the gate into the town.

The guard on duty winked wickedly at me. 'No time for your soup, citizen? I'm surprised at you. Forget how late it was, did you?'

I knew what he was thinking and felt myself flush in embarrassment. The man must think me desperate to resort to such extremes. Nevertheless, it had given me an opportunity. Roman guards are usually grim-faced and silent. This one was grinning widely, and, thinking he had me at a disadvantage, seemed willing to talk.

I glanced over my shoulder. The girl had gone back to her stall and was pouring the remains of the soup back into the cooking pot. I improvised wildly. 'I came here looking for my slave,' I said, sending up a mental plea to Junio for forgiveness. 'But she doesn't seem to have seen him.'

The guard shrugged. 'He won't have come here. She doesn't deal with slaves – unless they simply want a bowl of soup. Even if they had the money, which they mostly don't. Too much trouble if they are caught. No, she sticks to soldiers – auxiliaries mostly, they never have any money – and occasionally visitors to the city if they are short of cash and are not too fussy.'

I saw an opening, and took it. 'Like that red-headed fellow with the whiskers who turned up here yesterday? The one who had an argument with his coachman?'

The soldier grinned. 'You heard about that? I did not see it myself, I was not on duty at the time, but it was the talk of the barracks. Turned up in a hired coach, apparently, with not enough money to pay the driver, and then claimed he had business with Perennis Felix. We took him in for questioning, and locked him up for an hour, but it seems he was telling the truth. He insisted that we send a message to Felix, and the next thing we heard he was being invited to a civic banquet.'

I found myself grinning. 'So your commander let him go?'

'Quicker than Jove can hurl lightning. Did you see that Perennis Felix? And this man was an associate of his. We were expecting at any moment to be punished for our presumption. But who could possibly have supposed that the story was true? The man was half barbarian. He hardly spoke Latin, and could barely use an abacus. I saw him at the barracks when they brought him in. One cannot imagine why a wealthy Roman would have dealings with him.'

'I understand there is tin and copper involved,' I said carefully.

The soldier shrugged. 'That is what he said. Though he

refused to answer any of our questions, even when we threatened him. He simply said that Felix would vouch for him. Which in the end he did.' He grinned. 'Our chief of guard nearly prostrated himself with apology.'

'So you would have noticed if the man had passed the gate again?'

'Noticed? Great Mars! I think our commander would have come down and escorted him through it personally.' He grinned again. 'I suppose we should have guessed he was important. A man who can afford to indulge his private vanities like that is clearly a person to be reckoned with.'

'He certainly looked singular,' I said. 'In that plaid and that moustache.'

'Well, one sees that sort of thing often enough,' the guard remarked. 'In Isca, on the border, if not here. A lot of those peculiar Celts still wear their outlandish tribal fashions. No, what attracted my attention was the slaves. Apparently he has always done it. One of our centurions was posted in the south-west and he had heard of it before.'

'Always done what?'

'Surrounded himself with red-headed servants.'

The answer startled me. I tried to think back to the household of Egobarbus as I once knew it. There were red-headed servants, certainly, among them – as there always are when a vigorous leader keeps female slaves. But there were others with hair of every hue, and there was certainly no policy of any kind. Although, when I came to think of it, it was exactly the sort of petty tyranny the real Egobarbus would have delighted in.

I came back to the present, to find the guard staring at me. The friendly manner had gone and his voice was crisp as he lowered his spear and pointed it lazily in the direction of my vitals.

'And you, citizen? What is your interest in this Celt? You

are asking a lot of questions. You seem to know what he looked like. And yet you did not know about the servants? How do you explain that?'

It was a moment to exercise what little rank I had. 'I saw him at the banquet last night,' I said. 'I was a guest myself.' I saw the guard's jaw drop with incredulity. It would have been comic if it were not so serious. I pressed my advantage. 'And I have some property which belongs to him. His plaid cloak. He left it behind in a cupboard. And,' I added quickly as he made a lunge towards me, 'before you suggest locking me up in my turn, I recommend that you apply to Marcus Aurelius Septimus. He is my patron, and I am acting on his orders.'

The spear-point hesitated for a moment, and then moved aside. 'Your pardon, citizen,' the guard said. 'I did not realise. You do not look like a . . . Your toga . . .' He tailed off.

I stepped past the spear into the comparative safety of the city. 'No,' I murmured, 'that is the trouble with the peculiar Celts. Sometimes we wear the most outlandish tribal costumes.'

But, having a lively respect for Roman guards with spears, I didn't say it loudly enough for anyone to hear.

Chapter Thirteen

As I made my way back through the town I was not displeased with my progress. I knew the direction that 'Egobarbus' had come from, if not where he had gone. But what had he been doing on the road to Eboracum? I was beginning to believe that my enquiries should lead me in that direction. The fact that the trail to my wife also pointed towards that city had, of course, nothing to do with my decision.

The other information I had gleaned was quite suggestive too. I should have a lot to report to Marcus. I was so satisfied with the outcome of my enquiries that I was halfway across the city before it occurred to me that I had entirely omitted to discover whether anyone at the gate had seen Zetso.

It was too late now. If I returned to ask additional questions I was unlikely to be actually arrested, but I had no doubt that the guard would treat me with – at the very least – the utmost circumspection. Obtaining further information from him would be like trying to prise the flesh out of one of Marcus's oysters. And just as potentially dangerous.

I tried asking at the East Gate, where Zetso had collected me in the carriage, but I learned nothing. One of the guards was the handsome fellow I had seen flirting with Zetso the day before. I had hopes of him – I saw his eyes flash up at the description – but (perhaps because Zetso seemed to have fled the city) he became so belligerent and hostile that I very soon abandoned my attempt, and made my way back to

Gaius's house. There, I felt, there must be something that would shed light on this affair.

The queue of would-be mourners at the door was shorter now, and I was admitted quickly and without question. This time I did not wait for a slave to escort me, but made my way directly to the kitchens.

There were far fewer servants here than there had been on the night of the feast, only a handful of slaves stirring pots or basting meat over the charcoal fire while a pair of kitchen-boys chopped herbs on a marble slab. A couple of live chickens clucked in a coop by the wall, watched balefully by Gaius's remaining dog, which was lying under the table, gnawing scraps.

One of the cooks abandoned his bubbling pan and came fussing over to greet me, wiping his fat hands on his ample tunic. 'How can I assist you, citizen? We are busy with the grave-meats, as you see.'

I outlined my questions, but the slave shook his head. 'I really cannot help you, citizen. There were so many servants brought here during the feast. I scarcely knew any of them, because they came from a dozen houses round about. There were so many slaves in the kitchen that we were tripping over one another, but I was so busy with my own sauces and dainties that I had no time to take much notice. I doubt I would recognise any of them if I saw them.'

'Not even,' I suggested hesitantly, 'two big red-headed slaves?'

The cook smiled. 'The attendants of the Celtic gentleman? Yes, I did see *them*. Great hulking fellows with hands like dinner salvers. They came down to wait in the ante-room. We were so short-handed with the extra wine, I even thought of asking them to help, but when I went to speak to them I could hardly understand a word they said. So I abandoned the idea. I didn't want them creating embarrassment by serving the wine all wrong, pouring it out without mixing and filtering it. And they would have been useless in the kitchen.'

I could imagine that. Celtic cooking can be delicious – at least to my taste – but it has little in common with a Roman feast.

The cook shook his head. 'I didn't see where they went to afterwards. Waited to escort their master, I suppose. I did see him briefly, visiting the latrine.'

I nodded. That was possible confirmation of one of my theories, at least. I wondered if Egobarbus had taken advantage of such a visit to divest himself of his cloak. Supposing, of course, that it hadn't been seized from him by force.

'Ah yes, the latrines,' I said. 'I gather you have managed to correct the problem with the drains.' It was an unnecessary question. The difference was already evident. The stench of rotting fish had largely dissipated.

The slave looked at me doubtfully.

'Your master explained it to me. The piece of fish fixed there . . .'

The cook grimaced. 'It was more than that, in the event. I sent one of the boys down there this morning with a brush, and he found something else. It wasn't just the fish – some sort of animal seems to have died down there. Perhaps the fish attracted it, and it drowned. The lad found the tail wedged into a crack. There was no sign of the rest of the creature – doubtless it had washed away or been gnawed at by others. You find horrible things in the drain-stream sometimes.'

'A tail?' I said. A strange hypothesis had occurred to me. 'Only a tail? You are sure of that?'

He looked at me with distaste. 'See for yourself. We threw it out into the alley this morning onto the midden-heap, together with the remains of the fish. I imagine it is still there. You can't miss it. The length of a man's span, hard in the middle and tapered. It looked like a tail to me. I didn't examine it too closely.'

The idea of doing so didn't appeal to me, either, but I could see no help for it. I followed the cook's directions and went around to the side of the house where the stinking alley lay. In common with most of the houses in the *colonia*, Gaius's residence presented only blank walls to the outside world, at least on this side, and – lacking a sufficiency of courtyards – the household waste was simply brought outside and abandoned in the narrower alleyways until rains or the occasional desultory street-cleaners carried it away. In the meantime, it lay there festering, a haven for scavengers of both the two and the four-legged variety. Even now something furry scuttled away at my approach.

I could see the item I was interested in on top of the heap. The smell of putrid fish almost drove me back, but I picked up a stick and hooked up the dripping object. It was too wet and disgusting to handle, but I examined it as best I could. It might have been a tail. It was the right length, and it had the same knotted, hairy look. On the other hand it might have been the hairs, twisted together and held with some sort of wax, that had once formed one side of a long drooping moustache.

The whole thing was sodden and filthy with slime, but it was possible to imagine that the colour might once have been red. I let it slide back on the mire-heap and picked my way back to the house. The scowling doorman let me in again and, sending a slave for a bowl of water to rinse my hands, I made my way to the *triclinium*.

I had hoped to have a quiet word with Marcus, but he was no longer there. There was someone else, however, a huddled figure on one of the couches, who leaped up at my approach as though a snake had bitten him.

'We meet again, Octavius,' I said.

He did not return my greeting, but sank down on the couch again in a despondent fashion. 'I thought you were Phyllidia,' he said, reproachfully.

Since that is not an easy confusion to make, there was little I could say to this. I said nothing.

Octavius seemed to realise that he had been discourteous. He essayed a smile. 'Libertus, you startled me. I have been waiting a long time. Phyllidia sent for me.'

'They found you at the inn?'

He coloured. 'They did. I was looking for her. I had gone to her rooms. And before you ask, I didn't steal anything.'

I looked at him in amusement. 'I did not suppose you had. Is something missing?'

He sighed. 'Not that I heard. But I was surprised to find you here. I hurried over at once, as soon as I had the message, but now I am here Phyllidia hasn't come to see me. I must talk to her. Have you seen her?'

I nodded.

'What did she say? Did she mention me? Have you told her what you told me, about . . . you know. . .' he glanced about him like a spy in a Greek tragedy, 'about . . . Felix?' He uttered the last word in a penetrating whisper, so penetrating that it must certainly have reached the ears of the slave, who chose that moment to enter with my washing water.

'She is performing her lament for her father, even now,' I said, as smoothly as I could, to cover the moment. 'No,' I went on, when the slave had put down the bowl and retreated at my command, 'I thought it better to keep my suspicions private – though you seem to be doing your best to prevent it.'

Octavius had the grace to blush.

I moved to the bowl of water and began to wash my hands. In the light of where they had been, I took peculiar care, rinsing them carefully several times and wiping them meticulously on the napkin which had been provided.

121

Octavius watched me curiously. 'You are going to take a place at the lament?' he asked, at last.

For a moment I was surprised. 'No. I am not expected to join the mourners – not until the funeral, at least. What makes you ask?'

'I thought you were making ritual ablutions.'

I had to smile at that. I still felt a certain sympathy with this young man, and his appearance of clumsy guilelessness, though I was beginning to suspect that he was not quite as guileless as he seemed. 'Nothing so dignified,' I said. 'I was merely washing my hands because I made them dirty.'

He was still gawping at me like a sun-blinded owl, and I added, more to put him at ease than anything else, 'Raking through the waste-pile in search of evidence. Evidence about that secret you so nearly publicised to everyone.'

I intended to be merely facetious, but I had clearly failed. Octavius turned whiter than a fuller's toga, and said in a hoarse murmur, 'Did you find . . . anything?'

I was about to answer candidly, but his manner was so awkward and furtive that I said instead, 'I did. As you clearly knew that I would.'

For answer Octavius rested his elbows on his knees and buried his head in his hands. I could not imagine that a tail – or even a moustache – would cause him such manifest anxiety. So evidently there was something else out there that I should have noticed. I shut my eyes and gave an exasperated sigh. The prospect of digging about again in that odoriferous pile was not a welcome one.

Octavius misinterpreted my irritation. He raised his head wearily. 'Oh, very well,' he said. 'Since you have found it, I suppose I must confess. I put it there. Last night after the banquet. Before Phyllidia arrived. Is there . . . was there . . . anything in it?'

This was, in the circumstances, a difficult question to

answer. Whatever the woeful object had been, it was hard to image anything 'in it'. I said carefully, 'You put it there, Octavius. Should there have been anything in it?'

He buried his head again. 'So it was empty! I should have guessed. Oh, merciful Venus – I should have prevented this. Well, I suppose there is no help for it.' He straightened up, looked me directly in the eye, and got slowly to his feet. Then he stretched out his two hands, wrists together, like a captive waiting to be bound. 'Very well, Libertus, you are too sharp for me. You had best deliver me to the magistrates. I confess it. I murdered Felix – slipped poison into his goblet and threw the phial on the midden-heap. Here.' He thrust his hands towards me again. 'Call for a slave and have me bound and taken.'

I looked at him for a long moment. 'Why did you do it? Because he would not let you marry Phyllidia?'

'Marry her? He would not let me *look* at her. And he half ruined me, besides.' There was enough venom in the voice to have killed Felix twice over. 'Killing Felix was not a crime, it was almost a public duty.'

'I see. In that case . . .' I went to the door. 'A slave here!' The servant trotted obediently into the room.

Octavius swallowed and shut his eyes, his hands still outstretched.

'Take it away,' I said to the slave, indicating the water bowl. He did so, casting a startled look at Octavius as he went.

There was a silence. Octavius opened his eyes. 'You didn't . . .'

'No,' I replied gently. 'And neither, I think, did you. At least, not in the way you pretend. You were late arriving at the feast, I seem to recollect. When, exactly, did you manage to slip the poison into his drinking vessel?'

Octavius gulped, reddened, and gulped again. 'I had help,'

he said sullenly. 'That is . . . one of the servants . . . I did it before—'

He might, indeed, have told me the truth then and there and saved us all a lot of trouble later, but at that moment the door opened and Phyllidia arrived, accompanied by the fish-featured serving woman. Octavius leaped to his feet, like a startled sentry dozing at his post.

'Phyllidia, I have confessed.'

Phyllidia paled. 'Confessed?'

'I poisoned Felix, and threw the phial away.'

'Octavius! Surely . . .? You poisoned him?'

'This citizen found the phial,' the young man said, running a hand through his receding hair. 'So naturally I had to tell him.'

Phyllidia turned to me. 'Is this true? My father was poisoned?'

I could personally have poisoned Octavius at that moment. There would be no keeping the secret now. The aged maidservant was gaping like a dead carp, but there was little I could do about it.

I did my best. 'There is a rumour to that effect. Of course, most people have paid no attention to it. Perennis Felix choked on a nut, in front of witnesses. But if what Octavius says is true . . .'

Phyllidia said, 'Octavius! Why?' just as he exclaimed to her, 'But surely . . .?'

The old woman pursed her lips. 'I knew it!' she declared, in tones of vindicated triumph. 'I told my master that some of the poison was missing. But he wouldn't listen. Thought he knew best as usual. He even refused to pay me for the information.'

'What information is this?' Marcus had come in through the interconnecting door from the next room. 'What have you discovered, Libertus? I heard that you were looking for me.'

'It is my information, most revered Excellence.' The old crone was almost prostrate in her grovelling. 'Octavius has just brazenly confessed to poisoning my master. I heard him do it. Yes, and the citizen here found the phial. And I can tell you where Octavius got the poison. From this ungrateful daughter. My master Felix sometimes dealt in poisons – infusions of hemlock and the like. It was intended for the courts, for those condemned to hemlock, but he would also provide it, at a price, for people sentenced to more painful deaths. And Phyllidia found it out, the last time he visited the house. She must have done. I told him there was poison missing, but he was too trusting. And now, you see, they have poisoned him – this pair.'

Marcus turned to the girl. 'Is this true?'

'Of course it's true,' the old woman burst out. 'She brought a phial of it with her. She thought I did not know it, but I did. I am too sharp for her. Last night, I discovered it – she sent me away for water, but I spied on her through the door crack. I saw her unbind it from around her waist, under her clothing.' She gave Marcus a wheedling smile. 'That is the information, Excellence. That must be worth a *sestertius* or two.'

Marcus looked at her with distaste and then turned to me. 'Well, Libertus? What do you say?'

'I say,' I said carefully, 'that this is true. And, since the woman saw the phial last night, it cannot have been used to poison Felix.'

Colour came back to Phyllidia's face, but Octavius looked drained. 'In that case . . .?'

Phyllidia looked at him sadly. 'My poor, poor Octavius,' she said. 'I know you did it for me. But there was no need, in the end. And now see what you have done.'

'Citizen,' Octavius cried, turning to Marcus, 'it was a mistake . . .'

'Indeed,' Marcus said dryly. 'A bad mistake.' He turned to his slave, who had been listening, open-mouthed, at the doorway. 'Send for the guard. I'll have this young man under lock and key. In the meantime, secure him somewhere in the house. He has confessed to a murder. You agree, Libertus?'

I nodded. 'I agree.'

Two burly slaves were by now approaching the door, and Marcus handed Octavius over to them. He turned to the young woman. 'And you, Phyllidia. You were carrying poison. Do you confess it?'

She looked at him coldly. 'There is nothing to confess. I did not bring it in order to kill my father.'

Marcus frowned. 'Then why?'

'If my father had lived, and forced me to marry you, I should have taken it myself.' Her voice trembled. 'As it is, I shall be spared the necessity. Now, with your permission, Excellence.'

Marcus was looking at her, stunned, but he nodded in dismissal and she left the room.

The old crone edged nearer. 'And me? Do not forget me, Excellence.'

Marcus glanced at her with contempt. 'And you! You set out to offer false witness against your mistress. That is a punishable offence. I shall not forget you, never fear. Take her away, you can lock her up too.'

I have never heard my patron speak with such fury. Perhaps it was not surprising. The idea that someone would genuinely rather die than marry him must have struck a terrible blow to his self-esteem. His expression did not soften until the guards had left the room, taking their captives with them.

Marcus turned to me. 'I congratulate you, Libertus. You have achieved a swift conclusion to this business.'

'You think so, Excellence?'

He looked affronted. 'I suppose you are going to tell me

that Octavius did not murder Felix after all?'

'I think he is acting most suspiciously, Excellence, but I am not sure that he administered the poison.'

Marcus frowned. 'But the phial you found . . .'

'I did not find a phial, Excellence. I did not even suspect a phial until the young man himself mentioned it. We have no evidence against Octavius except his own word. And he is a citizen. Perhaps it would be unwise to commit him to the jail. He may appeal to the Emperor.'

'Then why did you agree to his arrest? I have enough problems with Commodus, without risking further rebukes.' Marcus's youthful face was flushed.

I considered my reply with care. 'I thought he should be locked up here, Excellence, before he caused any further problems for you. If you had not imprisoned those two, rumour that Felix was murdered would have been all over Glevum before nightfall. Now, even if any rumours do get out, it will seem that you have the murderer under lock and key.'

Marcus looked doubtful. 'That is all very well, but I am not Felix, to enjoy imprisoning the innocent.' It was true. My patron dislikes injustice, and he was tapping his baton dangerously.

I said, 'Besides, Excellence, I presume the woman is right. There is a phial of stolen poison somewhere, and Octavius knows that there is. Why else would he have concluded that I had found it?'

Chapter Fourteen

A brief silence followed this exchange. I knew better than to speak again. Marcus does not like to be confronted with the obvious.

At last he said shortly, 'No doubt you are right, as usual. However, since, as you say, Phyllidia's phial was not used to poison Felix, it seems that we have shed no further light on the mystery. Unless you have discovered anything else?'

I told him briefly what I knew. 'So, Excellence,' I finished, 'that is what I have gleaned in Glevum. I am, of course, at your disposal should you wish me to make enquiries further afield.'

He looked at me coolly. 'I know you, Libertus. You do not lightly suggest abandoning your workshop. What is it that you wish me to suggest?'

If I were not such an old man I would have coloured. I had not supposed that I was so transparent. 'Felix had visited Eboracum,' I suggested. 'And Egobarbus and his party came from that direction, too. What took the Celt so many miles from his home? It seems worthy of investigation, at least.'

He looked at me. 'That would be a long and expensive journey.'

I said nothing. If it were less long and less expensive I should have made it myself long ago.

He sighed. 'Yet I suppose you are right. It should be investigated. Fortunately I know the commander from the Glevum barracks. He is always sending messengers to

Eboracum – and they get there quickly, too. No more than three days sometimes. These military envoys always have the pick of the horses. I will have a word with him: since it concerns Perennis Felix, no doubt even the imperial post can be instructed to stop and make enquiries as they go.'

'Indeed, Excellence.'

He saw my face and broke into a grim smile. 'Did you suppose that I would agree to send you? With private transport no doubt, so that you could look for your wife? Well, I am afraid not, Libertus. I cannot spare you – there are matters I wish you to investigate here. I have my own wife to consider now, and she is most anxious that you look into the loss of her slaves.'

'Excellence?' I had almost forgotten the deaths in Corinium.

Marcus ran a distracted hand through his short blond curls. 'I know, Libertus. It is hardly an affair of state. But what can I do? I have been married only for a few hours. I can hardly refuse her. I have made arrangements to send her to my country villa shortly – I am afraid there may be trouble in Glevum when the Emperor learns of Felix's death – but she insists that she must see you first. It seems she has a high opinion of your abilities.'

From his tone, I gathered that she had been forceful on the subject. I said meekly, 'Of course, Excellence, if I can help . . . But there seems little I can do at this distance . . .'

'You know Delicta has brought her gatekeeper with her? She has her own ideas about the killings. She suspects a visitor who called at the house this morning – thinks he was one of a group of out-of-town fraudsters and thieves, come to spy out the house. Found out that she was intending to shop, she thinks, and lay in wait later to kill the servants for what they were carrying. Certainly the caller was a stranger.'

I nodded. 'Junio told me so. He said that someone

unidentified had come early with a wedding gift.'

Marcus looked at me wryly. 'In that case, you know as much as I do. As much as the gatekeeper seems to, for that matter. I had him questioned, while you were out in the town.'

'And did he remember anything?' I was doubtful. I hoped the man had not been 'questioned' too enthusiastically. Since such interrogation often involves flogging, it is not unknown for the victim to remember all kinds of things that never happened at all, just in order to make it stop.

Not this time. Marcus shook his head. 'He had nothing to add, beyond the fact that the visitor was cloaked and hooded – though that was not unexpected, with the rain. He did not wear a toga, though, and spoke Latin with a strange accent.'

I smiled. 'Conspicuous enough, one would think. Almost as if he was wishing to be noticed.'

Marcus grimaced. 'If that was the case he failed. The gatekeeper seems to have been paying more attention to the gifts than to the bearer. Costly bronze bracelets and a length of silk. Doubtless he was hoping for a tip. He didn't get one. But I am sure he told us all he knew. Even the promise of gold from me was not enough to sharpen his recollections.'

I smiled more broadly. This interrogation, then, had been of the more gentle kind. Marcus knows my views. Feeble purse-strings can often be as persuasive as the thickest lash, and no more unreliable. 'But you wish me to speak to him, all the same?'

Marcus's grin was almost sheepish. 'My wife wishes it, old friend. I do not know what you can achieve, but I am a married man. I am returning to my apartment, now, in a litter. Delicta is waiting for me. If you would attend us there?'

I bent my knee and bowed my head. 'With pleasure, Excellence,' and Marcus left. I could hear him summoning attendants in the hall. He would take Gaius's attendants, of course. Marcus had no doubt dismissed his own to wait on Delicta, and my poor slave had not yet returned to the building. When I went to visit Marcus, I should have to walk the streets unattended.

That would raise a few eyebrows. A citizen in a toga is conspicuous without slaves, but in other respects this arrangement suited me very well. Before I went to meet my patron I hoped to make some enquiries about that missing poison phial, and I could do that most effectively without a clutch of slaves at my elbow. Something told me that if I did not locate it soon, then I would never find it at all. Phyllidia was a determined woman.

I walked quietly back across the house towards the wooden steps which led upstairs. No one paid the least attention to me. From the atrium the wailing continued unabated, and as I passed I glimpsed the man Tommonius taking his turn beside the bier while the funeral attendants wafted him with burning herbs. He glanced towards me, and I saw his face as I hurried away. He looked consolable at the loss of Felix, I thought.

I walked upstairs, unattended by any slave and – as far as I could see – unobserved by any member of the household. It was a strange sensation. One becomes accustomed, in big Roman houses, to the constant presence of slaves. It was slightly unnerving to find oneself so unexpectedly alone. Yet presumably Egobarbus had contrived to do the same, last night, in order to divest himself of his cloak and – somehow – his whiskers. And yet it was a rare event. Not for the first time, it puzzled me.

I was up the stairs by this time. I was not actually creeping about, but naturally I was taking reasonable care that my footsteps were as quiet as possible. I paused for a moment outside the bedroom from which I had seen Phyllidia emerge.

There was no sound from within and no answer to my tentative knock.

I lifted my hand to the catch, and very gently lifted it. The door swung open at my touch.

I had been half prepared to find Phyllidia there, but the room was empty. Not a woman's room, despite the little row of ointment pots and powders lying on the wooden travelling chest. The covering on the slatted bed was of coarse wool, although a pair of thick fox skins had been thrown carelessly over the stool, as though the occupant of the room might find the British night chilly and damp after the warmth of Rome. A stained and crumpled *stola* had been gathered into a pile under the window space, presumably awaiting the ministrations of the fuller, and a belt-ring – oil spoon, scissors, ear-scraper and tweezers – lay on the floor beside the bed. There was a tiny travelling altar set up in a niche, with figurines of the goddess of the moon, but otherwise the room was bare.

I hesitated. I am not by nature a spy, and the idea of searching the room uninvited in the absence of the occupier was not a comfortable one. But the opportunity was too good to miss. I went over to the travelling chest and, setting aside the little containers of cosmetics, gently lifted the lid.

There was not much in the chest. A few tunics, *stolae* and linen shifts, a change of woven stockings and a pair of leather slippers, and – to my embarrassment – a hefty corset and a pair of sturdy open-work briefs with frilling at the legs and fancy lacing at the side. There was also a fitted wooden box containing a selection of brooches and decorative hairpins, and another of carved ivory which clearly was intended to contain cosmetics, but of the famous phial of poison there was no sign whatever.

I was returning the contents to the chest, ready to transfer my search activities to the bedding, when the door opened abruptly and Phyllidia came in.

I froze.

Slowly she took off her mourning veil and stood regarding me. She did not look upset as I half expected, but she was clearly furiously angry. Her voice was biting as she said, 'What are you doing here? Searching my things?'

Since she had caught me halfway down her luggage it was difficult to deny this. I said, 'Your pardon, lady. I was looking for the poison phial your servant spoke of.' It sounded feeble. It is hard for a man to appear dignified when he is clutching a bust-binder in one hand and a woman's underslip in the other.

She shut the door behind her with a bang. 'My father is lying dead downstairs,' she said, 'but it seems I am not to be free of his methods. Who paid you to do this? Or are you simply thieving?'

I flushed. Unhappy enough to be caught spying, but a charge of stealing could bring the might of the law against me. I said hastily, 'My patron Marcus has asked me to investigate. However, I have exceeded my instructions. He did not ask me to search here. I hoped to find the phial, that is all.'

Phyllidia's plain face darkened. 'Indeed? Then perhaps you should have had the courtesy to ask me. There is no mystery. I have strapped it under my garments, as my servant told you. You wish me to produce it?' She flung the mourning veil onto the bed.

'If possible, lady.' I tried to sound as humble as I could, in the hope of allaying her anger. Phyllidia in this mood would tell me nothing. But she was not to be pacified. To my horror, instead of asking me to go outside, she turned away, hoisted up her outer tunic and – with her back to me – began to fumble among her inner garments.

It was a protest, I understood that, designed to make me feel how much I had intruded on her privacy. I was agonised by the impropriety of it – as no doubt she had intended. I said, 'Lady, I will wait outside the door . . .' but it was too late.

Phyllidia let drop her skirts and whirled round, a small blue glass flagon in her hand. 'Why should you do that, citizen? It is clear how I am regarded here – a worthless female, with no more rights than a slave. I hoped my subjugation had perished with my father, but I see that I was wrong. Better I had drunk this, as I intended.'

'Lady, no!'

She withered me with a glance. 'No? Dragged here unwillingly by land and sea to marry a man I do not even know? Refused permission to see my friends, spied on and restricted at every turn? And even now, I cannot leave my room an instant without a stranger searching my intimate belongings. I should be grateful, perhaps, for your restraint. In your place my father would have had my woman strip me while he searched.'

I was genuinely horrified, and it must have shown in my face.

She raised her chin defiantly. 'Well, soon it will be so no longer. I shall have a powerful protector. Gaius the magistrate has agreed to approach the *praetor* and offer himself to be my legal guardian. We shall see who treats me as a servant then.'

I was astonished. It seemed that Marcus had lost no time in persuading Gaius to adopt the duty. But some apology was necessary. I had already alienated Gaius and if he heard of this latest outrage it could easily cost me my liberty, Marcus or not. I said sincerely, 'Lady, you have my most abject apology. I had no thought of treating you so ill – it was merely that I hoped to find the phial. Octavius—'

'Ah yes, Octavius.' The tone softened and for a moment

the stolid face looked almost tender. 'Where have they taken him?'

I saw an advantage and I took it shamelessly. 'I believe they are holding him in the house. I advised my patron not to send him to the jail. I do not believe that he poisoned your father.' I took the phial from her unprotesting fingers as I spoke. 'This may help to prove his innocence.'

This time there was a thaw in her manner. 'It may?'

I held the bottle to me. 'Of course. He knew there was a phial, but since it is full it could scarcely have been used to poison anyone, not even the dog.'

Phyllidia frowned. 'So, there is a possibility that my father was poisoned?'

'Not by Octavius,' I said. 'At least not personally. I was with him at the banquet and he would have had no opportunity.'

The frown lifted a little. 'You do not see him as a murderer?'

'On the contrary, I think he would do anything for you,' I said. 'Another reason why I think I should take away that phial of poison which you stole from your father. You did steal it, I assume? The maidservant was right?'

Phyllidia coloured. 'I told you the truth,' she said. 'My father ordered me to follow him to this province and meet him in Glevum. He had some business to see to in the north and then he intended to arrange a marriage for me. A political marriage – he had planned it with the Emperor. That alone would be enough to make me fear it. I tried to protest, wrote to him begging him to change his mind, but he would not listen. I intended to confront him here – threaten to take the poison, in public if necessary. I would have done it, too. I am not a chattel to be sold to the highest bidder.'

Poor girl, I thought – that was exactly how her father had regarded her, although as an unattractive daughter she was not even a valuable chattel. I said, in an attempt to be comforting, 'Your fate would not have been so dreadful. My patron Marcus is a just and honourable man.'

She turned on me. 'Then I would have been used to ruin him. My servants are all spies, and Marcus is known, in Rome, to be a friend of the Governor Pertinax. The Emperor fears him – no doubt in time my father's spies would have found some excuse to bring about his downfall. Already there are whispers in the court that Pertinax is to be moved from his command – to some other post, perhaps, where he is away from the disaffected legions.'

I was staring at her.

'You doubt me? Then you should talk to Zetso about it. Octavius heard him crowing about this to some handsome charioteer, one evening in the Circus Maximus – bragging of his master's influence. That is how I knew of it. I am not well versed in the intrigues of the city.'

'Octavius frequents the circus?'

She smiled. 'Not often, no. He went because my father was there. The foolish boy had heard rumours of an unbeatable horse and driver, and was hoping to win some money on the races in order to offer for my hand. Thought it would impress my father. Being Octavius, of course, he lost what little money he had.' She said it with affectionate irritation. If Octavius attained his wish, I thought, and took Phyllidia to wife, he would not have the easiest of lives.

I nodded, slipping the little bottle carefully into the folds of my toga. There was a cord threaded through a glass eyelet near the stopper, and I looped that around my belt where it would be safe.

'Well,' I said, 'I will do my best for him. I'll take this to my patron. He will be pleased.' That was true. Marcus was more likely to be impressed by a phial of poison, even if it had not been used, than by all the information in the world. For good measure, I decided, I would go back to the heap and take him the moustache, however malodorous it was. I could always hire a slave to carry it for me.

Phyllidia inclined her head. 'And I will send for a little bread and water to sustain me. There will be no meals served in this house, of course, until after the funeral, and I will observe the public fast – but I see no reason why I should go hungry.'

'You do not altogether mourn your father?'

She met my eyes then, and I was shocked by the fire in them. 'I will tell you the truth, citizen. I stole that poison with the intention of drinking it, but the idea of giving it to my father instead had occurred to me. I was almost ready to do it. Fortunately, I was spared the necessity – by accident or design. And I warn you, citizen, I do not greatly care which it was. Even if it was shown to be a murder, I should not wish to bring a case against . . . whoever did it.'

She meant it. Under Roman law there is no case without an accuser. 'I see,' I said softly. 'Though the Emperor himself might take an interest. I will send a servant with your supper.'

She had turned quite white, with little patches of scarlet on her cheeks. And with that I left her.

Chapter Fifteen

My first thought was to attend my patron. The interview with Phyllidia had delayed me, and Marcus is not in any case a patient man. Pausing only to collect my cloak from the alcove where I had left it and to glance into the servants' ante-room in case there was now a slave available (there wasn't), I hurried to the door with the firm intention of stepping through it and making my way to Marcus with all available speed.

The doorkeeper had other ideas. Instead of opening the door at my approach, he stepped out in front of me with a ferocious scowl, and the thick baton at his side found its way menacingly into his hand. 'You were thinking of leaving, citizen?'

It was not an encouraging opening. Obviously I was thinking of leaving or I would not have been making towards the door. However, over a long life I have learned never to quarrel, if I can avoid it, with a man who is bigger and younger than I am and armed with a baton.

I flashed the man a hollow smile. 'I am under orders to rejoin my patron, doorkeeper, but there are still no slaves in evidence. I was resigning myself to a long lonely walk through the town.'

The smile was strictly unrequited. I remembered with unease that the doorman had been suspicious of me from the beginning. I did not expect him actually to strike me – after all I was a citizen, albeit a unprepossessing one – and I was known to be a protégé of Marcus. That alone should afford me a little protection – which was indeed why I had mentioned him at all. But from the look on the doorman's face it would not take much to have him wield that baton.

'Have no fear, citizen,' the doorman said, with a nasty sneering emphasis on the final word, 'you will not be walking through the town, lonely or otherwise. My master Gaius wishes to see you. He is awaiting you in the *librarium*.'

'Gaius?' When I had left the old man earlier he had not seemed eager to keep up the acquaintance.

'I do not know what you have done to offend him, citizen, but he sent down his page a moment ago with orders to stop you leaving. I understand he is not best pleased with you. Now, have I to lock this door, and accompany you upstairs with this baton, or will you go up quietly yourself?'

I can make a choice, when it is presented clearly. I said, 'I will be honoured to attend upon him again.'

The doorkeeper looked unimpressed. 'Then I suggest you do it quickly, citizen. My master is an old man, but he can be fearsome when roused.'

It was hard to imagine the querulous old magistrate deserving that description, but I turned away obediently and retraced my steps up the stairs that I had so recently come down. I was, frankly, puzzled. What could have occurred to visit the wrath of Gaius on my head?

I tapped apologetically on the door. The young page opened it, and I was shown in to where Gaius was waiting.

The doorman was not wrong. Gaius was furious. He was sitting on a stool beside the table, and he rose to face me as I came in. His thin face was white with anger, and his eyes blazed. Even the dog crouching at his feet could sense the mood, and rose at my approach to growl at me menacingly.

'So, you have come.' The voice, customarily no more than a rusty whisper, had become a croaking bellow. 'Well, I warn you, citizen, I am most displeased. Asking intrusive questions of me is one thing – I am an old man and a magistrate and I am accustomed to defending myself in the senate. But this is different. Phyllidia is more than my guest, she is my ward – or will be very shortly. I will not have you distress her in this fashion.'

I was surprised that the news of my escapade had reached him so soon. Phyllidia must have gone to him at once. The dog was straining at me in an unpleasant fashion, only restrained by Gaius's hand upon the chain. I glanced at it nervously.

I said, as soothingly as possible, 'Most respected Excellence, I assure you there was no disrespect intended. I went to her room simply to attempt to find a phial of poison which I knew was in the building somewhere. It is unfortunate that she surprised me searching in her travelling chest, but I was acting under the orders of my patron—'

Gaius lunged towards me with a roar. 'You were doing what? Searching her possessions? Under my very roof? As if matters were not already bad enough! By Juno, if you were not a citizen I should have you flogged for this.' For a moment I feared that he would strike me himself, or loose the dog at me, but instead he thumped his bony old hand down on the table with such force that his writing papers rattled, and the page boy in the corner flinched. The dog howled and sat down, eyeing me with mistrust.

I was looking at *it* in a very similar vein.

Meanwhile, I was thinking hastily. I had miscalculated, clearly. Whatever had been the reason for my summons it had not been my searching for the phial, and rather than assisting myself I had now given Gaius additional cause for displeasure. I tried a different tack.

'Excellence,' I said, in the best imitation of Marcus's manner that I could muster, 'this house has been the scene of a most unfortunate event. More unfortunate, perhaps, than you suppose.' I saw his features change, and I pressed my advantage. 'I am merely obeying the orders of my patron. If aspects of this reach the Emperor—' I stopped dramatically and nodded towards the door. 'Between ourselves, perhaps . . .?'

Gaius was not a magistrate for nothing. At the hint of international intrigue his manner altered abruptly. He nodded sharply to the page and gestured to him to leave, so peremptorily that the slave went scuttling from the room like a startled chicken.

The old magistrate sat down on his stool again, and his hound skulked under it to lie at his feet. That at least was a more favourable sign. 'Well?' Gaius said sharply. 'Tell your tale, pavement-maker, and make it plausible, or I shall see that you never lay a tile in this town again.'

That was a threat which worried me more than a beating. I made a rapid calculation. Rumours that Felix had been poisoned could not now be long in starting, at least in this house – the arrest of Octavius had seen to that. Indeed, if Gaius had spoken to Phyllidia, he had presumably heard it already, and my own blurted explanation a moment earlier had mentioned a poison phial.

I took a deep breath. 'It appears, Excellence, that the death of Felix may not have been quite the accident that it appeared.'

He had been white with fury, but I swear he paled. 'Nonsense!' he said shortly. 'The man choked. I saw it myself.'

'And your dog?' I said.

The old man glanced towards his remaining animal with such affection I almost warmed towards them both. 'Poisoned,' he said sulkily. 'I would like to lay my hands on the scoundrel who did it. Felix, I dare swear. He has always hated this household. Unfortunately he is—' he broke off suddenly. 'Is this something to do with that poison phial you mentioned?'

'I believe it is not entirely unconnected.'

'You cavil like a Greek. Is it, or isn't it? In any case I cannot believe that Phyllidia is involved. Why should she want to poison my dog? And how? She was not even at the feast.'

'That was fortunate for her,' I said carefully. 'I have reason to believe that the poison was not intended for the dog.'

He thought about that for a moment. 'You are telling me that there is some connection? Felix was poisoned too?'

'I believe it is a possibility. And my patron is of the same opinion.'

'Juno and Mercury!' the old man cried. 'No wonder he was urging me to hold my tongue. But surely . . . you saw Felix take the nut. That idiot Tommonius cannot have contrived to poison them all. Even if he had planned that Felix should be offered nuts, how could he know which one the man would take?'

I thought again of the scene at the banquet, Felix with his goblet in his hand lurching forward, flushed with drink and lust, to seize a nut, while the young acrobat swayed forward, teasing him, with the nut bowl balanced on his upturned feet. So it was Tommonius who had put the bowl there. That was something I had not realised until that moment.

'An interesting point,' I murmured. 'Perhaps I should tell you that, according to the maid, Phyllidia did have poison in her possession. She had stolen it from Felix himself.'

'You think that she intended to poison her father?'

'An interesting question, magistrate. You say "intended". That suggests that you are certain she didn't. Is that, perhaps, because you know who did? You yourself had no cause to love him, and you were very defensive, a little earlier, when I asked you about meeting Felix once before in Rome.'

He flashed me a glance. The anger had gone out of him

now, and he was clearly frightened. 'You really believe this? That the man was poisoned? Here, under my roof? Dear gods! But he was an imperial favourite.' He buried his head in his hands.

I said nothing. Experience has taught me that silence is sometimes a formidable weapon when a man is gripped by terror. I continued saying nothing long enough to allow Gaius to conjure graphic pictures of what might constitute a fitting punishment for a man who had allowed – perhaps had caused – one of Commodus's favourites to die of poison at his table.

It was enough. Gaius gave a little whimper of despair. I almost moved towards him, but the dog at his feet growled warningly and I thought better of the impulse.

'It is true,' he said at last, 'I did meet the Perennis family once, in Rome – Felix among them. He was an objectionable man, even then, and treated us badly, but I was forced to have dealings with him. His wife, however, was very good to mine.'

'Indeed?' I was surprised, remembering Marcus's scornful dismissal of the lady.

My voice must have betrayed me, for Gaius hurried on, 'When we arrived in the Imperial City and my young bride was exhausted by the heat and the journey, it was Phyllidia's mother who befriended her.' To my embarrassment, his voice was shaking with emotion. 'Of course, she was much scorned by Roman society – she was no beauty and she had few graces – her father had to dower her well to get her married at all – but she was a kindly woman. Her husband held her in open contempt because she had never given him sons – but she took my wife into her own home, treated her like a sister and was with her when she died.' He looked me squarely in the eye. 'For her sake alone, I would have hated Felix. And for her sake I will make Phyllidia my ward.'

'Felix treated her badly?'

'Appallingly. There are some in Rome who think he murdered her, though naturally this is not a rumour one would dare repeat. Certainly, he sent her a gift of wine and she died shortly after, but the connection would be hard to prove. She would have watered the wine, and there was a problem with the well. Others died at the same time, who drank from it.'

'I see.' I did see; there were often epidemics in Rome. 'Does Phyllidia know of this rumour?'

He glanced at me sharply. 'You are persistent in this, citizen. You seriously believe that she murdered her father? How could she have? She had not even arrived in the town. I cannot believe the maid servant. She has a spiteful tongue. No doubt she hopes to implicate her mistress and claim a reward from the Emperor. I wager ten *denarii* you will find no poison phial in Phyllidia's possession.'

I could not resist it. 'You are right, magistrate,' I said. 'I will not find it. I have found it already. She gave it to me with her own hands. But the maid's accusations are in vain. Her poison has not been used. Octavius has confessed to the murder.'

Gaius paled. 'That is why you have had him locked up in the attic?'

'Indeed.' A sudden inspiration came to me. 'I take it Phyllidia complained of that – and that is why you had your doorkeeper detain me?'

'Octavius is detained in my attics,' he said, with some dignity. 'Naturally I made enquiries. Phyllidia swore that *you* had had him arrested – for a crime that you knew he had not committed – and that you had locked up her maidservant with him. She came to me in distress.' He sighed. 'She did not tell me on what charge Octavius was being held. It seems, citizen, that I owe you an apology.'

'On the contrary,' I said. 'You have been more helpful than

you know. And, honoured magistrate, if I might suggest – Phyllidia was rightfully discreet. It is expedient that no one else should hear rumours of poisoning. Better that everyone assumes that Felix choked to death as it appeared.'

He nodded. 'I understand. Although, if it was a murder, I do not know even now exactly how the thing was managed.'

I grinned. 'Neither do I,' I said cheerfully. 'Though I intend to find out. But Phyllidia was right about one thing. I am perfectly sure that Octavius didn't do it.' The expression on his face was comical, and I gave him a swift bow to disguise my smile. 'And now if you will excuse me, magistrate, my master awaits me.' And before he could prevent me I had opened the door, let in the page, and made my way downstairs. I glanced into the atrium. Tommonius was still wailing dutifully.

There were still no slaves in evidence, and I did not stay to look for one. I had meant what I said to Gaius. Marcus would have been impatient long ago. It pleased me, however, to say, 'Good afternoon and thank you,' to the astonished doorkeeper before allowing him to open the door and see me out.

Outside there were still a few long-suffering mourners waiting. I threaded my way through them and set off walking briskly. I did, though, take a moment to make my way reluctantly to the waste-pile. Marcus ought to see that moustache, I felt – if that indeed was what it was.

But I could not find it, not even after poking around diligently with a stick. For a moment I was despondent. Perhaps it had been a tail after all, and some animal had dragged it away to gnaw on. I scratched around a little deeper, and came upon something which might have been another fraction of the same. Part of the other side of the moustache, perhaps?

I picked it up dubiously. It was even smellier than the

other, and I devoutly wished for a piece of stout leather in which to wrap my find. I could find no such thing, however, and I was obliged to content myself with a piece of old stained linen which I could see, just out of reach upon the heap. I availed myself of my stick, and scratched it closer.

As I did so, however, something caught my eye, and I abandoned all thought of delicacy. Wrapped in the piece of linen was another little blue glass phial, exactly like the one I already held.

Except that this one was empty and smelled of almonds.

Chapter Sixteen

For a moment I simply stood and gaped. Then, I leaned over
and grasped my smelly trophies in both hands, bundled them
into the filthy linen, and, abandoning all thoughts of dignity,
a moment later was rushing like a war envoy through the
streets towards Marcus's apartment. My head was spinning
with my discovery.

The quickest route to Marcus's house lay down the wide
central avenue but in spite of my haste I avoided it, not least
because the sight of a respectable elderly citizen in a toga
rushing wildly through the town – especially when bearing a
stinking linen cloth full of items from a waste-heap – is
calculated to arouse unwelcome interest. I was already late
for my meeting with Marcus, and I had no wish to be further
delayed by embarrassing explanations to the town guard.

I avoided the attention of the *vigiles*, by some good fortune,
but I was aware of startled faces as I passed. It is difficult to
hurry in a toga, and my frantic attempts to keep my drapes
together was the subject of great glee among the street
urchins, who jeered and pointed mercilessly. When I noticed
a couple of fascinated spectators in tunics, whispering to
each other and then following me at a distance and melting
into doorways if I turned to look, I concluded that I had
made an exhibition of myself and slowed my pace to a more
accustomed stride.

All the same, I was impatient to see Marcus. He would be
delighted with my discovery, and although I was unlikely to

receive financial reward he would almost certainly offer me a little food and drink. I was hungry. It was already long past midday, but a house of mourning offers its guests no refreshment until the funeral feast.

I turned my thoughts to the events of the day. To whom did the second poison phial belong? To Octavius, seemed the obvious answer. Had I entirely misread the motive for his 'confession'? I was beginning to become much more suspicious of that young man.

I turned the corner into a narrow alley which would take me to the street where Marcus lived, a mere unpaved footpath between the houses. The rubbish here had been recently cleared, and – keeping a watch upwards, lest anything be tossed from an upstairs window – I was able to pick my way easily along it. I was hurrying, too – my patron would be losing patience altogether.

It came as a surprise, therefore, to suddenly become aware of running footsteps behind me. These unwholesome alleys are rarely frequented. I turned my head to look, but even as I did so something powerful caught me behind the knees and I found myself collapsing forwards on to the paving. At the same instant a strong arm seized my wrist and twisted my forearm painfully behind me, jerking my head downwards while powerful fingers clamped across my mouth.

I could not have cried out if I dared, but a harsh voice behind me muttered, 'Keep your mouth shut – and your eyes too, if you know what's good for you,' and I felt the cold metal of a blade-point pressed into my neck.

I knew what was good for me. I am an old man and the hands that forced me downwards were strong. I did not attempt to struggle, but did as I was told, kneeling obediently where I had fallen. I tasted dirty sacking as a bag of rough cloth was pushed over my head and the drawstring tightly bound around my mouth, cutting into the corners of my lips and effectively gagging me. My other arm was forced back and I felt the bite of leather as a thong secured my wrists none too gently behind me.

My heart was thudding at my ribs. I had been foolish to come this way in a toga and without an escort. I would not be the first foolish old man to lose his life for the sake of a few *sestertii*.

As if in answer to my thoughts I felt the pressure of the blade withdraw, and a moment later something flicked at my belt, cutting loose my purse-pouch. I had dropped the linen bundle as I fell, and I sensed rather than heard the clink of glass as my attackers scooped it up.

I wanted to plead, to explain, but the bag was gagging me. I was pushed roughly forward, losing my balance so that my forehead grazed the pavement. A foot caught me ignominiously in the rear and a moment later I heard the running footsteps disappear. It was all over in an instant.

For a moment I lay there, too dazed to move. I could scarcely believe what had happened. I had been set upon and robbed in broad daylight in my own city. I rolled uncomfortably over, and struggled back to my knees. It was not easy, with my hands secured, but I managed it at last, and turned my attention to the awkward business of trying to free my wrists.

There are endless legends of escaping slaves and runaway wives who twist their hands and loosen their bonds, or find some sharp projection nearby and ingeniously saw them through. The reality is a little different. I was stiff, bruised and uncomfortable, and ridiculously aware of the ignominious figure that I must present, kneeling helplessly in a muddy alleyway with my head in a bag. For a moment I was almost glad that there was no one nearby to witness it.

Then common sense prevailed, and I was aware of panic. There was no reason on earth why anyone should venture down the alley for hours – perhaps for days. I had a miserable picture of myself drenched and starving, found half dead by the very town guard that I had been so anxious to avoid.

Or, if I was unlucky, twice as dead as that.

This reflection sharpened my responses, and I did at last manage to move my fingers sufficiently to find the knot in my bonds. I sent up a swift supplication to all the gods I knew and began to pluck at it, in the hope of loosening it. At last I felt it move a fraction, but it was an agonising business.

I tried to think as I worked. It is a means of suppressing panic.

My attackers first. Who were they? I had heard footsteps echo away down the alley, and I thought I knew which way they had turned, but that was little help. They would have vanished into the crowds long ago.

They. I was sure that there were two of them. Yes, certainly, there must have been: one to hold me down, the other to bind me. And there had been two sets of running feet. That was a beginning, something to hold on to.

A pair of random thieves perhaps, lying in wait beside the narrow alley, ready to pounce on any unsuspecting passer-by. Well, I wished them joy of their booty. So much effort for so little reward. My purse contained only the smallest of coins, after Junio's foray into town and my own purchase of soup, and the thieves would hardly be delighted by the objects in my linen parcel. The leather thong that bound me must be worth more than they had gained. For a moment I almost smiled at the absurdity of it.

Almost as if my mind had cleared, another thought struck me. Suppose this had not been a purely random attack? Those two shadowy watchers – I had been aware of them almost ever since I left Gaius's house. What had I glimpsed of them? I searched my memory. I could curse myself for having paid so little attention.

Men. Certainly men, and, I rather thought, wearing brown tunics, although I could not be sure of that. Not cloaks, certainly, and neither did I recall seeing anything in their hands, though one of them must have been wearing a dagger. They were big men, too: I seemed to envisage them filling a small doorway as though they were both tall and broad. But the rest was shadows. Try as I would, I could remember nothing more.

I had loosened the knot a little by this time and with a little working I could feel the leather moving on my wrists. It was a mixed blessing – as the blood rushed back to my hands the numbness ebbed, and I could feel the ache begin. My fingers, though, had recovered their feeling and I worked more dextrously.

I was still plucking at the leather when I heard the noise. Footsteps – hesitant footsteps behind me in the alley. Light footsteps, as if it was a child. I wriggled myself around in that direction, and tried to call for help, but the sacking in my mouth reduced my words to a muffled roar. The footsteps stopped.

Idiot! I tried to imagine the picture I must present. If I frightened him away I might lose my chance of rescue. (I assumed it was a him – few girls would venture alone into such an alley.) But the footsteps had not retreated. I toned down my roar to what I hoped was a more comforting sound, and turned round so that my bound hands were visible. I lifted them as best I could, hoping that he would understand and help me to free them.

A voice. Clearly a child's. 'What are you doing?'

I almost sobbed, and muttered something muffled through my sack.

'You want me to undo you?'

That was better. I nodded, enthusiastically.

'Are you a citizen?'

I nodded again.

'You must be rich. What will you give me? Twenty *asses*?'

It was just my misfortune, I thought bitterly, to find myself in negotiation with a calculating beggar child. On the other hand, I would cheerfully have promised twenty *denarii*. I nodded so vigorously that my sack shook.

The footsteps approached, gingerly, and I felt a small hand touch my bonds. I moved my fingers and he drew back sharply, but a moment later I felt the leather twitch. For a moment I was hopeful, but then the voice said plaintively, 'It is too tight, citizen. I cannot move it.'

I longed to urge the child to fetch his parent, if he had one, or at least to take the news of my predicament to someone. But I could only roar incomprehensibly.

But he had a suggestion of his own. 'I could take that sack off your head, citizen. I cannot untie it, but it is torn, here, at the back.' I felt the tug of little hands and suddenly the cloth behind my head parted, and there was daylight and air. I blinked open my eyes.

He was a small, ragged child with the big eyes, thin legs and bloated stomach which spoke of having far too little to eat. Not a slave, or he would have been better cared for – more likely the starving offspring of some poor freeman labourer. Yet the child was loved – it had not been sold, but kept, living in a hovel somewhere, to help pick a thin living on the land or work from dawn to dusk to earn a *quadrans* or two. No doubt one of the scavengers I had dismissed so lightly earlier.

He was staring at me speechlessly.

I used my shoulder to work at the end of the sack, which was still tied tightly around my mouth. It was painful, but I must have gained strength from desperation, for I managed to move it just sufficiently to say, 'Ar . . . uh . . . Ar-uh oh-ee-iuh eh-ih-uh.'

The child went on gazing. 'Marcus?' he said, suddenly understanding. 'Marcus Aurelius Septimus?'

I nodded, gratefully. 'O!' I managed. 'O ah eh ih.' I signalled frantically with my eyes.

His stare widened. 'Me? Go and tell Marcus?' I thought for a moment that he would refuse, out of simple awe, but the grubby face broke into a grin. 'That should be worth an *as* or two. You wait here!' he added, unnecessarily, and set off at a canter.

There was nothing to do but wait, as the boy had said. I shuffled over to the wall and leaned my weary head against it. My jaw ached from the gag and from where the heavy hand had clamped it.

The heavy hand. I had glimpsed it, in the split second before it clamped across my mouth. A big work-hardened hand, devoid of rings, and a thick muscular wrist. And on the hand and wrist and arm, a scattering of thick red-gold hairs. I took a deep breath. Was it possible? A red-headed man? I had been looking for Egobarbus and his red-headed slaves, but now I began to wonder if perhaps they had found me.

Who else would have cause to steal my linen parcel?

I was still contemplating this when there was a shout from the street. 'Master! Oh, master! What have they done to you?'

It was Junio, rushing towards me with the child at his heels.

Chapter Seventeen

There can be few things more agreeable, when one is shocked and shaken, than to find oneself in the hands of a faithful slave. Junio untied me in a trice, and, far from finding my predicament ludicrous, assisted me to my feet with such anxious solicitude that I found myself suddenly shaking and treacherously close to tears.

Perhaps that is why I said, more testily than I intended, 'That is sufficient! There is no need to support my arm. Now that you have seen fit to release me, I can manage perfectly well.'

Junio, however, was not deceived. 'I see that your temper is undamaged, master. But there is a nasty graze on your forehead and your knees are by no means stable. If you do not permit me to assist you, you will have me arrested by the market police on suspicion of having failed in my duties. Besides,' he gave me an understanding grin, 'Marcus will be much more impressed and solicitous if you arrive at his apartment limping on my arm.'

I couldn't resist his blandishments. In spite of myself I found myself grinning shakily in return. 'Oh, very well then. I suppose I must submit to your attentions. I shall have to impress Marcus – I am dependent on his bounty. My purse is stolen so I have no coins, and I promised this young scoundrel twenty *asses* for his help as messenger.'

In fact, when I began to walk, I was grateful for the steadying arm. I ached abominably from head to foot, and I found myself weak with the shock of it. Junio did not hurry me, but as I limped along he listened to my account of the event.

'So you think these were Egobarbus's slaves?' he said, when I had finished. 'You have made progress in your enquiries, master, if that is so. It proves that they have not left the city. And they will not escape now. Marcus has watchers at every gate.'

I nodded. Junio was trying to humour me, but he had a point. I had been too fuddled to think of that.

'It should not be too difficult to find them,' Junio went on. 'Glevum is a big place, but it will be hard for them to remain hidden for long. They will have to eat, and with looks like that they will be conspicuous. A pair of big red-headed strangers might pass as traders once or twice, but sooner or later they will attract attention.'

I managed a faint smile. 'No doubt they are having to steal to eat. Egobarbus had no money when he arrived. He could not even afford to pay the coach-driver, and I do not imagine Felix ever paid him.' I sketched in the events I had learned of at the gate.

'You think that is why they robbed you? In order to buy food?'

I didn't, but before I could say so the urchin, who had been dragging along behind us in the expectation of a tip, suddenly stepped forward and tugged at my toga sleeve.

'Your pardon, citizen . . . the money you promised . . .'

I stopped my stumbling progress and looked at him bleakly. Was I to be subjected to threats, I wondered, now that the child had worked out that I had no money with me? 'What is it? You will get your money. Marcus Septimus will engage for me.'

A pair of too-wise eyes flickered shiftily in the grimy face. 'I have no doubt of that, citizen. He promised me money when I arrived with my tidings. No, it is about the red-haired men. I think I could tell you something about them – at a price.'

I glanced at Junio, but he was looking impassive. 'Go on.'

'How much is this information worth?'

Of course, that depended on what the intelligence was. Yet from the cunning look in his eye I suspected that if I refused to pay, the boy would try to sell his information elsewhere – perhaps to the red-haired slaves themselves. I was debating how much money to offer when Junio, who remembered what it was to be young, and besides had not been shaken up by a street attack, solved the problem for me.

'A whole basket of food – bread, cheese, fruit and meats – plus a hot pie and a honey-cake from the street vendor. Just for yourself, in exchange for your information. What do you say?'

I breathed again. That was a reward I could find (albeit with difficulty) from my own resources if necessary. And it might be necessary. My patron pretended to disapprove of my offering bribes for information, although it was a method he often employed himself. I might easily have to put up the reward myself.

And Junio was right. The offer of immediate food was of more value to this pauper child than money, which he might have been bullied out of or, worse, accused of having stolen himself. A good meal, when you are starving, is quickly put beyond the reach of thieves.

'Settled!' The boy's eyes were luminous with greed.

'Well then?' I demanded.

'I'll see the basket first!' the child rejoined. I reflected again on the wisdom of this scheming little innocent. He had lived too long in the back streets of Glevum to give anything on trust.

I nodded, and we limped the rest of the painful way

towards the building where Marcus had his rented apartment.

It was a sumptuous suite of rooms, the finest in Glevum. It occupied the whole of the first floor of a large building, but – like most other apartments – still suffered the inconvenience of being contained vertically between a wine shop at street level and a cluster of smaller flats above, and over that again a collection of squalid crowded rooms in the attics under the roof. The communal staircase, as usual during daylight hours, was crowded with comings and goings.

With Junio still supporting my arm, we picked our way through the throng: malodorous honest inhabitants from the upper floors, stiff official supplicants and messengers having business with Marcus, and the usual sprinkling of the slightly nefarious and simply curious. At the door of the apartment, a smartly tunicked slave admitted us, and leaving the urchin to attend us on the stair Junio and I made our way into the spacious room where Marcus and his new wife were waiting to greet me.

It was a fine room, with balconies and tiled floors, painted plaster frescoes, woven rugs, mirrors and braziers. Marcus was reclining on a gilded couch and his lady, as is the custom with women, sat on an upright chair beside him, looking more beautiful than ever in a glowing deep blue over-tunic girdled with gold. The silver-blonde wig was elegantly coiffed, and a cluster of jet beads at her lovely throat was her only other adornment. A greater contrast to the unfortunate Phyllidia could hardly be imagined.

As I was ushered in, still leaning on Junio, my patron rose to greet me. His face was a portrait of the most flattering alarm.

'My dear old friend. I rejoice to find you safely here.' Junio was right about my reception. An attendant slave was commissioned to fetch me a stool, another to bring food and wine, and Delicta, who had once had a private physician in Glevum and prided herself on her medical knowledge, herself ordered salves and warm water and maidservants to bind up my wounds.

I felt like a visiting emperor as – waving aside my proffered obeisance – Marcus oversaw the siting of the stool and watched solicitously as I lowered myself onto it. 'You were attacked, I hear?' Junio, in deference to my shaken state, was motioned to stand behind me. Normally he would have been sent away to wait in the servants' quarters.

'Attacked and robbed,' I said ruefully. 'I had found something I wanted to show you.'

'You see?' Julia Delicta turned to her husband with a smile which would melt bronze. 'Attacked and robbed, just like my unfortunate slaves this morning.'

Marcus gave me an awkward smile. 'Delicta is convinced there is some group of itinerant robbers abroad, and these events are part of a pattern. Unlikely, don't you think, on the evidence of just two attacks? And in different towns?' He picked up a jug of wine and a morsel of bread from the laden trays which had miraculously appeared before us and, to my surprise, dutifully placed a little of each on the household altar. Then he took his place on the couch and picked at a date himself. It was a formal signal that I could eat, and (having had my head, hands and feet bathed by Junio in the bowl provided) I did so ravenously.

Secretly I was amused. The arrival of Delicta had already effected a change in the household habits. Such strict social conventions had never been observed before when I had eaten informally with Marcus.

The lady herself ignored the refreshments, as well-bred women do. Instead she said firmly, 'These are just two attacks we know of. There may be many more. We have seen this before in Corinium. Some family of thieves moves in on market day and mingles with the citizens. Then, when they have filled their pockets, they disappear.'

'But this attack was not in Corinium,' Marcus said in a tone of amused patience, raising his eyebrows slightly in my direction.

Delicta was not to be subdued. 'Of course by the time the authorities are searching for them, they are far away. What more likely than that they should come to Glevum? I tell you, husband, if you do not apprehend the culprits swiftly, they will move on to the next town and never be caught. And they have robbed me of two valuable slaves and some expensive goods. I am your wife. They must be brought to justice.' She turned the torchlight of her smile on me. 'Do you not agree, Libertus?'

I may be an old man, but when a woman like Delicta looks at me in that confiding way, I am almost ready to agree to anything. However, I had the presence of mind to say, 'I believe, lady, that this attack was directed at me personally. I have come to think they wanted what I was carrying. It was of no value to thieves, but I had found something which I thought might throw some light on the events surrounding the death of Felix.' Briefly, I outlined the finding of the supposed 'tail' pieces and the empty phial.

Marcus nodded thoughtfully. 'It seems a likely explanation.'

Delicta, although still smiling, was unwilling to abandon her theory. 'So you think the incident in Corinium was unconnected?'

I was about to answer that I did, but upon reflection I modified that. 'I do not think,' I said carefully, 'that the two attacks were carried out by the same people. But as for being connected in some way, that is another question. Two attacks, so close to Marcus, may be more than coincidence.'

Whether I was right or wrong, it was a diplomatic answer. Marcus looked suitably grave and thoughtful, and murmured that the culprits must be caught, while his wife glowed at me more warmly than ever.

'You are so shrewd, Libertus,' she said. 'And you are hurt. If you have finished your meal, I will have my maidens tend your head.'

I indicated that I had, and the girls stepped forward.

The next moments were delightful. I might have been a young man again, submitting to Gwellia's ministrations. Whether an ointment of agrimony and hog's grease is really a useful specific against cuts and bruises, I do not know, but the effect of having my forehead and then my knees softly bathed and salved by smooth willing fingers would have cured me of worse injuries. I was beginning to wish I had more grazes to tend.

Marcus brought me out of my reverie. 'Now then, old friend, is there anything more that you require?'

It seemed churlish to ask for money, but the urchin was still on the stairs. Diffidently, I suggested, 'With respect, Excellence, could you lend me a little money? No great sum, merely some coins for the child who acted as messenger? I regret to have to ask you, but my own purse was stolen.'

'My dear old friend, feel free to ask for more than that. I would do as much for a beggar.'

He spoke with such warmth and alacrity that I was moved to add, 'Of course, on reflection I will have to take the child home with me, in any case. He thinks he has some information about my attackers. I promised him a basket of food if it was useful.' I hoped, of course, that Marcus would volunteer the reward, but I knew him too well to ask him for it outright.

I was lucky. Marcus was still feeling benevolent. He smiled. 'Leave it to me,' and he sent one of his slaves scurrying. Mentally, I blessed the gods. That little exchange would save me a week's provisions.

The urchin was brought before us, his eyes wider than

disci, so overwhelmed in the presence of Marcus and his broad purple edgings that I believe he would have parted with his information for nothing.

We didn't ask him to. Marcus fingered some coins from his purse and said, 'You are the boy who brought the message here?'

The urchin nodded, too terrified to speak.

'You say you have some information? About the men who attacked my poor old friend here?'

The urchin glanced at me. Being called a friend of Marcus, however poor and old, had raised my status considerably in his estimation. He stammered, 'It . . . it is nothing, Excellence.'

'Nevertheless,' Marcus said, 'we shall hear it.'

The boy gulped. 'It is merely . . . I thought I had seen them before, selling trinkets near the market, outside the temple of Mars. They'd spread a cloth under one of the outer pillars, and had laid out their wares. They were blocking the alleyway. I saw the *aediles* move them on.' No talk now of needing to see the basket first: he was gabbling in his eagerness.

'Trinkets?' I said, at the same time as Marcus demanded, 'You are sure it was the same men?'

The boy babbled, 'I saw them dash out of the alley. Two of them. I thought they were the same. They are not easy to miss. Big men in brown tunics, with red hair and Celtic boots.'

I nodded. That made sense, if my theory was correct. 'What were they selling?' I asked again.

The boy shrugged. I did not cow him as Marcus did. 'Bracelets, armlets, mirrors – that sort of thing. Bronze, they looked like. I am no judge of these things. People were buying them.' He turned to Marcus. 'I swear it, Excellence, that is all I know.'

Marcus looked at me. We were not much further forward, but I was sure now that my attackers were the servants of Egobarbus. I nodded.

A servant was sent out to fetch the basket, and I saw the boy's eyes widen as he looked inside. There might not be honey-cakes, but the child looked pleased with his bargain. Marcus drew out the coins, and I saw the tip he proffered. I was not displeased to know that the urchin, for all his scheming, had earned much more than his twenty *asses*.

Well, I would think about it later. For the moment, I had other concerns. I closed my eyes again, and, proffering my hands, let the handmaidens rub ointment into my wrists where the leather thong had chafed them. There were some advantages, I thought languorously, to having had my patron become a married man.

Chapter Eighteen

My patron's indulgence and concern, welcome as they were, could not be infinite. In having him pay off the urchin I had, naturally, depleted the supply. It seemed a very short time before he was saying abruptly, 'Well, well, that should be sufficient. Surely, Libertus, you are feeling better by now? You will remember there are matters to discuss.'

I could do little more than acquiesce.

He waved a lofty hand and at once the sybaritic ministrations halted, and my enchanting handmaidens picked up their balms and potions and drifted away. Their mistress, at a signal from her husband, followed them, and – apart from the inevitable attendant slaves – I found myself alone with Marcus, who was now sitting almost upright on his couch and tapping his thigh impatiently with his baton. Any dream that I was the Emperor Commodus (or Jupiter himself) enthroned in some earthly paradise tended by willing votaries had instantly vanished.

'Excellence?' I ventured, trying to sound briskly intelligent. 'What do you wish me to do first? Interview Delicta's gatekeeper about the trouble in Corinium, or report first on the progress I have made here?'

He looked at me gloomily. 'Is there more to say about that? You spoke of finding those items on the pile. Have you found other evidence of which I'm unaware?'

'Not evidence,' I said carefully. 'But there are some important impressions. Suggestive incidents.' I moved my

167

stiffened fingers discreetly to touch the little phial hanging by its cord inside my clothes. The attack had driven it out of my mind. But my fall had not broken it. I was reassured.

I was debating whether this was the most auspicious moment to show it to Marcus when he solved the problem for me by saying impatiently, 'I cannot act on your impressions, my old friend. Give me the facts, when you have discovered them. In the meantime, speak to this gate-keeper of my wife's. She will give me no peace until you have. Here, my slave will show you the way.'

Junio helped me to my feet and we followed the tunic-clad servant out of the fine public chambers and into the humbler quarters at the rear of the building, where a cluster of shabby rooms led off from a smoky passage, and a still more smoky vented space with a large charcoal fire, set on an iron stand, in the centre. This clearly was the makeshift kitchen. Most Glevum apartments have no cooking facilities at all, and upstairs in communal blocks like this such things are actively discouraged, following the tragic blazes in Rome. Apartment owners these days either dine out or content themselves with meals brought in from the better class of hot-food stalls.

This uncertain device was therefore an indication of Marcus's stature. No wonder men of means, like Gaius, preferred to buy a house where possible, so that their cooks could prepare meals – and even banquets – without the constant risk of either asphyxiation or conflagration.

The kitchen slaves, half stripped and wheezing with smoke and heat, were too busy skinning a goat and placing it on a turnspit to pay us attention as we went by. The slave-boy with the bucket, whose job it clearly was to douse the flames and cool the walls in an emergency, looked up and nodded.

Junio was led off to the slaves' waiting room, where doubt-less he would win himself a few *quadrantes* playing at dice with the others. My servant has an innocent face and an uncanny talent for gambling. I don't know how he contrives it, but the fall of tile and dice seem to favour him much more than chance alone allows. I left him to make his fortune while I was taken to the gatekeeper.

I found the man in one of the cell-like rooms which were reserved as sleeping spaces for the servants. He was a large, brawny man with huge hands and even bigger feet – as befits a gatekeeper. I had seen him before at Corinium, and I smiled encouragingly, but if he felt any pleasure at seeing me he was quick to disguise it.

'Oh, you've come at last, have you?' he grumbled. 'They said you were sent for. Why, is what I want to know. I've told them everything I can, a dozen times over.'

'And what exactly could you tell them?' I said affably, squatting beside him on the bundle of reeds which was provided as a bed. The room was small, but otherwise it was no more humble than my own.

He looked at me savagely for a moment, then fetched a great sigh. 'Oh, very well. If I must go through it all again, I suppose I must. He came to the house early this morning. I hadn't seen him before that I remember. He brought a parcel of silk and some bracelets, and said they were a gift for Julia Delicta, on the occasion of her marriage. Then he left. I paid no great attention to his face. That is all I know.' He produced it all in the fashion of a recitation.

'I see.' I thought about this for a moment. 'How early did he come?'

He frowned. 'I don't know. Do you think I am a councillor to have water-candles by me? Very early. The sun was hardly risen in the sky and I could hear the schoolmaster scolding in his pupils.'

'And it did not surprise you that he brought a gift?'

The man shrugged. 'I suppose a little, since he was a stranger to me. But there have been gifts arriving ever since

Delicta arrived home from the forum yesterday.'

Of course, once the marriage was solemnised it was no secret. 'No doubt the witnesses had spread the news,' I said.

For the first time the gateman almost smiled. 'More than that,' he said. 'The old *auspex* was delighted by being asked to perform the ceremony – he must have told half the town. And since it was Marcus that she married, everyone was anxious to come and make a gift – and be seen to do it.' He paused. 'I suppose that is why I remembered the man. There was nothing with the gift to say who the giver was.'

'Did you ask him?'

The man grimaced. 'I did. He said it was from an old friend of Marcus's. I could hardly argue. I know who calls on my mistress, but His Excellence has a dozen friends in Corinium that I have never seen.'

It was hard to argue with that. I changed the subject. 'So what made you suspicious of the man?'

He shrugged. 'I would not have suspected him at all, if there had not been this stabbing of slaves from our household in the town. Of course, when I heard of that, I began to wonder about the stranger who had called. But truly, citizen, I can remember nothing else. He was wearing a dark cape and hood, but I thought nothing of that. It had been raining and the man was very wet. He came to the gate and asked to be presented to Delicta. I had to tell him that she was in the town.'

'Surely the shops were barely open?'

That brought a reluctant smile to his face. 'Delicta is a wealthy woman, citizen. The shops would open for her.'

I nodded. Delicta was unusual in doing her own shopping. Wealthy Roman women are not like Celts, they prefer to send their husbands or their slaves, even for cloth and jewels. But Julia Delicta was accustomed to having her own way. No doubt the shopkeepers of Corinium would hurry bleary-eyed down the stairs at midnight to open their shuttered stalls if they had found her on their doorsteps. I said, 'So the caller left the parcel. Did you get a look at him?'

'Youngish, and dark, and he had a strange, clipped sort of accent – or at least he seemed to have. I have wondered since if he adopted it on purpose. He had a fine horse, I remember.'

I nodded. That at least was new information.

He said, after a short pause, 'My mistress thinks there was a company of thieves in the town. It has happened once before. Men calling with messages when the house-owners were out and – when they were admitted to wait – sending the slaves away on fruitless errands while they looked around for something to steal. Nothing large, of course, only a golden statue or two, which they would hide under their clothes, and walk out later as calmly as you please. The thefts were not noticed until afterwards.'

'That hardly seems the case in this matter.'

'Fortunately for me, since it would have been on my head if I had let him in. But there are always other thieves, attacking helpless people in the street and stripping them of their purses – as I hear they stripped you, citizen.'

I could hardly deny this, but he said it with a grin which was almost insolent. I did not care for the turn the conversation was taking, and having learned – as I supposed – all there was to learn, I took my leave of him and returned to Marcus.

My patron had a string of *clientes* waiting for his attention by this time, but he had lingered to speak to me.

'So, my brave pavement-maker, did you learn anything new?'

'No real facts, Excellence, since that is what you required.'

'Well, I have facts for you. You heard that my poor herald's body has been found?'

I nodded. 'Junio told me so.'

Marcus sighed. 'I have had him collected. It is vexatious. Worse than I thought. Deliberately insulting. Not only did Felix have him tied to a stake for the birds to pick at, as if he were a common criminal, he also had a notice nailed up above him: "Here is a nameless, insolent slave who insulted the great Perennis Felix." Who did Felix think he was? A Roman governor?'

I made a sympathetic noise. I knew what he was referring to. Some senior magistrates and provincial governors routinely labelled criminals in this way before their executions, and sometimes made them parade the streets wearing their placards of indictment, as a humiliation to them and a warning to the rest of the populace. I have known Marcus himself have a notice nailed over a crucified criminal, but Marcus was a senior magistrate. Felix had had no such authority.

'Insulted the great Perennis Felix, indeed!' Marcus fumed. 'It is I who am insulted, if anyone.'

It passed through my mind that perhaps the herald himself had a certain claim to having been insulted, but naturally that was not a thought that I could voice. I said, 'But you have had the body moved, Excellence?'

'Of course. We cannot have his spirit unquiet and haunting the town. I intend to have him disposed of decently. But therein lies the problem, old friend. I should have had them bring him here, to be properly bathed and anointed, since this is where he lived and worked, but I am in official mourning for Felix. It would be disrespectful to host another funeral, especially of someone whom Felix himself put to death.'

'But surely, Excellence,' I ventured, 'the slaves' guild would bury him? I know you normally make provision for your slaves, like a thoughtful master, but in the circumstances surely you could have *them* cremate him? It would be all over before Felix's funeral. They could do it at once. He was only a herald. There is no need for a mourning period.'

'There will be no problem with that,' Marcus said. 'The herald is a guild member – I have always paid his dues. I have done it for all my servants. I never can be certain that I will not be recalled to Rome and be unable to provide a proper funeral when they die. No.' He furrowed his brow. 'The difficulty is where to take the body now.' He looked at me speculatively.

I knew Marcus. He was working up to something. I said cautiously, 'Of course, Excellence, if there is anything whatever I can do . . .'

Marcus smiled. 'Libertus, you are a true friend. I will not forget this when it comes to assigning public commissions. Very well, then, I accept your offer. The funeral guild can take him from your rooms. That way you can attend the ceremony in my place. I will not have Felix contrive to have my herald sent to the other world with only slaves to mourn him.'

I opened my mouth to protest. Playing host to a funeral, especially as chief mourner, is a burdensome business. It would necessitate not only giving up a room to the corpse – and goodness knows there was little enough space as it was – but also all manner of cleansing rituals afterward, including a sacrificial offering, a period of fasting, and another series of personal purifications at the end of nine days. To say nothing of a cold nocturnal procession outside the city walls – no funeral is permitted within them. But one cannot argue with Marcus.

He was smiling at me. 'I was certain of your good offices, old friend. I have already had them take the herald to your workshop. The guild has agreed that they can bury him from there. And you need not fear ghosts – they will not use your sleeping room. They will do the thing tonight. I have spoken to the foreman already.'

He meant he had offered the man a bribe. I said feebly, 'But, Excellence, I had planned to go to the North Gate tonight, and meet the driver of the conveyance that brought the Celts.' It was not exactly a firm plan of mine, in fact I had just thought of it, but it seemed a reasonable undertaking, and preferable to a funeral. I added, winningly, 'He was promised payment this evening, and I hoped—'

Marcus interrupted. 'Do not concern yourself with that. I will have the man questioned myself.' He clapped me companionably on the shoulder. 'The guild is expecting you. And do not look so downcast. There will be little fuss.'

I was not so sure. No doubt, if the corpse had been delivered, the gossip would already have started – and for the next half-moon my neighbours would avoid me with the wary politeness which always follows the presence of a dead body in the house. And there would be no hiding the funeral.

I have attended slave-guild funerals before. The bier is only of gilded wood, and it is rescued before the cremation, the urns are of cheap pottery instead of gold and bronze and the mourners are paid slaves, but there is no lack of ceremony. To a man who has nothing in this world, the entry into the next is an important occasion, and slaves will often set aside every *quadrans* they own to ensure that they pay their dues and so avoid the communal pit which is otherwise their lot. Even so, more than one slave is often cremated at a time – it halves the cost, and increases the show. I could envisage a very large cortège arriving at my door.

Marcus saw my look. 'I assure you, Libertus, tonight will be a quiet affair. There was a great slave funeral last night, apparently. One of the dead actually worked for the guild at one time, so they made a huge ceremony of it: a senior priest, proper orations, pipers, dancers and scores of mourners following the corpse.'

I nodded. 'We saw the procession ourselves, Excellence, on the way to the banquet.'

Marcus waved the remark aside. 'Indeed. Well, there will be nothing like that tonight. I have requested that it be discreet, although I am assured that the guild always does these things very well.'

I must still have looked doubtful.

There was a hint of impatience in his voice as he continued, 'And there will be no expense. They are providing the sacrifice, and the funeral meal afterwards. I have made the arrangements.'

Which is more, I reflected, than anyone would do for me. Except perhaps Junio. But I must not annoy Marcus. I said, with as much dignity as I could muster, 'My pleasure, Excellence.'

In fact, of course, it was no pleasure at all. But there was no help for it. Already it was getting dark, and I would have to go home and prepare myself. Coarse cloth, ashes on the forehead and then a cold vigil in the night air when I was already stiff and bruised from an attack. And it was raining.

As I summoned Junio and made my way back to the street I wished, not for the first time, that Felix Perennis had never come to Glevum. I was so concerned with my resentful thoughts that it did not occur to me that I had been given the solution to at least a part of the problem I was trying to solve.

Chapter Nineteen

The evening was as dismal as I had feared. The poor old herald was a sorry sight, stretched out on a makeshift bier on my workshop table, with the ritual candles burning around him. He had not been a pretty spectacle when he was dragged away behind the carriage, and a day and night pegged up to a stake had not improved him – even the bits of him which one could see. I was glad that the guild, contrary to custom, had covered his face with a cloth.

They had done their best with him, bathed his appalling wounds and clothed what they could in a new robe which Marcus had provided. They had also provided a weeper, whose moans could be heard from the alley outside, and put up a wreath of funerary green on my entranceway to show that there was a corpse within. So, as I had half expected, people were already crossing the street to avoid the house. I would be lucky to have any customers call for days, after this.

Marcus was right about one thing. When the moment arrived there was comparatively little 'fuss'. The guild had provided a mere four bearers, and they turned up almost before I was ready for them. I was still clothing myself in the *lugubria*, the dark-coloured robe expected of the closest relatives or chief mourners. I hadn't worn mine since my own master died, and that was more than ten years earlier. Fortunately, since I had increased in girth as well as age, Roman fashion is not close-fitting.

I arranged my folds, with Junio's help, and dashing the

required ashes on my forehead I hurried down to meet the funeral workers.

Marcus's bribe had clearly done its work. The foreman of the guild was there in person, together with a little wizened man I recognised as a priest of Diana, although I am not sure if the local slave guild has some affiliation with that cult, or whether this religious functionary merely happened to be available. Either way he looked pleased with this assignment – perhaps he too was benefiting from Marcus's purse.

The guild foreman came wheezing over, wringing his thin hands, to instruct me in my 'duties'. I was surprised. I have attended slave funerals before, and normally everything is performed by the guild.

The old man looked at me with rheumy eyes. 'Oh no, citizen. You represent the slave's owner – a rare honour at these occasions. And since the slave's owner is His Excellence Marcus Aurelius Septimus of course it is doubly so. Naturally you must help officiate. You could begin now, perhaps, by calling on the spirit of the departed?'

This was awkward. I knew what to do – I was supposed to call the herald's name, to ensure that his spirit really *had* departed, but this was difficult because I didn't know it. I had to content myself with simply calling 'Herald of Marcus' three times, in ringing tones. It seemed to satisfy my audience.

It did not occur to me until afterwards that, since I represented Marcus, they were unlikely to be critical of me, whatever I did. And it made little difference. The poor fellow's spirit had clearly escaped the body long before, and given the manner of its going, I doubt it was anxious to be recalled.

These formalities complete, the bearers hoisted up the bier, and took it outside. I saw them place it on the more ornate carved carrying stretcher they had brought with them, for which there was no room in my cramped workshop. Instructed by the priest I doused the candles, 'purified the room with fire and water' (a whirled censer and a quick sprinkle from the ewer provided) and we were off: myself, Junio, the pall-bearers, two professional keeners, the officiating functionaries and a couple of skinny torch-bearers.

My habitation, of course, is on the west side of the city on the marshy margins of the river – not a suitable place for cremations and inhumation. To reach the cremation site necessitated a long damp procession through the town. Fortunately the guards at the gates were used to funerals, and let us through without a murmur.

It was still drizzling.

'We shall be lucky if he burns at all,' Junio murmured at my side, and I was obliged to silence him. As chief mourner I had to maintain an appropriately lugubrious expression.

We crossed the town – taking the narrower lanes, to avoid the night-time traffic – and as we did so our procession lengthened, until by the time we reached the eastern wall there must have been twenty people in the retinue.

I glimpsed Junio's face in the torchlight.

'Who are they all?' he mouthed.

I recognised some of them as other servants of Marcus. No doubt my patron had sent them, as he had sent me. I frowned severely. 'People who knew the herald or belong to the guild, naturally,' I whispered, in my best pompous manner.

Junio grinned. 'Or who have contrived to attach themselves to the procession in the expectation of a free meal afterwards.' He cocked an eye skywards. 'Given the weather it is fortunate that we don't eat the funeral feast at the graveside in these islands, as they are said to do in Rome.'

He spoke so softly that only I could hear him, and he almost made me smile. That would be unforgivable for a chief mourner and I had to scowl fiercely to put a stop to his levity.

We had passed through the far gates by this time, and reached the site where the guild held its cremations. Despite the damp evening the pyre was dry – it must have been covered with something – and a member of the guild was already standing by with a torch to light it, and an amphora of something liquid to pour onto the faggots to help them burn. Oil and fat perhaps, or distilled wine: I wish I knew their secret.

It was time for me to pay attention to the ceremony; according to the priest it was my job to scatter a handful of earth on the corpse before it was consigned to the flames.

I did so, and was preparing to take my place in the crowd again when the foreman of the guild came bowing over.

'An oration, citizen?'

Of course! I had forgotten that. I was also expected to make some sort of flattering speech about what a good herald this had been. Without, of course, alluding to the manner of his death, or appearing to criticise Felix. There would be spies everywhere. Once more I mentally cursed Marcus for getting me into this. If one of the guild were making this oration I would have felt a great deal safer.

I cleared my throat. 'Fellow . . .' – I was about to say 'citizens' but stopped myself in time – 'Glevans . . .'

It was not a good speech, but I managed something.

Then I had to be witness as a part of the corpse was cut off to be ritually buried – a grisly concession to custom which the average mourner is spared – and finally the bier was lifted from its gilded stretcher and placed rather clumsily on the pyre.

'Not too close, citizen,' the foreman murmured, gesturing me back.

He was right. The moment the torch was applied the flames sprang up, and once the liquid was poured onto them the heat and smoke became even more intense. Perhaps the cloth that covered the face had also been doused in something because, despite Junio's fears, the whole corpse was soon burning fiercely.

'Grave-goods?' the foreman asked, in an undertone.

I shook my head, feeling foolish, but he was clearly not surprised. A slave does not often have possessions and a man cannot take into the next world what he does not own in this.

The aged priest muttered a prayer to his goddess, pausing and smiling to me at intervals. I muttered something inaudible which I hoped sounded appropriate, and soon the immediate formalities were over. I have always disliked the smell of burning flesh and I was glad when I was permitted to stand back with the crowd. Most of them had pulled their hoods over their heads against the drizzle. Gratefully I did the same and resigned myself to wait.

It promised to be a damp evening. Even the appearance of a drummer and piper did nothing to enliven it.

All the same, the pyre-builders knew their trade. They had developed combustion into a fine art: the fire and the torches were skilfully kept alight, and indeed it was not much more than an hour before the mortal remains of Marcus's herald were reduced to ashes. They were then doused with wine and water and swept up – at least partially – into a funeral pot. To my relief I was not expected to take any part in that.

They handed the urn to me, though, when they had finished, and I was obliged to lead the procession and carry it – still warm – to the communal tomb building recently erected by the slave guild. I had not seen the edifice before, although there were already a number of burials within it. They call it a *columbarium,* a dovecote, because of the dozens of little niches set into it, and they are very proud of it. Besides, it saves money. Slaves die every day and a communal resting place removes the need to sacrifice a pig each time to consecrate the grave.

181

I put my pot warily into the recess the foreman indicated, and a guild functionary fixed it into place with damp mud. It would be sealed more firmly later.

I was afflicted by a terrible desire to wipe my hands on my dark-coloured toga, after handling the pot, but it would have been disrespectful to do so. I forced myself to stand still while the old priest muttered a quick blessing, first on the grave itself and then on the bread and wine which the foreman handed me.

'No other grave-meats?' he enquired, and again I was forced to say no.

He nodded. 'There rarely are,' he said, in his peculiar wheezing whisper. 'And don't worry, once the urn is in this grave, you won't need to feed it further. There will be other funerals, with their own foodstuffs, and we sacrifice a bit for everyone at regular intervals.' He stepped back and allowed me to place my humble offering in the appropriate place.

I regretted not having provided some grave-meats, if not to be cremated then at least to be offered now. This dry crust and dribble of thin wine did not seem much sustenance for the long journey into the next world, but it was all that the herald was likely to get.

I hoped there would be something more substantial offered to the living. I was cold and hungry and still stiff from my ordeal and I knew a funeral supper was to be provided. Knowing the guild, it was likely to be a single dish of stewed river eels and barley, a meal which I have never liked, probably accompanied by that revolting fish pickle. I told myself that after my eventful day I should be grateful to eat almost anything – and in any case, as chief mourner, I could hardly refuse.

Well, I would soon know. The priest was invoking the moon-goddess again and then it would be time for us to return to the city. Already the more impatient mourners at the back were beginning to drift away in the direction of the gates. At last the mumbling stopped, I added my '*Vale*' to the dead man and the obsequies were over.

The guild foreman fell into step behind me. I ventured an enquiry about the funeral supper.

'Eel stew, citizen? By no means. There is pork stew tonight, and fennel. I have had the kitchen slaves prepare it specially. Last night, with such a huge attendance, it was different – though of course not everyone attended the banquet.'

'There were many mourners?' I said, with more politeness than interest.

'Crowds,' he said. 'I couldn't tell you how many.' In the flickering torchlight he smiled thinly. 'Of course, with a big crowd like that there are always hangers-on. One fellow had to turn back at the gate because his father had been jostled to the ground in the crowd, and another came to me this morning saying that he'd been robbed. No doubt there were outlaws and thieves among us.'

And then, at last, something meshed inside my brain. The foreman went on chatting to me all the way into town, about this funeral and that, and what distinguished servants he had been called upon to bury, but I confess I was scarcely listening.

Never mind that the pork and fennel was poorly cooked, and that it was served smothered with the vilest kind of jelly-fish pickle-substitute, or that the speeches and eulogistic poems went on for far too long – my mind was on other things.

If Zetso or Egobarbus had left the town last night – and I was fairly sure that at least one of them had – I now knew how they had done it. It had been so blindingly obvious that I was ashamed of myself for not thinking of it before.

I was even more ashamed a little later when, as we were walking home again, Junio turned to me. He was trotting along beside me, holding a taper.

'Master?' he said thoughtfully. 'Forgive me if I sound presumptuous, but it occurs to me . . .'

'Well?' I said.

'If I were a stranger to the town, and wished to pass the gates after sundown without arousing suspicion . . .'

'You would put on a cape and pretend to be a mourner at a funeral. And there was a huge funeral last night, anyone could have gone to it. Yes, Junio, I am very slow. The same thought has just occurred to me.'

He frowned. 'Only . . .'

I waited.

'Only, from what you say, Zetso and Egobarbus both left the banquet late. The funeral would have been over by then. One would have to move with the crowd. A lone mourner would have attracted attention.'

'You think so?' I said. 'Watch this.' We had almost reached the city gates and, as we approached, the guard, seeing my mourning clothes, grudgingly opened up the inner door and permitted us to pass.

Junio thought for a moment. 'You mean, he would have to be hiding here, in the western suburbs? But then he would be trapped between the walls and the river, once the guards were alerted.' He sounded excited, suddenly. 'But in that case, he must still be here.'

'Either that,' I said, 'or he found another way. Joining at the East Gate when the mourners were returning, for instance, and pretending to "turn back" to find his father.'

Junio looked at me.

'Somebody did,' I said. 'The foreman told me so. And I was too stupid to have thought of it. And now Zetso or Egobarbus – whichever it was – has a whole day's start over the searchers. It is very unlikely we shall catch them now.'

It was no comfort, when I got home, to find the whole

house still smelling of herbs, candles and corruption. Dismissing Junio's offer to bathe my bruises, I threw off my damp *lugubria* and called rather petulantly for a blanket. As I did so, ready to lie down in my tunic as I always did, my fingers found the cord loop of the little bottle. I had forgotten all about it again.

Junio brought the cloth to cover me. 'What is that, master?'

I told him. 'But if she poisoned her father,' I finished, 'she did not do it with this.'

Junio chuckled. 'Then it is as well you didn't show this to Marcus. He is so fearful of the Emperor's wrath that he would have had half Glevum under lock and key. That old crow of a servant was taken to the jail and began singing like a blackbird. Claims that Phyllidia always hated Felix – even before the Octavius affair – because she thinks he poisoned her mother for bearing him no sons.'

It bore out what Gaius had told me, but I had not expected Junio to know. 'Where did you hear this?'

Junio grinned. 'In the servants' room, while you were interviewing that gatekeeper. One of the slaves had visited the jail and came back bursting with gossip. All I had to do was listen – as you have always taught me, master.'

I aimed a playful cuff at his ear, but he evaded me easily. He curled up at my feet, blew out the taper and was asleep in an instant.

But I couldn't sleep. The more I learned about this affair, the less sense it seemed to make.

Chapter Twenty

'Well, old friend?' Marcus said indulgently next morning, when I presented myself, bright and early, to tender my report. He had allowed me into his presence before any other of his *clientes* and was reclining on his couch eating a breakfast of hot bread and spiced fruits. There was no sign of his new wife, but a thin secretary-slave squatted on a stool beside him, scribbling frantically on a wax tablet. Marcus waved him away at my approach, and gestured me to the stool.

I gave him an account of the funeral, hinting – not without a touch of satisfaction – that I had deduced something significant. He went on eating his spiced fruit and regarding me with amusement. I reflected that the advent of a wife seemed to have improved his early-morning mood. Marcus was often bad-tempered at this hour.

'So,' he said, when I had finished, 'you think you have the key to the mystery?'

'Part of the mystery, Excellence,' I corrected humbly. 'A very small part, I am aware.' I explained my theory about the mourner.

'Very astute of you, my old friend.' Marcus nodded sagaciously. This affability was beginning to worry me. I knew from experience that when Marcus addresses me with that air of good-natured condescension, he is about to produce a thunderbolt from somewhere.

He did it now. 'However, pavement-maker, I fear that the

matter of how these men escaped the city is no longer as significant as it was. Last night, while you were at the funeral, I received some important news.'

He paused theatrically. I knew better than to interrupt when my patron was making one of his dramatic declarations. I waited.

'You will recall,' he went on, 'that I asked the commander of the garrison to make enquiries on the road to Eboracum? About that so-called Egobarbus and his party?'

'You said that you would.'

'Well, my friend, he was better than his word. Yesterday he sent a courier with a message to a little *mansio* halfway to Letocetum, an official way-station for the military post about a day's march away. It was a short distance, for a horseman, and he had time to ask some questions in the area. There were some interesting results.'

He pushed aside his platter and gestured to the slave at the door, who hurried forward with water and napkins.

Marcus extended his fingers to be washed, and went on, 'It seems that Felix took a house near there for a day or two, before he came to Glevum. Paid gold for it, and insisted on solitude. The owner was to make it ready for him and then go away and leave him undisturbed.'

The slave poured him a cup of watered wine and offered some to me. I took a little – to refuse entirely would have been insulting – and the servant retired. Marcus raised his drinking dish and looked at me questioningly over the rim of it. 'What do you make of that?'

It was so unforeseen, I could make nothing of it. But Marcus was clearly waiting for an answer. 'The solitude you might expect,' I ventured. 'Felix would not care to share his lodgings with anyone. What surprises me is that he should rent a house at all.'

Marcus's grin broadened. 'A most unlikely house it was

too, by all accounts – a modest freeman's dwelling less than four hours' drive from here.'

I frowned. 'Why should he do that, Excellence? He had a carriage, and an imperial warrant too – the *mansio* itself would open its doors to him, offer him the best it could, and it would cost him nothing. Why would he choose to sleep in some rented hovel?' I took a sip of sour wine.

Marcus smiled. 'That is just the point, my dear Libertus. He did not sleep there. Perhaps he never intended to. It seems he took the house for someone else. Or at least someone else stayed there. The owner did not know the name, and – after his instructions – did not dare approach, but he glimpsed the man, he says. A big red-haired Celt in a plaid with a long drooping moustache.' Marcus tossed down his wine in a victorious gulp.

I was so startled I almost choked on mine. 'Egobarbus,' I exclaimed, as he had no doubt hoped I would.

Marcus set down his drinking cup. 'You see what that suggests? The two men did know each other. Felix arranged the house himself, although he pretended only to have dealt with Egobarbus through an agent. Of course he would expect Egobarbus to come to him, and not the other way about, but why select a place like that, instead of arranging to have him quartered at a military inn at no cost to himself? He was carrying an imperial warrant. Or why not simply summon him to Glevum? I never trusted this visit. I knew he was plotting something – no doubt with the help of his bewhiskered friend.' He glanced at me. 'What are you frowning at?'

'I was merely wondering, Excellence, why – if Felix met the man at the house, or even simply sent word where it was – he did not invite him to the banquet then. Of course, Felix did not know whose mansion he would have here, but he was clearly intending to demand a feast as soon as he arrived. But the guard at the gate was quite specific on the point. Felix sent his invitation only when he learned that the Celt was being held for questioning in Glevum.'

'I cannot answer that,' Marcus said tetchily. 'But there was clearly a secret meeting between them. There is confirmation of that, from an unlikely source. The driver of the hired carriage, you remember?'

I remembered only too well. I had hoped to question him myself.

'You were right to think of it,' Marcus said, magnanimously. 'He did come back for payment, as you suggested. I had one of my guards waylay him and bring him in for interrogation. He was most co-operative.'

I felt sure he was. My heart went out to the poor fellow whose only crime was first to carry a party of Celts who failed to pay him properly, and then to return to claim what was his. It was likely to have proved a painful experience. But Marcus does not share my doubts on such matters. I said, briefly, 'What did you learn?'

'That he was engaged by one of Egobarbus's slaves in Letocetum. That is where he comes from. On a given day he was to drive along the Glevum road, pick up Egobarbus and his party from a house – the same house from his account of it – and bring them here.'

'But not to take them from Letocetum to the house?'

Marcus looked startled. 'I had not thought of that. You are right, my old friend – it is a little odd.' He motioned to the waiting slave to come and refill his cup. 'Although the Celt was expecting to receive some money. The driver kept repeating that, whatever they did to him.'

I winced.

'He was promised a large sum,' Marcus went on, 'and payment for his return journey too. He arrived as arranged, but he had agreed a premium for a fourth passenger, and there were only three. When they got here the Celt refused to pay it.'

'I have been thinking about that,' I said. 'That is odd too. Why should he demand an additional fare? Does he not have one of the devices on the wheels which counts the times they turn? I thought that was the agreed basis of all hiring charges now?' The widespread introduction of the simple machine from Rome some years ago had enormously simplified the business of travelling – up to then the price of a carriage depended largely on chance, and how vulnerable you were to threat and extortion.

'He needed to bring a bigger carriage, he says, instead of his usual lighter one. Three he could have managed, but not four. He swears he explained to the slave who hired him that there would have to be an extra charge. And then the Celt could not pay it – or would not. Instead he referred him back to Felix. And, remember, Felix arranged for the use of that house, and paid for it.'

I took another sip of my own watered wine before I ventured, 'Do you suppose, Excellence, that they arranged to meet there, and somehow failed to do it? That would explain the fourth place in the carriage. Intended for Felix, do you suppose?'

Marcus looked at me. 'Felix would have his imperial carriage. Why would he want to travel in that way?'

I had no answer to that. 'Perhaps it was not Felix himself,' I suggested feebly. 'There are others of his party. Phyllidia, for instance – or that maid of hers. Her *custos* – the guard who travelled with her. Zetso Octavius even.' I did not believe it, even as I spoke. Perhaps the wine had fuddled my brain – I am not accustomed to strong drink in the morning. 'Though of course they had their own transport too. We must find Egobarbus, Excellence, and ask him. He cannot have gone far.'

'You can ask him, my old friend, but I doubt that he will help you.' Marcus's face took on the satisfied look of an arena lion after a tasty snack. He knew something that I didn't, clearly, and he was making me work for it.

I struggled for inspiration, and it came to me at last. 'You have found him?'

Marcus shook his head. 'I have not found him, no, but it seems that someone may have.'

'Dead?'

Marcus raised his drinking cup as if to say, 'Correct.'

I was, frankly, surprised. That attack in the alley the day before had convinced me that the counterfeit Egobarbus was still alive, and presumably in the city somewhere. 'Where?'

'In that self-same house I was talking of. He must have done as you suggested, crept past the gates disguised as a funeral mourner, and made his way back there. It is not impossible to walk at night, if one is desperate.'

'But, Excellence – those ruffians yesterday – I am convinced they were his slaves.'

'I presume he went alone. He could hardly smuggle his servants through the gates with him.'

It is dangerous to dispute with Marcus, but I could not let it pass. 'But it is a day's march. You are sure it is the same man?' It occurred to me that this might be the missing passenger.

'As sure as I can be. The owner of the house was questioned this morning when he returned to his home. A little later he came running to the *mansio*, saying that there was something in the well. A red-haired body, in plaid leggings.'

It was not one of the slaves then. They wore simple tunics. And it was a Celtic gentleman. No one else in these islands wore trousers. But I was still doubtful. 'Have they examined the body?'

Marcus shook his head. 'The owner tried to pull it up on his bucket but the weight broke the rope. But he thought he should report it, since the courier had been asking questions. I think he was hoping the military would help him to retrieve the body. It will poison his water supply.'

'And did they?'

'I imagine so. I do not know with what results. The messenger was just leaving, as it happened. He galloped straight to Glevum and the commander sent word to me. However, since you were so keen to visit Eboracum, I thought of sending you. You can confirm it is the same man. I will give you a letter, with my seal, and they will entertain you at the *mansio*.'

But this was not Eboracum, I wanted to shout. This was a poky military inn only a few miles away. But if my patron ordered me to go, I would have to do it.

Marcus saw my face. 'Cheer up, old friend. At least, if you make the journey, you will escape the necessity of attending another funeral. There will be a *funus publicus* for Felix in two days' time. I have decreed it. The Emperor will expect some such public gesture.'

I nodded. For these great state occasions a herald goes about the streets summoning all the citizens to attend and – whatever one's dealings with the deceased – it is generally prudent to do so. It occurred to me with a shudder that at any other time it would have been Marcus's herald that made the proclamation.

'It will be a huge affair, with a decorated bier, trumpeters, hired dancers and a sung dirge,' Marcus said. 'I have given the instructions. If we are going to do it, we will do it properly.'

I could not have escaped it – trailing along in the procession with the magistrates and dignitaries, the Vestal virgins, crowds of soldiers – horse and foot – and every citizen in the town. Always at the back, too, so that when the golden litter stopped (as it inevitably would) for fanfares and panegyrics, it would be quite impossible to hear a thing. Suddenly the prospect of this journey seemed much more attractive.

'So,' I said. 'You have no idea who this body is? Or was?'

Marcus looked inscrutable. 'I have some suspicions. The courier brought us this.' From under the cushions at his side he produced a small parcel wrapped in linen cloth. He watched me as I opened it. It was a small glass bottle with a loop at the lip. A faint aroma of almonds still lingered about it.

If it was not the poison phial which had been stolen from me the day before, it was one most extraordinarily like it.

I stared at Marcus. He was grinning triumphantly.

'The soldiers found it hidden in the ditch a little way from the house. Conclusive proof, do you not think, that this is our missing murderer?'

I did a little rapid calculation. 'But surely this cannot be the same phial, Excellence. This was recovered yesterday, you say, halfway to Letocetum. But it was only yesterday afternoon that I was robbed. Egobarbus might have gone there, but he did not have the phial. It cannot have been in two places at one time.'

Marcus's face fell. 'You think there are two phials?'

The moment had come. I slipped a hand into my folds and untied the knotted cord about my belt. 'Not two, Excellence,' I said, sadly, producing the little bottle. 'Three. I found this yesterday at Gaius's house.' I could see the questions forming, so I hurried on. 'Of course, this phial has poisoned no one. It has not been opened. But I think I should go and identify this body.'

'Very well. You had better return home and collect your slave. I have requisitioned a carriage for you. My driver will take you to the *mansio*.' He got to his feet and motioned to the slave to show me out. 'Now, excuse me, I have *clientes* to receive.'

The interview was over. I was dismissed.

Chapter Twenty-one

I shall gloss over the journey that ensued. I am getting too old to be joggled about the countryside, never mind doing it twice in three days. Suffice it to say that any bruises I had sustained in my fall in the alley were reinforced by the lack of springing, and that any threat of a chill after the funeral was redoubled by a dreadful river crossing, where the carriage wheel got stuck in a shallow ford, and Junio and I were obliged to clamber out and wade, with unpleasantly damp results for our footwear and lower garments.

I was glad I had forgone my toga for the occasion. The events of the previous day had taken their toll on my already pathetic garment. I reasoned that interviewing a freeman peasant did not require my formal badge of citizenship and I had sent Junio to the fuller's with it before we set off, in the forlorn hope of having it cleaned and mended. Since even my long tunic and cloak were clinging damply to the backs of my knees, I blessed the gods at least for my decision. Marcus's warrant and this carriage would give me all the authority I needed at the inn.

For once Junio's company did not cheer me. He was miserably anxious himself. The further we got from the familiar roads around Glevum, the more nervous he became. He had been cast down since the stabbing of the fair-headed maid, and this journey seemed the final straw.

I could understand it. Places like Letocetum were merely names to him, and I doubt he would have been surprised if the road had suddenly vanished and we found ourselves galloping briskly into oblivion. Even I, who have travelled half the island (albeit most of it in chains), was sobered to reflect that Roman horsemen routinely cover fifty miles in a single day, and the army can do almost half as much as that on foot, with their heavy kit on their backs.

We were making for the *mansio*, an official inn and staging post, just such a day's march away, where weary riders of the post could obtain fresh horses, travellers on official civil business could find a bath-house and accommodation, and even a contingent of marching soldiers could rely on food, water and a place to camp. I was looking forward to the food and water myself: it was long past midday by now, and I was beginning to understand why travellers complain of thirst.

We reached the place at last, a smallish building with stables and a large enclosure, situated near to a crossroads. It was the centre, not exactly of a settlement, but of a number of civilian farms and houses close enough to be in view. A grumbling servant sweated out to meet us, looking very doubtfully at my mere tunic and cloak.

I will say this for Marcus – the presence of his seal on a letter does wonders for the warmth of one's reception. One glance at the document I carried, and the military innkeeper opened his doors as though I were a visiting tax inspector, and offered to fetch the soldiers who had retrieved the body. A small contingent of guards commanded by an *octio*, it appeared, were using the facility en route to Letocetum, and the grisly task had fallen to them.

I agreed that meeting the *octio* would be helpful, and a servant was dispatched to find him.

Meanwhile, Marcus's letter continued to work its magic. The horses and the driver were taken off to be refreshed, while we were shown into a small but pleasant room with a central table, surrounded by stools, not couches, but comfortable enough. Cold meats and cheeses were rapidly produced and a hunk of fresh bread for each of us. Junio caught my eye. We would have lunched much more frugally at home.

They left us alone while we ate it, which we did sharing my knife and sitting companionably side by side – though, obviously, when the commander of the guard looked in a little later Junio leaped to his feet and tried to pretend he was behaving in a properly servile manner.

The *octio* looked at me severely. 'We have retrieved the body again, for your inspection . . . citizen,' he added, after a pause.

'Again', I learned, because being an anonymous body without mourners (and therefore no one to pay for a funeral) the corpse had been flung on a cart, ready to be taken to the town and thrown – literally without ceremony – into the nearest paupers' pit. In deference to my appearance, however, it had been brought back to the *mansio* and was now lying on a trestle in the entrance, awaiting my examination. I washed my hands in the bowl of water provided, brushed the cheese crumbs from my mouth and followed my guide.

It seemed to be my month for unpleasant sights. The body before me seemed to have bloated with the water, and some of the grotesquely wrinkled skin was beginning to hang loose on the bones. It had been dressed, as Marcus reported, in a pair of plaid trousers, but there was no retaining belt and the cloth had been stretched and torn as if stones had been stuffed down into it to weight the body. The face was brutal, even without the gruesome pallid swelling, and almost clean-shaven, but there were abrasions on the forehead and chin and a clump of short reddish hairs on the upper lip. The chest was badly abraded, too.

What drew my attention, however, was the hand which dangled, bloated and water-swollen, by its side. It was a squat, ugly hand, with curling red hairs still visible upon it, and a cluster of fine bronze rings – so tight they had cut into the flesh – on every finger but one. There was no ring upon the little finger, because the digit was wizened and misshapen. I might not have recognised the face, after that sojourn in the water, but I would have known that deformity anywhere.

'Yes,' I said, to no one in particular. 'This is the real Egobarbus.'

'A rich man, by the look of it,' the *octio* remarked. 'There's some fine work in those rings.' He turned to one of his men. 'Did he not have a buckle, too, when we brought him in?'

The man turned scarlet and vanished, to return a moment later with a magnificent belt of ox-hide, with a great bronze buckle worked in the shape of a dragon eating its tail. It was a work of art.

'It must have fallen off him when he was moved,' the soldier said, but no one was deceived. It occurred to me with a jolt of horror why the flesh above the rings had been so cruelly torn. Perhaps, if I had not arrived in time, my old enemy would have been tipped into his pit without any fingers at all. Though one could hardly blame the guards. The clothes and ornaments of executed criminals are routinely shared among their executioners. There is no point in wasting valuables.

The owner of the rented house was sent for (he had not been permitted to leave the *mansio*) and I heard the story from his own lips. My lack of an official garment may have won his confidence, but in any case he was garrulous with fright.

His story was simple. He had returned to the premises the previous morning, as he had arranged. 'I'd had my money from the Roman gentleman in advance, you see, and after what he'd said I expected to find the house empty. Never thought anything of it until that courier arrived asking questions. Course, being a law-abiding sort of man, I told him what I knew.'

I made no answer to this, although he glanced at me hopefully.

'And then, going out to draw water for my own purposes, I found the body in the well. And it didn't fall down there, either,' he concluded. 'I've got a slab covering my well, to keep the pigs from slipping down it, and the cover was back in place when I came to it. No, someone pushed him in and drowned him, that's what I say.'

I doubted it myself. The grazes on the face and chest suggested to me a body that had been dragged to the well after death, and stuffed down it – perhaps as a crude means of disposing of the body. That also made sense of the poison bottle. What I did not know was who had done it.

'There was a bottle found on the road,' I said, 'a mile or two from here. It had some liquid in it. Do you know anything about that?'

His expression of injured innocence was replaced by a look of pure surprise. 'A bottle? No. I did put out an amphora of wine – same wine I always give my visitors – and there was a jug of something of his own on the table. I don't know anything about a bottle.'

'Well, citizen,' the *octio* said to me, when the interrogation was over and our informant – at least temporarily – released. 'What do you want to do with the body?'

It had become my corpse, I realised, because I had endowed it with identity. I hesitated. Egobarbus was not a man I mourned, but he was a fellow Celt. Somehow I could not consign him to a paupers' pit. In the end I gave instructions to have him buried, Celtic fashion – curled like a newborn baby and facing the rising sun – wrapped in a piece of linen with his buckled belt at his side.

The soldiers, impressed by my official warrant and seal,

and accustomed to obeying orders, complied immediately, although visibly bemused by the idea of daytime burial. They watched in bewilderment as I murmured a prayer over him – to the ancient gods of earth and stone – and left my old enemy under a mound of rocks. I did not weep.

'Well, master,' Junio whispered, as we made our way back to the *mansio*. 'What will you do now?'

It was a good question. The house-owner had been present at the burial – not entirely from choice – and for want of any clearer plan, I suggested that I might begin by seeing the house. It had begun to interest me. The owner was a fat, grimy man, with an expression of foolish cupidity and a certain flabbiness of stomach which suggested that however he earned a living, it was not chiefly from labouring on his land.

I was right. The house was sizeable enough – two large draughty rooms on the ground floor and a couple of lofts above, both with frowzy curtains on one wall and crude straw palliasses on the floor. Downstairs there was a scattering of plain battered furniture. The place was not dirty, exactly, but there was a general air of dinginess: even a woven rug before the fire, which might once have been cheerfully coloured, had faded to a dismal grey over the years with dirt and soot. Outside, a scruffy field was home to a thin cow and a mangy sheep.

An odd place, I thought again, for Felix to have hired as his own.

'Tell me about it,' I said. 'From the beginning. Who asked you to rent out the house, and when?'

The oily face assumed a patient frown. 'I have been telling you,' he said. 'It must have been a half-moon ago. That Roman fellow turned up here, wanting to take the house. For two people, he said – there would be a friend. Well, I knew how to interpret that.' He gave me a hopeful smirk. He had

learned of my citizen's status at the funeral, but he still seemed
to regard me as a sort of fellow-conspirator against authority.
'He didn't just want a room, the way they sometimes do, but
the whole house. I had been recommended to him, he said,
by some of the guard at Letocetum, so he knew I was discreet,
and he was prepared to pay – more than the usual rate.
Naturally I agreed.'

Junio glanced at me, grinning widely, and enlightenment
dawned. 'Did you offer . . . entertainment?'

The fellow smirked. 'I offered him a pair of girls, of course.
Clean as a whistle my girls are, no disease and no rotten
teeth. But he wasn't interested. Didn't look like that sort of
fellow, if you understand me.'

I understood him all right. I realised all of a sudden what
kind of house this was, and what kind of pictures might be
screened behind those uninviting curtains upstairs. Clearly
the intelligence from Marcus's spies had not included that
information.

The man took my silence for encouragement. 'All he
wanted was a tray of food on the table – good food and wine
for two, and a bite of something simple for the servants. I was
to leave the door ajar and keep myself well away.' He smiled,
oleaginously. 'I knew how to do that. You learn to hold your
tongue, in my trade, and he paid me well.'

'But nonetheless you spied on him?' I suggested. He began
to look aggrieved, and I added quickly, 'You saw the Celts
arrive.'

'It's my house, citizen. It isn't where I live, but I own it.
Naturally I kept a watchful eye. I always do.'

In the hope of extorting money from his customers later, I
surmised. 'So what did you see?'

He shrugged. 'That Celtic fellow with the moustache
turned up with his servants, and I saw them go in. Worn out
with the walk, they looked, and glad to be here. I was

expecting to see the Roman, but he never came. I think he sent a message, though, later in the evening, as I heard horses, and when I looked out I saw someone at the door.'

'You saw the messenger? What did he look like?' I was expecting a description of Zetso. It was not hard to guess whom Felix would have entrusted with that task.

Disappointingly, the fellow shook his head. 'I couldn't say, citizen. I couldn't see. It was dark and he was cloaked and hooded. One of those fancy fringed military capes, not a simple woollen *cucullus* like yours.' He nodded at the one I was wearing. 'Gifted horseman, though – I heard him set off again, and he rode off galloping – at night too. Must have been fearless.'

'Did he go in?'

'No. I'm sure he didn't. He wasn't there long enough. Just came, delivered a message at the door and left. I thought his master was obviously delayed. I didn't wait any more. I went to bed. When I looked out in the morning, the carriage was outside and the Celts were leaving. I waited until yesterday, as I promised, and then I went in to clear up the place. The rest you know.'

'And when you went in,' I said urgently, 'what did you find?'

He shrugged. 'Nothing. Nothing you wouldn't expect. Someone had eaten half the food, drunk all the wine, and the beds had been slept in. Nothing else. No signs of a struggle, if that is what you thought.'

It was what I had thought. I shook my head doubtfully. 'And Felix took the house. You are sure of that?'

He spread his hands in a gesture of despair. 'Lucius Tigidius Perennis Felix. He told me his name himself, and I saw his seal. I wouldn't forget him in a hurry. I don't get many customers like him.'

That made me smile. 'I imagine not.' Clearly the Perennis

name meant nothing to him: he was merely aware that Felix was a very rich man to be interested in such squalid entertainment. 'No wonder you were tempted to spy. A man with that much purple on his edges must have aroused your suspicion.'

The brothel-keeper shook his head. 'I don't know about his toga-edges, citizen; he was only wearing a tunic and cloak. Mind you, he looked well in them. A flashy sort of gentleman.'

I stared at him. 'Perennis Felix,' I said carefully, 'is – or rather was – a squat middle-aged Roman with an ugly face. He wouldn't look well in anything.'

My informant shrugged. 'Not this Perennis Felix, citizen. He was as handsome a young man as I have ever seen astride a horse. Though I have heard a rumour he is dead.' Suddenly he tugged my arm and pointed through the open door behind me. 'But the rumours can't be true. There is no "was" about it, citizen. Here he is now, riding up the lane. Ask him yourself.'

I turned in the doorway and looked at the horseman.

It was Zetso, naturally. For a moment he clearly did not recognise me – the last time he had seen me I had been dressed in a toga. Then recognition dawned, and from the expression on his face he was as shocked and astonished to see me as I was to see him. Indeed, if it had not been for the guard waiting at the gate, who quick as thought zipped out his sword and laid a hand on the bridle, I believe that Zetso would have turned round and galloped away as fast as his horse would carry him.

Chapter Twenty-two

I don't know what I had expected. Remorse, perhaps, or revealing confessions. I got neither. Zetso had nothing at all to say, and continued to say it even when, at my request, the *octio* had him taken under guard into the *mansio* and held there.

'A difficult case,' the *octio* informed me uneasily, when I arrived at the *mansio* a little later (a man of my years cannot keep up with marching soldiery). 'In my position it is hard to know how to proceed. I am caught between the Governor's orders and the Emperor's. Perhaps you would like to question him yourself?'

They had him in an outbuilding, a little room with stone walls and high slit window spaces – not a cell exactly, but all the same a place which the passing military occasionally used to secure less willing members of their company. Zetso was sitting on a stone bench by the wall. He was unchained, but with his flamboyant looks and scarlet cape he looked like an exotic bird in a cage.

When he saw me he raised his head defiantly. 'On what authority do you hold me here?'

I began sincerely to wish I had my toga with me. In these simple garments I hardly looked a person of influence. I tried to bluster it out of him. 'I carry a warrant from my patron, Marcus,' I told him. 'It carries his personal seal and will be honoured by the Governor Pertinax – and he represents imperial authority anywhere in these islands.'

Zetso gave me a look of curdling contempt. 'To Dis with Pertinax,' he informed me, shortly. 'I carry an *imperial* warrant. It was issued by the Emperor Commodus himself, and *is* his authority anywhere in the Empire. It will be honoured by everyone – including yourself, my pavement-making friend – or else His Imperial Excellence shall hear of it. I do not think you would enjoy the consequences.'

He reached into a large leather pocket at his belt and briefly took out a scroll. He did not offer to show it to us. He did not need to. It was sealed with a purple ribbon and a seal which must have been the size of a man's hand, though I could not actually see that, since it was protected by the most elaborate enamelled seal-box I have ever set my eyes on. The *octio*, who had accompanied me to the room, ran an uneasy tongue around his lips.

'And this,' Zetso said, indicating the pile of dirty straw, the reeking candle and the crude water pot which was all the furnishings of his cell, 'is how you dare to treat me? I am sure the Emperor will be very interested.'

The guard turned the same sickly shade of yellow-grey as the straw and shifted from foot to foot. He gave me an agonised glance which said, more clearly than any words, that he wished devoutly to be somewhere else.

I made one last attempt. 'The warrant which you carry was issued, surely, not to you but to your master – Felix?'

Zetso looked at me as Felix had looked at the shattered corpse in the forum, with distaste and disdain.

'I have my master's authority to wield it,' he said. 'And it is especially framed to allow me to do so. My master had a number of affairs to see to in this province, some of them of imperial importance. He could not attend them all in person. He arranged with Commodus that I should be specially named as his proxy.'

'And now that he is dead?'

'Dead?' Zetso stared at me in astonishment.

I nodded assent. 'The evening of the feast, when you were so conveniently absent.'

That stunned him. He leaped to his feet. 'Of what am I accused?'

I thought about that warrant in his pouch. 'You are not accused of anything. At least, not yet. But naturally I wished to question you on this matter. In such circumstances any man may lawfully be detained for questioning.' I did not add that men carrying a warrant were usually exempt, at least if the questioner had any respect for his own safety.

The fight had gone out of him. 'Dear Jupiter! I had not expected this so soon. I must consider what to do.' The news – if it was really news – appeared to have shattered his lofty disdain. He turned to me urgently. 'By the strength of Hercules,' he said, 'I had no hand in this. How could I have? I was miles away. You saw me yourself.'

'You left the feast,' I said, more savagely than was strictly necessary. 'Unexpectedly.'

He flushed. 'My master gave me an urgent message to deliver. It often happens, when he does not require me to drive him. Felix was never a man to brook delay – once he has thought of a matter it must be done immediately. I arranged a horse and attended to the business at once.'

'But you did not return? Where did you go? I had thought that rumours of the death and funeral would have been the talk of the province.'

'It is true that I have been . . . out of the public eye.'

'Where? Do not try concealment. It will be easy to discover. I will have the couriers ask at every door if necessary – on the order of my own warrant which you despise so much. Others respect my patron's name, if you do not.'

Zetso collapsed like a punctured boil. He sat down lamely

on the bench again. 'There is no secret about it. I have been enjoying the hospitality of an old acquaintance of my master's, a retired centurion from the eighth Augusta. He has a handsome villa just outside Glevum, further down this road. We stayed there briefly on our journey south—'

I interrupted. 'Ah!' A tiny piece of mosaic which had refused to fit the pattern slipped neatly into place. 'I wondered where Felix spent the night before he came to Glevum. I thought for a moment that he had stayed here, in that house he rented – but once I got here I saw that was impossible. It was early in the morning when I met him in Glevum. He would have needed the horses of Jupiter to have travelled from here in that time.'

Zetso shrugged. 'There is no mystery. We had made good time from Letocetum, and my master preferred to enter Glevum in daylight. He sent me to the villa to ask for lodging. The ex-centurion agreed at once.'

I nodded. The poor fellow must have been tripping over his tunic-hems in his anxiety to offer hospitality. One glimpse of that imperial warrant, and any man with a sense of self-preservation would have turned his dying mother out of bed in order to comply. 'And when Felix moved to Glevum you went back to the villa?'

'There was unfinished business to attend to, and I returned to the villa afterwards. Is it significant? The facts are easily verified.'

I sighed. Inwardly I was convinced that Zetso had some hand in all this mystery, but it seemed he had not only a warrant to protect him but a witness too.

I tried again. 'Yet the news did not surprise you? You said you had not expected to hear of his death "so soon". And do not think to deny it. I am sure this gentleman' – I indicated the *octio* who was still standing, terrified, at the entrance – 'would testify to the truth.'

The guard looked baffled but, taking my cue, gave an unwilling nod.

'So you were expecting to hear of his death sometime?'

Zetso shot me a look which would have withered oaks, but at least he was talking now. 'It is true that he had many enemies. I have expected for many months that one of them would find him. There have been plots against him before – it is no secret in Rome. Have they arrested the killers?'

'What makes you talk of killers?' I said carefully. 'Rumour has it that he choked to death on a nut.'

The effect was astonishing, but it was not the guilty stammer I had half expected. Zetso leaped to his feet as though lightning had struck him. All deference had left him and he was his old arrogant self again.

'In that case, you have nothing to hold me for.' Zetso turned to the *octio*. 'You! Fetch me a stool and writing materials here. You will find them in my saddlebag.'

The soldier looked at me and hesitated. It was not the kind of instruction he expected from a prisoner.

'Now! Or by the imperial deities I shall have you strung from the nearest oak bough!'

The *octio* cast a frightened look in my direction.

I could hardly object. A man without a charge against him was entitled to send a letter if he could. What impressed me was that Zetso could. Most members of the army can read enough to interpret their written orders, but few do it willingly and fewer still can casually summon wax and *stilus* to pen a letter for themselves.

I nodded, and the soldier scuttled away.

Zetso rounded on me. 'Now, you may arrange for my release from here. I have unfinished business to complete. I was delivering letters from my master when you dragged me in.'

'All in good time. I have unfinished business of my own. It

was from the villa that your master sent to Marcus? With the results I saw?'

'Ah yes, the herald.' Zetso was unabashed. 'The ex-centurion sent one of his own messengers to the town, but Marcus's herald returned to say he was not available.'

'Marcus was in Corinium,' I said. 'The herald could hardly help that.'

Zetso sneered. 'My master did not like the tone in which the news was delivered.' His hand strayed again to the pouch which contained the imperial seal. 'Does that offend you, citizen?'

The *octio*, who had just come back through the door with the leather saddle-pouch in his hands, caught his breath sharply.

This was absurd, I thought. Zetso was a suspect in at least two murders, yet here he was effectively defying authority – threatening us almost – because he held an imperial warrant in his pocket. Such is the power of the Emperor.

But it was real power. A single wrong move might be the death of either of us. News of this incident would certainly reach Rome, and the Emperor is not a man to reason with. I said, 'That was not the purpose of my questions, carriage-driver. I heard that Perennis Felix had rented a house near here, the day before the feast.'

Zetso looked startled, but he said nothing. He sat down abruptly on the bench.

I sat down companionably beside him. 'Or rather,' I went on, 'it seems you rented it. Using his name. That is not quite legal, I think.'

That was an understatement. For a slave to impersonate any citizen – let alone a purple-striper of Felix's rank – is a capital offence. Not a neat death either, but often an unpleasantly gruesome one, involving floggings and stab wounds and then slavering wild dogs in the arena.

Zetso was not cowed. 'I was acting as my master's agent, as I am entitled to do by the warrant. I did nothing against the spirit of the law.'

I saw the *octio* smile faintly. It was not the spirit of the law which counted in the courts. Zetso scowled at him, and he subsided.

'There was no impersonation. I was acting on Perennis Felix's express instructions. He learned of the house from a friend in Letocetum, and told me to come ahead and hire it in his name. He gave me gold and that is what I did. I never claimed to be him. I simply did not deny that I was.'

I could not argue with that. 'What did he want it for? He could have had any accommodation he wanted – here or with his ex-centurion. And for nothing too. Why did he want to rent a bawdy-house?' The *octio* looked up with sudden interest, and I finished hastily, 'He didn't even want the girls.'

A dozen expressions chased each other across Zetso's handsome face. At last he said, 'It was . . . for a business acquaintance.'

'Egobarbus? The Celtic gentleman?'

Zetso seemed to have forgotten his reluctance to talk. He said simply, 'The Celt demanded a meeting with Felix, and my master arranged it. It was very generous. He paid for the accommodation out of his own purse.'

'A meeting about what?' I asked. I moved a little closer on the bench. 'The money that your master owed to him?'

He edged away from me. 'I was not party to the business. You will have to ask him yourself.'

'I can hardly do that. You know that Egobarbus is dead? His body was found yesterday, in the well.'

I surprised him, if I am any judge of men. His jaw dropped and his eyes widened like a startled man in a mural.

He sounded more startled still. 'Here? But I saw him in Glevum at the feast.'

'That was not the real Egobarbus,' I said. I explained about the little finger.

'Then . . .' Zetso began. He seemed to be thinking frantically. 'After all he must have . . .' He tailed off.

'Must have . . .?'

'Must have been murdered by one of his servants. Someone must have poisoned him, thrown his body down the well and taken his place in Glevum,' Zetso said. His confidence was increasing as he spoke. 'Not an easy task with that moustache.'

I had come to much the same conclusion myself. 'You had seen him before?'

Zetso shook his head. 'Never. He tried to barge in once, when my master had a meeting in Letocetum, but the servants chased him away. We never saw him, except at a distance, but he was a startling figure, with that red hair and plaid. I would have recognised him by those things alone.'

'A fact which his impersonator depended on,' I said reflectively. I was sure of it now. I wondered how the moustache had been managed. Hot wax would have held it, at least for a few hours. And, now I came to recall it, the Egobarbus at the feast had been constantly dabbing at his mouth with his napkin. I had remarked on it at the time.

'You did not see him when you called at the hired house again? It was you, I presume? The hooded rider who called that evening at the house?' I got to my feet. 'The owner heard the horse's hooves and saw you.'

He looked up at me. 'Then he will tell you that I never entered the premises. I merely brought the message that Felix could not come. And no, I did not see the Celt himself, although I heard his voice – I assume that it was his voice – bellowing at a servant. One of his slaves opened the door. I simply delivered my package and was gone. Ask the slaves, if they are still alive.'

'I shall do that,' I said, 'as soon as we have found them. For the moment they have eluded us. So, my friend, I have only your word for this.'

'I swear by all my childhood gods,' Zetso said. 'The Celt was alive when I left here. And as for Felix, he was miles away. The ex-centurion will vouch for that.'

I was sure he would. I would, however, ensure that he was given the opportunity.

'Egobarbus was singularly ill-fated in his appointments with your master,' I observed. 'Felix must have passed this very door on his way to Glevum, and yet he did not even pause to contact the man for whom he had rented the house. It seems a little calculated to me.'

Zetso flushed. 'The Celt was importunate. He had almost caused a scene in Letocetum, trying to burst in when my master was in conclave with important officers from the northern legions. I think my master thought to punish him.'

It would be like Felix, I thought, to exact such a vengeance: keeping the man here, miles from anywhere, and failing to pay him the money that he owed. 'And you have not returned here since? You did not come here after the feast?'

He shrugged. 'I returned to the ex-centurion's house, as instructed. My master had left some further letters there he wished me to deliver – as I was doing, when they brought me here.' He opened the leather saddle-pouch to reveal two small sealed vellum scrolls and a fine hinged wax writing tablet and stilus.

I thought of demanding to see the scrolls, but the memory of the warrant deterred me. I contented myself with asking, 'Who are these for?'

'The men he was talking to in Letocetum. I do not know their names. I am to deliver these to the house, that is all. Now, with your permission, I have a letter to write myself.'

He took the writing tablet from the bag, together with a wax stick and a flamboyant seal-press.

He turned himself away so that the tablet was hidden from me and scratched a few lines hastily upon it. Then he folded and latched it, and with a contemptuous glance in my direction made a great performance of sealing it, tying the cords of the tablet so that the knot lay in the recess provided and then warming the wax stick in the candle-flame and dripping it over the knot to hold it. Then, for ultimate security, he took the seal-press and impressed it onto the hot wax, saying with satisfaction, 'This seal is still effective, citizen, whoever may be dead. And I am still empowered to wield it.'

Only then did he hold the tablet out to me. I hesitated.

'A letter to the ex-centurion, to let him know what has happened. He lives apart and does not hear the rumours. It will be a shock to him. Perhaps you will see it is delivered. No doubt you will wish to interview him, in any case.' He gave me a brief description of where to find the villa.

I wondered what welcome awaited me if I arrived there bearing this letter. I did not trust Zetso a thumb's-breadth but I took the tablet without a murmur.

'Now if I am to deliver my own messages before nightfall, citizen, I suggest it would be wise to let me go. Very wise. I still carry a warrant, and these letters are of imperial importance.'

I looked at the *octio* and he at me. I was defeated. Faced with the Emperor's orders, I could only let him go. I nodded, and the door was thrown open. We all blinked fiercely in the sudden light of day.

'My horse!'

The *octio* scuttled to fetch the animal. It was a handsome brute. I have not possessed a horse since I was taken into slavery, but I had once loved to ride and I knew good horseflesh when I saw it. I was seeing it now.

Zetso slung his saddlebag over the neck, took the reins and swung up effortlessly onto the animal's back. He looked down at me. 'Your servant, citizen.' It was a sneer. Then, with a clattering of hooves, he was gone.

I stood there for a moment, clutching the writing tablet. I knew in my bones I should not have let him leave. But I could not hold him longer with impunity: I dared not even open his sealed letter. And he knew it.

I turned away and went back into the *mansio*.

Chapter Twenty-three

Junio was waiting for me. Wine was on offer at the inn, but he had obtained from somewhere a flagon of honeyed mead and a handful of spices, and was in the process of heating them up in a borrowed pan over the communal fire, preparing my favourite drink.

'Where did you get this from, you young scoundrel?' I asked, taking the proffered drinking vessel with real relish and pretended severity. In fact, knowing Junio, I guessed that he had probably won them from some unsuspecting player of twelve stones.

Junio grinned. 'There is a tax-collector newly arrived in the *mansio* from Glevum, with his slave. The others in the inn have kept away from him' – I nodded, tax-collectors are generally as popular as lepers – 'but I am not too proud to play a game of dice with his servant. Especially as he had a flagon of mead about him. I know your preferences, master. And there was little risk – they were his dice.'

I smiled, indulgently. Gambling in inns is technically forbidden, except on public feast-days, but provided there is no fighting over stakes the law is rarely enforced – one might as well attempt to stamp out an ants' nest with a pin. 'I see the Fates have favoured you again.' I poured out a little of my mead in front of the hearth. 'There, I have given the gods an oblation in gratitude.'

I was jesting, but there was method in my action. I am not a superstitious man, but my dealings with Zetso had frightened me severely. And it had distressed me to fail. I felt some sort of offering was necessary.

Junio knew me. 'You let him go then, master?'

I sighed. 'I had no option, really.' I knew what Junio was waiting for, and (as is my custom on these occasions) I told him all about it, word for word as nearly as I could remember. Merely telling him is sometimes enough to give me insights, and he will occasionally notice details which I had missed.

He did so now.

'Killers.' He interrupted my recital. 'Why should Zetso think of killers? In the plural? That is suggestive, don't you think?'

I forced myself to smile. I have tried to teach Junio my trade, and I should be pleased when he is more observant than I am.

'He talked of earlier plots, in Rome,' I answered feebly. My pleasure at my servant's skill does not necessarily entail drawing his attention to my own lack of it.

Junio grinned. 'I am not surprised. Felix must have made many enemies. He had not been in Glevum above a day, and already I can think of people who would cheerfully have killed him.'

I sipped at my mead. 'But who would have dared? Or had the means and opportunity?'

'You think Zetso killed him? If Phyllidia could steal poison from her father, presumably his slaves could do the same. Or perhaps Zetso plotted with others, and his fellow conspirators struck sooner than he expected? That would explain both his surprise and his remarks.'

'It is possible,' I said. 'He has the mentality for it. I saw his face when he recalled the herald. I think Zetso enjoys killing.'

'Then he found himself the right master,' Junio said.

I nodded. I might have said more, but at that moment the door opened and a short, thin, self-important man in a vulgar vermilion-dyed tunic and voluminous cloak looked in. He glanced at my dishevelled tunic with a mixture of disdain and astonishment, said, 'Good evening, countryman,' in an affected, but imitation, Roman accent and disappeared again. I didn't need to be a rune-reader to recognise the tax-collector.

'There goes the most hated man in all Britannia,' I said, raising my drinking cup again. 'Now that Perennis Felix is dead, that is!' The mead tasted all the sweeter now that I had seen its rightful owner. It is rare that tax-collectors find themselves on the receiving end of improper extortion.

Junio refilled my goblet, with a grin. 'I thought your Celtic friend with the damaged finger was your favourite contender for the title?' My slave was doing his utmost to lift my mood.

I was ungracious. 'Ah yes,' I said. 'Egobarbus. Another unsolved mystery.'

'Do you suppose that Zetso murdered *him*?'

I sighed. Even my spiced mead could not console me on this one. 'I would have sworn he did it,' I said. 'That would explain the poison bottle in the ditch. But Zetso himself does not believe that he did. That was obvious from his manner.'

Junio shrugged. 'If you are right, he brought poison. You hardly murder a man in that fashion without knowing it.'

'He did not push that body down the well – the house-owner was watching him. Nor did he return to do it later. He clearly has witnesses that he returned to the villa that night.'

'Suppose that Felix had Egobarbus murdered because he owed him money,' Junio said. 'If he will kill a herald for bringing bad news he would do no less to escape a serious debt. Could it have been a plot, to substitute one Egobarbus for another?'

'I had thought of that,' I said. 'But how, in that case, did he silence the slaves? They were not bribed. They had scarcely an *as* between them when they came to pay the coach-driver.

And that was no pretence, they were almost imprisoned for it.'

'Perhaps Felix promised to give them what he owed to Egobarbus,' Junio suggested. 'After all, they appealed to him from the jail.'

'In that case, why murder Egobarbus at all? Felix would still have to pay. He could not hope to cheat the slaves, if they knew where the body was. And why invite them to the feast where everyone could see them? It makes no sense.'

'Nothing in this *mansio* makes sense,' the high-pitched, affected voice broke in from the doorway.

I glanced at Junio. Our tax-collector was back.

'All I require is a roasted fowl and a goblet of decent wine,' the newcomer went on, approaching the fire. I saw to my alarm that he was carrying a wooden gaming box. 'And all they can offer me is some frightful Gallic vintage and a dish of some revolting local stew.' He settled himself on a seat not far from me, and placed the box conspicuously in front of him. The laws on gambling do not extend to board games. Clearly, despite my dishevelled appearance, I was to be tolerated as a gaming partner. 'I hear you are a Roman citizen, after all. Do you play?'

I don't, if I can help it. I am not like Junio, and I am as likely to lose a gamble as to win it. But there was little I could do. It was too late to travel further that day, and clearly we were to spend the evening together. To refuse would be discourteous.

I do not care for tax-collectors, but since I am a citizen, and therefore liable to tax, I am generally careful not to offend them. If there is a shortfall in collection, as there often is, I prefer not to be an individual target for additional levies. Besides, he had not waited for an answer: asking the average Roman if he gambles is tantamount to asking if he breathes. The man was already laying out the inlaid board and counting out the coloured glass tiles into two heaps.

'I should have stayed in Glevum,' he grumbled conversationally. 'At least I should have been assured of a clean bed and a respectable meal. But one might as well try to catch the clouds as attempt to collect any taxes there at present. What shall we play for, citizen?'

I had been afraid of this. After the expenses of the day I had little money with me. I placed a few brass coins on the table. 'This, to begin?' I knew that it was hopeless. The board itself was worth more than I possessed.

He glanced at Junio, and for a moment I thought that he was about to suggest the slave as a stake. In that case, offended or not, I would have been obliged to refuse him.

But I was safe. 'That flagon of mead, perhaps, against another? I have acquired one, though I rarely drink it. I can sell it in Eboracum. At least there I shall be away from that confounded funeral.' He placed his first playing piece on the board, and waited for me to place mine. Behind him, Junio had caught my eye and was signalling numbers with his fingers.

'The funeral?' I supplied, helpfully. Junio had signalled three, four, and I held my piece speculatively over the fourth square on the third rank. Junio shook his head. I moved it to the third square on the fourth rank and Junio smiled. I placed the piece. 'I imagine there are lavish preparations.'

'Wreaths and statues and Jupiter knows what,' the tax-collector said, pausing only as we laid out our tiles one by one. 'They are talking of having the whole garrison marching in procession. Gladiatorial games and spectacles in the arena ... all funded from the public purse. And you know what that will mean, don't you, citizen? More taxes, more trouble, more travelling for me. Why the Governor has to come at all I cannot see. They could hold the funeral perfectly well without him.'

'The Governor?' The board was almost complete by now, and I paused with my last piece in my hand. 'Helvius Pertinax is coming to Glevum? In person?' Under Junio's discreet instruction, I laid down my counter. It was, appropriately enough, the *dux* – the high-ranking piece, like Helvius Pertinax himself. Marcus's patron and friend was no more than a name to me, but I could well understand what a stir his arrival in the *colonia* would produce.

The taxman moved one of his coloured counters to jump one of mine. 'Of course,' he said, importantly, whisking my tile from the board. 'This Perennis Felix was a powerful man. An intimate of the Emperor, it is said.' He moved again; another of my tiles disappeared. 'Of course, messengers were dispatched to the Governor at once, riding night and day, and they returned yesterday with the information.' A third tile was taken from the board, and I glanced at Junio. He winked reassuringly.

It was my move now, and taking my cue from my slave I moved my *dux* into an open space. It looked feeble after our beginning, and the tax-man grinned hugely. He moved one of his own pieces forward to attack. 'As soon as Pertinax received the news he set out towards Glevum with all speed. He is already on his way.'

Suddenly I saw what Junio had planned. 'They will delay the funeral till he arrives?' I said, and suddenly it was all over. One by one his pieces fell to mine, and I was left triumphant with more than half my tiles untouched. 'My win, I think, my friend,' I said. 'A lucky chance. I think you said a flagon of mead?' Next time I took Junio to the market, I thought, I would buy him a dozen honey-cakes if he chose, and I apologised mentally for having doubted his skill.

The tax-collector was glowering. He clapped his hands impatiently and a skinny slave appeared. The tax-collector gave his orders in an undertone, and the slave, with a reproachful glance at Junio and the pot of mead which was now bubbling aromatically on the hearth, murmured something back and disappeared again. The taxman cleared his throat.

'It will have to be coins after all,' he mumbled. 'Our mead has apparently been stolen while we sat here, by a bunch of unscrupulous villains with cudgels.' He looked at our flagon suspiciously, but Junio gave him the most innocent of smiles.

I could not repress a grin myself, but I saw an opportunity to ingratiate myself. It is not always expedient to win a game of chance.

'Have a little of our mead in any case? My slave has made it hot and spiced, in the Celtic fashion. I warrant you will find it excellent.'

He hesitated for a moment, but temptation was too strong. He accepted the brimming cup which Junio offered him and, rather unwisely, drained it at a gulp. He was not used to mead, which can be potent when warmed, so I won the second game quite easily, even without Junio's help. And the third. It did not matter. In a very short space of time our companion had become quite remarkably confiding and garrulous.

'It's my belief,' he assured us, rather indistinctly, 'that Pertinax is only coming to Glevum because that fellow Marcus has got married. He is threatening an enormous feast as soon as this funeral is over.' He pondered over a move. 'An attractive widow, so they say, and already ruling him like a general. Ah! My game, I think.'

I had with some difficulty managed to place my *dux* where he could not fail to take it. It was important that he win something. Tomorrow, when he was sober, he might regret his losses and I would still be liable for tax.

'They say,' the taxman said, reaching out for the coins on the table and sweeping them with one unsteady hand in the general direction of the other. The affected Roman accent was slurred with drink and it was with difficulty that I made out what he was saying. 'They say,' he lifted a drunken finger at me, 'she is sulking . . . over some slaves of hers who were killed and refuses to leave Glevum until the murderer is found. Though Marcus,' he smiled a stupidly beatific smile, 'has somebody in cust . . . cust . . . has somebody locked up. Stupid fellow confessed. Silly sort of chap from Rome.'

Octavius, I guessed, and blessed whichever gods were responsible for that particular false rumour. I might have asked the taxman more, but he was already slumping forward on his stool, and leaning his head upon the table. Four or five beakers of hot mead had taken their toll. I made a mental resolution to leave the building next morning before the headache awoke.

I tiptoed off with some relief and availed myself of the bath-house. It was small, but adequate, and the sensation of hot steam and cool water – to say nothing of a quick oil and scrape-down from the bath-house slave – made me feel more human than I had done for several days. If I had only had a clean tunic to put on, I would have felt almost myself again. This one was becoming as battered and travel-weary as I was.

We returned to the communal eating room, where a cheerful stew was being served, and I made a comfortable meal. Junio, in the servants' quarters, ate more simply, but quite well. The tax-collector had disappeared, though the sound of reverberating snores from one of the sleeping rooms suggested what direction he had taken.

After dinner I had a short discussion with the *octio*. He offered his contingent as escort for our carriage as far as Letocetum.

I was tempted. I knew that Egobarbus had been at Letocetum and Marcus had sent me (hadn't he?) to investigate the death. Even if I took his carriage, I wouldn't be exceeding my authority – much – and if I achieved results my patron would forgive me. Indeed, he would be likely to claim that it was all his own idea. However, I could not be in two places at once. I still had to deliver Zetso's letter to the ex-centurion, and that would answer the question of where Felix spent the night. Regretfully, I was obliged to decline.

'You were lucky tonight, master,' Junio said with a grin, as he assisted me, still dressed in my tunic, to the floor.

'On the contrary,' I said testily. 'I have failed. I have not solved the question of Egobarbus, and now Zetso has slipped through our fingers. But what could I do? Zetso was carrying an imperial warrant, and without evidence it is more than my life is worth to detain him. But it is a tiresome business. I should not have let him go. I am still convinced that he was involved in the death of Egobarbus.'

Junio looked at me. 'It would be possible, master, for you to accept the *octio*'s offer. You could accompany the soldiers, perhaps in one of their carts, and I could take the carriage and deliver the letter. You could seek out Zetso and we could meet tomorrow evening in Letocetum.'

There was some sense in the suggestion, but I shook my head. 'I do not trust him a thumbs breadth. For all I know this letter carries instructions to throw me in irons as soon as I arrive.'

'But it will name *you*, it will not apply to me,' Junio said. 'And even if it does, better he imprisons me than you. You could go to Marcus – or even Pertinax – and sue for my release. It would be much more difficult to do the same for you. They would take days to grant me an audience. And I will have Marcus's carriage-driver with me.'

'Oh, very well,' I said reluctantly. 'I will think about it.' I lay down on the straw and put the tablet under the pillow at my head. I had been clinging to it all evening like a nervous sailor clinging to a oar. 'All the same, I wish I knew what that letter said.'

Junio finished arranging blankets over me. 'You should get some sleep, master. You will have to rise very early to avoid the tax-collector. He might want another game with you, and you would never beat him, sober. At least, not without me.'

He gave me a cheeky smile, and blew out the candle and curled up at my feet. I wanted to think of a reply, but it had been a long day and he was already asleep. I lay a long time on the straw, the events of the last few days swirling through my brain like unconnected pattern pieces for a pavement. Then I too, drifted into sleep.

Chapter Twenty-four

I awoke next morning with a jerk and sat up so suddenly that I banged my head sharply on the wall. Something (apart from the wall) had struck me. Why had I not thought of it before? I felt for the writing tablet beneath the straw and held it up hopefully, but it was still too dark to see.

My movement had awoken Junio, and he raised himself with a groan. 'Master, what is it? Even the sun is not yet out of bed. Can I not stay in mine a little longer? There is time yet to escape before the taxman wakes.'

'A candle, Junio.' I scrambled out of bed, pulling stray pieces of bedding from my hair. 'If am right there is no time to lose.'

'Very well, master.' He hauled himself to his feet, dusted himself down and disappeared through the door. I glimpsed him, a slim shadow in the darkness, groping towards the main building of the inn. Like every other establishment, they would not let the fire die if they could help it: if nothing else there would be a bucket of hot coals in a brazier where he could light his taper.

It seemed an age, to my agitated mind, before I saw him return, the light glimmering like a beacon in the darkened yard.

'Come here, Junio,' I greeted him. He brought the lighted candle closer, and held it aloft. I held up the wax tablet, and saw with a rush of triumph that I had been right. 'You see that? I should have thought of it before. Look at that seal.'

Junio gazed at me. 'The seal, master? What is wrong with it? It looks impressive enough to me.'

I found myself grinning at him. 'It is the seal of Perennis Felix, and that cannot be lawfully used, because the man is dead.'

'Felix's seal? You are sure?'

My grin widened. 'As sure as I stand here. I saw the seal on Felix's ring the first time I met him. One could hardly miss it. He meant it to be noticed. I marked the design at the time – I am not a pattern-maker for nothing. Three crossed swords and curlicues over a sheaf of wheat. I wonder I did not recognise it before. Give me my knife from the table there.'

Junio gulped, but he obeyed and watched as I carved at the cord that bound the tablet together. He did not voice his anxiety, but I could hear it in his tone as he said, nervously, 'So why did Zetso have it? You think he stole it from his master?'

I shook my head. 'In that case he would not use it so openly. More likely that Felix gave it to him, or even had the seal-stamp made for him. Zetso told us that Felix used him as an agent in business matters.' It was thick cord and my knife had not been sharpened, but I had almost sawn it through.

'Men do not often lend their seals.' Junio was still sounding doubtful. 'Felix must have trusted him implicitly.'

I thought again of Felix's pudgy face. 'That man would not willingly trust his own reflection in a mirror, unless he held it firmly by the neck. He must have had some additional hold on Zetso – or perhaps Zetso had a hold on him.' I moved aside the cord, taking care not to disturb the seal – I might need that later, if I was called to account for my actions – and opened the latch on the writing tablet. Junio held the candle closer.

The message was short, scratched out in a bold but uneducated hand. 'We are too late. The man is dead. Send word to Glevum. I ride to warn the rest.'

'So!' Junio said eagerly. 'You have it in your hands, master. Conclusive proof that there was a conspiracy. Zetso may not have killed his master, but he certainly planned to.'

'This message certainly puts a new complexion on the matter, Junio, though I confess I still do not altogether understand it. However, on one point I have been peculiarly stupid. I should have noticed the seal. Go quickly now and find the *octio*. We will have need of his soldiers after all.'

Junio gave me another startled look and disappeared again, while I tried rather ineffectually to rouse myself by rinsing my face and neck in a bowl of water which my slave had set in readiness the night before. If I was right I needed my wits about me, and I was beginning to regret the several goblets of spiced mead that I had allowed myself the night before.

We were none too soon in reaching the *octio*. Soldiers keep early hours. The contingent was already afoot and preparing for the day's march.

The *octio* came in, his natural air of assertive bustle restored now that Zetso had left us. He was ready to be obliging, though – I still held Marcus's warrant in my pouch. 'How can I assist you, citizen?'

I outlined what I wanted, and the affability flowed out of him like dye from an octopus. A little of his confidence went with it. 'Citizen, I already have my orders. This is impossible. We could escort you to Letocetum if you wished it – but to arrest that horseman again, with that warrant still in his pocket? And then abandon our march and return with him to Glevum? That is more than my life is worth.'

I could hardly blame him for this. He was speaking literally, if a charge of disobeying orders was proved against him. He was not even a centurion, only a second-in-command. If I was wrong in my deductions I was risking not only my life, but his. And, although he did not know it, I was about to flout the Emperor's own warrant. My only hope lay in an appeal to rank.

'Listen, *octio*,' I said, with as much authority as I could muster, 'Helvius Pertinax is governor of this island. Every soldier in it is under his command. I issue you this order in the name of Pertinax, on the authority of the seal I hold.' I held up the wax tablet. 'I assure you it has more authenticity than this one.'

He glanced at the little recess on the tablet-cover where Felix's seal still nestled on its broken cord, and his jaw dropped – for all the world like a mime at a banquet caricaturing surprise. For once I had occasion to bless the ugly Roman's taste for ostentation. One could almost see the *octio*'s brain working. I could not have cut an impressive figure at that moment, in my tousled tunic with pieces of bed-straw still adhering to me – but if I had the authority to unseal that tablet, and boast of it in front of witnesses, I must be more important than he thought.

I said, to encourage him, 'I have doubts about that warrant he was carrying, too.'

He ran a thoughtful tongue around his lips. 'Of course, citizen, when you put it that way . . . But surely, by the time we get to Letocetum, the man may easily have gone? He is an excellent rider, and he has a night's advantage on us, and in any case my men are on foot.'

He was right, of course, and I acknowledged that. 'Nevertheless, it is my guess that he will stay there for a while. He speaks of "others" in that tablet – it will take him a little time to find them all.'

The *octio* looked doubtfully at the unsealed tablet again. 'But, citizen, even if he is still in the vicinity, how will you know where to look? Letocetum is not a large settlement but it is far bigger than this. There was most of a legion stationed there at one time, and a whole little *vicus* grew up around it. Besides, Letocetum is a meeting of the ways. If he has left, how will you know whether he went to Deva, Danum or Londinium?'

He was right, again. The fellow had more knowledge of the roads than I did. 'There is a good chance that he will not have left,' I said, with more certainty than I felt. 'He does not expect to be followed. Once he has found his contacts, there is no need for hurry. And as for finding him in the village, that should not be difficult. Zetso spoke of Egobarbus bursting in on a meeting "in the house". Glevum is a large *colonia*, but any inhabitant could tell you everywhere that Felix visited. He was not an inconspicuous person. I imagine in a small village, even on a crossroads, such information should be easy to obtain.'

The *octio* swallowed and nodded. He was clearly very unhappy. 'In a while then. I must see my men are fed, and then we shall be on the road. Your servant, citizen.' He went out, looking like a religious prisoner on the way to the arena.

I too had breakfast to attend to, although here it would be a miserable Roman affair of bread and water, with an apple if one was lucky. Oatcakes are a Celtic taste. I could find it in my heart to envy the soldiers their morning issue of thin, watery vegetable soup – the army, at least, recognises that a man must eat before he marches.

I was swallowing my crust of bread (no apples), and hoping that the taxman would not waken and join me, when the *octio* burst in on me again.

'Apologies, citizen,' he blurted, looking askance at Junio who was scrambling to his feet from my side with his mouth full of breadcrumbs, 'but I have a solution. You could send ahead to Letocetum – there is a postrider newly arrived from Isca, with urgent orders for the garrison there. He will pause only to eat and to exchange his horse, and – although it is irregular – no doubt he could alert the garrison of your wishes. There is still a small *vexillation* posted there, in case of any repeat of that regrettable Boudicca affair.'

He was so delighted with his solution, which would relieve him of the necessity of arresting Zetso, that he forgot I was a Celt and that for me the ill-fated revolt of the fearless queen of the Iceni was less regrettable than tragic. However, I did not dwell on that. I had the courier sent for, and gave him instructions for the commander of the little holding garrison at Letocetum. On the assumed authority of Pertinax, naturally. All the gods preserve me, if I was wrong.

'The fellow claims to be holding a warrant,' I said. 'But I believe that the seal is worthless. He is to be arrested and held until I arrive with the guard, and then I will take him back to Glevum to face trial. I believe he poisoned one of my countrymen, and perhaps conspired to kill his master besides, although I cannot prove it at the moment.'

It was all one to the courier; he was not required to arrest Zetso himself. He repeated my message faithfully, word for word, and assured me that it would be delivered to the *vicus* before noon. With a little help from the Fates, he added, that should ensure that Zetso was captured and waiting for me when I arrived in the evening. If he thought it odd in any way, taking these outrageous orders from an elderly civilian in a tunic, he did not betray it by so much as the flicker of an eyelid.

After he had departed, I finished my meagre breakfast and we were ready to depart ourselves. It was a slower business, moving in concert with the marching soldiers, but for a man of my mature years it was a good deal more comfortable. It was amusing too, bowling through little hamlets with an armed escort – more than one labourer, under the impression that I was some important personage, stopped to throw leaves of tribute under our wheels and half prostrate himself as I passed.

It was late afternoon before we came to Letocetum. The *mansio* was not much bigger than the one we had left, and only partially completed, although the enclosure here was more elaborate, a paved compound protected by a rampart and ditch with the road running through the middle of it. I left Junio to settle in at the inn, while I drove on to the fort which was built on a commanding hilltop nearby.

The courier had been better than his word. I was expected, and with urgency. As soon as our contingent came in sight – obviously the soldiers would spend the night at the camp rather than the *mansio* – the commander of the post came bustling out to meet me, in full regalia: an effect rather spoiled by the sight of his armourer scuttling after him to tie up one of the leather bows that held the polished chestplates at the back.

If he was surprised to see a togaless old man emerging from the carriage he did not show it – perhaps the courier had alerted him. It was clear, however, that he was in some agitation.

'Hail, citizen.' He raised his hand in salute as though I were indeed representing Helvius Pertinax in person. 'I have good news to report. The individual you were seeking has been apprehended, and is in confinement awaiting your arrival. He had no letters with him.' He avoided my eyes in obvious embarrassment. 'I presume you are aware that he appears to be travelling under an imperial warrant? He keeps referring to his "seal". I hope you are right about him. I am holding him solely on your supposed authority.'

I gave a short laugh, which was supposed to sound dismissive. The officer's manner left me in no doubt of the dreadful consequences of error. 'Have you examined the seal?'

'No, citizen, that was not in my instructions. I have left that to you. I prefer to involve myself as little as possible. If it proves authentic . . .' He did not complete the sentence. He did not need to. If I was wrong the only question remaining was which agonising death awaited me: being burned alive for treasonably ignoring the imperial warrant, or being crucified for bringing false accusations against its bearer. Commodus was not only the most powerful man in this world, he was (according to the law) an incarnate deity.

I tried to still my thumping heart by reminding myself of the equally unpleasant consequences – at least for a non-citizen like Zetso – of passing off a lesser seal as the Emperor's. That made me feel a little better until I remembered that I had rashly claimed to have the governor's authority, in a not dissimilar fashion. I took a deep breath.

'The matter is soon settled,' I said. 'Lead me to the man.'

They had tried to ride both horses, as the saying goes. Zetso had been detained, but in a warm and well-aired room in a little outbuilding beside the tower. He was unfettered, and had been allowed to keep his possessions, with a stool, blanket and pillow at his disposal. Bread, cheese, fruit and watered wine had been thoughtfully provided. If Zetso were proved innocent, he could not complain to the Emperor about his treatment at the hands of the guard.

He looked up sullenly at my approach, and from the look on his face I was certain of my victory. I wasted no words.

'That worthless warrant you carry,' I said, with a dramatic flourish. 'Give it to the officer.'

Zetso said nothing, but produced the scroll and handed it to the soldier. I have never seen a man look more defeated.

The officer looked at the elaborate seal-box in dismay.

'Open it,' I said. 'And let us all see how valueless it is.'

The man obeyed. I saw his hands tremble as he forced the box open and revealed the flamboyant seal within. His face, when he saw it, was a picture of amazement. Wordless, he handed it to me.

I took it with a little smile, which died upon my lips. The warrant that I held in my hands was sealed, beyond a doubt, with the great imperial seal of the Emperor Commodus himself.

Chapter Twenty-five

They threw me into a cell, without light or water, to shiver miserably on the stone floor, while they considered what to do with me.

I learned later that I was lucky to escape execution. Only the protestations of Marcus's carriage-driver that I was indeed a Roman citizen, enjoying the personal protection of Marcus Aurelius Septimus, saved me a brutal flogging there and then. At my age I would have been lucky to survive it. As it was, the testimony of a terrified Junio, marched up from the inn, and the production of the all-important document from Marcus, saved my life.

Of course, I did not know this at the time, so I did not know whether to hope or despair when they came for me a little later. Two silent and surly guards hauled me to my feet. They bound my arms, and – ignoring both my questions and my explanations – took me in silence to the jailer's own quarters, to spend an uncomfortable night on his lumpy mattress with a regiment of fleas for company, and a lump of sour bread and sourer wine for sustenance.

It did not matter. I could not have slept or eaten if all the pleasures of Bacchus were spread out at my feet. In the brief intervals between the bouts of terror I was racked by a kind of self-reproach. I had been so sure that the seal was worthless and that Zetso knew that it was. And I was convinced, on every rational ground, that he had poisoned Egobarbus. Yet he had equally convinced me that he did not think he had.

The man must be a consummate performer. That was, perhaps, why he had been so useful to his master. Whom he had in the end, it seemed, conspired to murder. And now they would let him go. I would be executed; even if I could send to Marcus and he commuted the sentence to 'interdiction', by which a man is legally refused the necessities of fire and water, that would come to the same thing in the end, only more slowly. I could not flee into exile like that citizen in the matrimonial case. The tribunes would never let me go, and I should die in prison, a nasty lingering death of cold and thirst. But there was no certainty that I could even send to Marcus.

And Junio, what would happen to poor Junio?

My thoughts tormented me almost as much as the fleas. Through the little window space above the bed I strained my eyes against the dark until the stars faded and the chill light of dawn began to brighten the sky. I wondered whether I should ever see it again.

I was soon to know.

It was hardly sunrise before the *secundarius* marched into the room. He was boiling with truculence and indecision, though he tried to hide it, and I realised that I had created a dilemma for my captors. Free Zetso, and they risked offending Pertinax: free me, and there was likely to be a complaint to the Emperor. The officer's solution was born of desperation.

'I'll pack you both off to Glevum,' he announced. 'Shackled and under guard. Pertinax has gone to Glevum; he can take care of it. I shall send that so-called imperial warrant with you, to be used as evidence. Then we shall see if that authority was real.'

I felt myself pale. Since I had claimed the governor's authority, without his approval, I was guilty of a crime myself. I had usurped his authority, and in his name defied the

Emperor. That would endanger Pertinax and I could expect no mercy. But there was still a glimmer of hope. Pertinax was a friend of Marcus, and my patron at least would intercede for me.

Or would he? The Emperor was not a man to cross.

The *secundarius* shook his head like a maddened bear in the arena. 'I do not understand you,' he roared, suddenly. 'You bear false witness in front of witnesses: he carries an imperial warrant which should prove his case. Yet you look hopeful and he seems in despair. I shall be glad to see the back of both of you.'

I had feared a long weary march to reach our destination – wearier yet under the weight of chains – but it appeared that after all this was not to be. They tied us in ropes, not fetters, and put us in a cart – standing, it is true, but a considerable improvement on the heart-straining, foot-blistering trudge I had envisaged. Instead it was our guard that would have to march, four armed soldiers ahead and two behind. Fortunately, being soldiers, they were trained for it.

Junio, bizarrely, was permitted to return to Glevum with Marcus's coach and driver, although without me he obviously could not ride inside the carriage. Instead he perched up on the seat beside the driver, carrying my patron's warrant in case of being stopped and questioned.

I was being hoisted into the cart as they pulled away, and I stood there helpless, hands bound to my sides, and watched my servant go, until the carriage disappeared from sight and the rattle and the hoofbeats died away. Without slave, toga or warrant I was triply vulnerable: just an unknown ex-slave being hustled onto an open waggon. I had never felt so bereft since the day I was taken into servitude.

Then Zetso was hauled up after me, and it was our turn to set off. No swift horses for our cart, only a pair of plodding army mules, and as soon as they were urged into action we discovered the shortcomings of our position. We were loosely tied to rings high up on the front end of the cart but – though this kept us more or less upright – every rut and pebble meant a buffeting, since we had no hand free with which to steady ourselves. Almost before we were out of the fort Zetso and I were falling painfully against each other, exchanging looks of mutual hostility. I set myself the task of keeping silent, whatever the bruising, and found that the concentration helped me to bear the jolts.

An escort of soldiers has advantages. At the junction where the two roads crossed we met a convoy of waggons bound for Londinium, but since we were military traffic and they were civilians, despite their larger numbers they had to clear the road to let us pass. There was a brief respite as a score of carters, sweating and swearing, urged their heavy waggons onto the uneven verge.

'Taking all this collection down to sell.' The driver of the leading cart addressed one of our escort apologetically. 'Belonged to a wealthy widow who died of the pox, and her son has ordered it. Better price in Verulanium Londinium, he says, though I cannot see it. Who would want to buy this load of junk? Older than the old lady herself, most of it, and more decrepit. And as for the slaves, there can hardly be one under thirty.'

The guard ignored him, and we rattled past. I saw the cart of slaves, at the end of the procession. They were roped as we were, though a little more secure since there were a dozen of them, all of them with faces of dull despair. All female, of course – any useful manservant would have found a home at once with the heirs – and all of them faded. Only one had a face which might once have been beautiful – might be so yet if that terrible weariness left it.

As we rumbled past she lifted her eyes, and looked towards

us expressionlessly. Embarrassed, I averted mine. And then looked back. Something – the curve of the cheek, the shape of the brow – stirred recollection in me. I forgot my vow of silence.

'Gwellia!'

I leaned forward, almost losing my balance as I called, and lurching into Zetso. The guard behind me muttered a curse and swiped at me with his baton. I did not care.

But it was too late. Our cart was lurching onwards. But she did turn, at the name, and for a moment our eyes met. She knew me. I saw it in her face. A fleeting moment only, and she was gone.

Gwellia. She was alive. On any other day I would have stopped the coach and offered everything I possessed to buy her from her owners. But today I was a captive, with no rights, and every lurch of the cart was carrying us further apart. My spirits, which had soared for an instant, sank lower than the dusty road and stayed there. I was almost glad when it began to rain.

Both Zetso and I still had our cloaks, and a kindly guard pulled up our hoods for us. We stood there, two shivering statues in a waterfall, as we ploughed on helplessly through the deluge. The weather made the cart-floor slippery and increased our misery all the way back to the halfway *mansio*.

But I did not cry out again, and any water coursing down my face could simply be mistaken for the rain.

Chapter Twenty-six

It took us two days to return to Glevum. Even then it was late afternoon before the cart drew up before the North Gate. From the nature of our arrival you would think us captured rebel generals at the least. Our escort stood in formal ranks around us, daggers drawn, while their leader went to interview the guard. I could hear the murmur of voices, and then hobnailed sandals crunched towards the cart. I sensed Zetso stiffen but I avoided his eyes. We had not exchanged a syllable since leaving Letocetum.

The footsteps stopped beside me. I continued to stare fixedly at the floor of the cart.

'Great Hercules!' exclaimed a voice. 'I might have known that we would have trouble with that one. Hanging around here in a toga the other day, pretending to be a citizen and asking too many questions.' I looked up and recognised the guard with the spear, whom I had spoken to after my visit to the *thermopolium*. He had the spear again, and he was looking none too friendly with it.

I said nothing. He would never believe I was entitled to that toga, and I was in enough trouble already. I could only wait until Marcus could be found to vouch for me.

The guard poked at the fringe of Zetso's hood, lifting it back from his sodden cloak. 'And here is another one. There has been a lookout for this fellow on the gates for days. Oh, dear Mars, our commander is going to be delighted with this little cargo.' He nodded to our escort. 'Get them down. We'll get them locked up in the guardroom straight away.'

Our descent from the cart was just as humiliating as our entry into it. I was released from the restraining ring, a soldier grabbed the rope which bound my arms and I was hauled to the back of the cart and lifted unceremoniously down like a bundle of hay. Zetso followed shortly after and we were marched, though none too steady on our feet, through the gate and into a cell in the bowels of the watchtower.

It was merely a holding cell, but the Romans know how to construct a prison. It was calculated to instil despair. Dank floors, cold stone, damp bedding and bleak walls with only the smallest slit above our heads to permit the entry of reluctant daylight. The smells of human terror – sweat and urine – mingled with the sour odours of decay.

'I appeal to the Governor of Britannia,' I exclaimed, as I was shoved half staggering into the room. If Pertinax were here he would be lodging with Marcus. 'I am a Roman citizen . . .'

'With traces of a slave-brand on your shoulder? Tell them all that at your trial,' the guard said, jeeringly. 'You will see the governor soon enough.' He gave me a final push and tied my bonds loosely to a shackle on the wall. Zetso was propelled in after me.

I had expected Zetso to protest as well, to refer to his warrant and demand immunity or at least an audience with the commander of the garrison. He did neither. He gave a sneering laugh as the door swung to behind us, then as the key turned in the massive lock he shouted, 'You will pay for this!' Then he lapsed into silence again.

I marvelled that he could find anything to laugh and sneer at, although he was better placed than I was. Once that warrant was proved he would certainly be released. I might never see the outside world again, except perhaps when I was taken out to die.

I did not look at him, nor he at me. We had brought this misery on one another. We stood, each in his own stinking corner, leaning in fettered silence against the filthy wall. I do not know how long we stood there – perhaps an hour, though it might have been far more. Through the narrow slit in the wall we could see the sky grow darker, and the gloom of our prison grew more gloomy yet. I was hungry and thirsty, tired and bruised, but there was nothing to eat or drink, and nowhere to sit except the pile of damp and fetid straw on the floor.

However, after what seemed a thousand years, a duty soldier unbolted the door and opened it a crack. A thin shaft of light streamed into our cell and he pushed a stale loaf and a shallow bowl of water at each of us.

Zetso made a move, so sudden that he startled me in the darkness. 'Guard!'

The soldier paused. I saw his hand move towards his sword, but Zetso was no threat. He, like me, was still bound about the arms.

He strained at his bonds urgently. 'I wish to send a message. I can pay.'

The soldier sheathed his dagger, hesitantly. It is not uncommon under Roman law for prisoners to send messages, even letters, from their cells. Especially if they can pay the messengers. 'Well?' He left the door open and moved towards Zetso.

Zetso's voice dropped to a murmur. He intended that I should not overhear, but around those empty walls even a whisper echoed. With a little effort I could make out every word.

'A message, urgently, to Gaius's house. Look at my hands. See, there is a ring on my second finger. It is the finest onyx. Remove it and take it to the citizen. Tell him that I am held here and ask him to arrange for my release. Do that, and the jewel is yours. Bring me my release within the hour and you shall have another to match it.'

I did not need to hear the soldier's reply. In the light from the door I saw him remove the ring, and a moment later he disappeared. The door shut and Zetso shuffled back against his corner in the darkness, but already I could sense a more confident air about him.

If only I had a ring with which to bargain, I thought, perhaps I could send a message to Marcus. Although of course there was no guarantee that Zetso's plea would ever reach Gaius. Gaius? I jerked myself upright. Why was he sending messages to Gaius? Had he conspired with Gaius from the start? That was a possibility I had not considered. And yet, now that I had thought of it, I wondered why it had not occurred to me before.

There were so many factors which suggested it. Felix had died in Gaius's own house. Who would have such opportunity to poison his food? Or perhaps not even food. There was that so-called cure which Gaius proffered. Supposing that had contained the poison? Far more secure than meat or drink which anyone might share. And Gaius hated the man. Not merely with the kind of general loathing which anyone who had met him felt for Perennis Felix, but with a more personal hatred. Something, surely, connected with his wife?

I tried to piece the story together, as I had heard it from my several witnesses. Gaius had visited Rome, together with his wife – the young and beautiful bride whom he had loved. She had been affected by the journey, he had told me that himself, and Phyllidia's mother – Felix's unwanted wife – had been good to her. And then?

I shrugged. I did not know. Felix's wife had died, supposedly from drinking bad water from a well. That was not surprising; there were often deaths from contaminated water sources. Yet Phyllidia – and Gaius too it seemed – believed that Felix had arranged her death. 'He sent her a gift of wine and she died shortly after.' Why should they suspect him of that? Others had perished from drinking of the same well.

Then, like a thunderbolt from Jove, a solution occurred to me. Supposing Gaius's bride was one of those 'others'? What had Gaius said? 'She was with her when she died.' If Felix had sent poisoned wine, had he killed both women at a stroke? That was a motive for revenge, if I ever heard one. A sweet revenge, if Gaius had contrived to serve Felix with a little of his own medicine. Provided by Zetso perhaps, stolen from Felix's stores? It was Felix's own poison, I was sure of that from the empty phial. It was the image of the one that Phyllidia had stolen.

It would explain so much. Why Gaius had been so ready to adopt Phyllidia. Even the hapless dog, perhaps. A painful sacrifice to test the effect of Gaius's mixture?

I was so pleased with the elegance of my solution that I had almost forgotten the discomfort of my surroundings. Even when a duo of guards arrived a little later and took Zetso off 'upstairs' – presumably to more congenial surroundings – I was sustained by the realisation that, if I could prove my theory to the court, not even the imperial warrant was likely to save his life. The penalty for a slave who conspires to kill his master is always death. And for all his fancy uniform, Zetso was still a slave.

Little by little, though, my enthusiasm waned. Even his silent presence in the cell had been some company, and without him the darkness seemed more threatening and every instant an hour. I tried to console myself anew by imagining the case I would present to Marcus – supposing Marcus ever sent for me. As the weary night drew on I began more and more to doubt it. I had nothing to offer to the guard; how should Marcus learn that I was here?

I had reckoned without Junio.

It was late – very late. So late that hunger and fatigue had forced me to gnaw a little at the musty bread. With my arms bound to my sides, I could only do so by lowering myself painfully to my aged knees and leaning forward to it like an animal. I understood now why they had provided water in a bowl – there was no way that I could lift a cup. I was obliged to lap at it, like the abject creature I was. Nor, once down, could I regain my feet. I was beginning to resign myself to the necessity of spending a dismal night down there, grovelling on the stinking straw, when I heard the key in the latch.

The door was opened, and two things happened at once. Junio came in, accompanied by two guards whose blazing torches flooded the cell with sudden blinding light, and on the instant – as if that same illumination had lit the dusty corners of my brain – I saw the flaw in all my careful reasoning. If ever a man could smile and groan at once, I did it then.

Junio ran to me. 'Master? What have they done to you?' He set down the cloth-wrapped parcel he was carrying and turned to the guard. His voice was trembling with what may have been anger, but sounded treacherously close to tears. 'Release his bonds at once. Have you no fear of the authorities? This man is a Roman citizen. More than that, he is under the protection of Marcus Septimus. See, here is his letter of authority.' He stooped and produced Marcus's warrant from his parcel.

The younger soldier looked sheepish. 'We learned that one of these two was a citizen. We thought it was the other prisoner. He has rich clothes and carries seals to proves he works for the imperial court. That is why your master has been held. He questioned and ignored the seals, and stands accused of treasonably failing to honour the Emperor.'

Junio looked at me. 'Did you not appeal to Marcus, or to the Governor? I tried to let them know you were arrested, but they are at this funeral feast tonight. They have been involved in the rituals all day.'

Before I could reply the soldier started babbling again. 'He did appeal – to the Governor, and we have made arrangements for him to be heard. He asked for the Governor, and the Governor he shall have. He is to be taken before him first thing in the morning. We are simply holding him here, waiting for the court, like any other prisoner. There was nothing to mark him out. He has no . . .' whatever he was going to say – toga, rings, money – he thought better of it, 'marks of status,' he finished lamely.

The other guard said nothing, merely leaned forward with his dagger and cut my bonds. 'I'm sorry, citizen,' he muttered gruffly, as I attempted to move my numbed fingers and my stiffened arms. 'But how were we to know? A tattered tunic and work-hardened hands. You don't look like a citizen.'

Junio meanwhile had opened up his bundle more fully to reveal my toga, darned and mostly clean, freshly fetched from the fuller's. I have never been so glad to see the wretched garment in my life. He shook it out and held it towards me. I saw the two soldiers exchange frightened looks.

'You'd better fetch the captain of the guard,' said one, and the other disappeared. I could hear his footsteps clattering on the flagstones. Junio helped me to my feet, and taking off my still-sodden cloak began to wrap me gently in my toga. Its heavy folds were warm and comforting, and perversely I began to shiver.

All the old gods of earth and stone, bless Junio! Suddenly, the soldiers could not do enough for me. I was taken upstairs – or rather I was assisted there – to a small room with a stool and a narrow bed, and a bowl of warming soup was brought to me. I was still a prisoner, of course, with a guard at the door, and would be tried tomorrow, but I recognised anew the privileges of citizenship and patronage. Even when I was found guilty of the charges – as I doubtless would be – I would die a more dignified death.

They were so apologetic at my previous treatment that they allowed Junio to stay with me awhile. 'If only I could prove a case against Zetso!' I said. 'There might yet be hope for me if I could show that he conspired to kill his master.' I outlined my ideas concerning Gaius.

Junio beamed. 'But, master, that is wonderful. Gaius was famed for having loved his wife to distraction. If Felix poisoned her, even by accident, he would have had a splendid motive for poisoning Felix.'

'Except,' I said gloomily, 'that he didn't do it. There is the dog, for one thing. I attempted to convince myself, but while I can accept that Gaius would murder Felix, I do not believe for a moment that he would harm his dog.'

Junio was not to be quelled. 'Perhaps the dog was killed by accident. When Felix dropped his drinking cup, perhaps? You told me that everything was split upon the floor.'

'Yes,' I conceded. 'I believe that something of the kind destroyed the dog. But not at Gaius's hands. Supposing that everything I said is true. Gaius had prepared a poison mixture, and was ready to proffer it as a medicine. How could he hope to ensure that Felix would conveniently require it, by choking on a nut?'

Junio stared at me. 'Tommonius . . .?' he suggested, feebly.

'Tommonius had no grudge against Felix. Against Marcus perhaps, for upsetting his private affairs, but he had never met Felix. He came to the feast hoping to arrange some trade with him. In any case, when he placed the bowl on the acrobat's feet, how could he guarantee which nut Felix would select, to have it stick in his throat – or, indeed, that Felix would select a nut at all?'

Junio sighed. 'So, what do you suppose? Octavius is guilty after all?'

'Of course he isn't. He clearly thought that Phyllidia had killed her father. Presumably he knew that she had stolen the poison, and deduced the worst. The poor idiot made a confession in the hope of saving her. But he could not have done it. He was not even in the house until the banquet was begun, and I myself was with him after that. And Phyllidia did not arrive until the gates were closed.'

'One of them might have bribed the servants.'

'When? Unless Phyllidia was in collusion with Zetso. I considered that. It remains a kind of possibility – we know that she had succeeded in stealing poison – but I cannot make sense of it. Why come to Britannia to murder her father? She might have done it much more readily at home. She still had her phial of poison intact – and what did Zetso stand to gain from it?'

'Then it remains a mystery?'

'There is something missing in my reasoning,' I said. 'I don't know what it is. Perhaps it really was a judgement of the gods, as Tommonius said. There must be many vengeful spirits in the afterworld who would seek Felix's downfall. Marcus's unfortunate herald, for one. And I am as convinced as I can be that Felix engineered the death of Egobarbus, simply in order to avoid paying him the substantial sum he obviously owed. But it seems that I will never prove that either. I face trial in the morning – on a charge of which I am clearly guilty.'

'I will try to help you, master, even if they will not let me stay with you,' Junio said. The guard was already signalling that it was time for him to leave. 'I will work at it all night if necessary.'

'So shall I,' I promised.

But I was wrong. I am an old man and the buffetings and depredations of the day had left me bruised and exhausted. I lay upon the simple bed to rest, shut my eyes for a single moment to help my concentration, and when I opened them again I found that – despite the threat of execution hanging over me – it was already morning and I had slept till dawn.

Chapter Twenty-seven

A Roman court is always an impressive business, even when one does not find oneself the subject of it. The lofty chamber, white-robed magistrates, the bevy of scribbling slaves and scuttling attendants, the tap of sandals on the pavement floors and the swish of togas – all these things create a sense of awe. Even the babbling crowds of the curious and ghoulish, who are forever clamouring at public places, feel it and are hushed.

When the court is to be presided over by the provincial Governor, the awe is increased a hundredfold. As I was conveyed to the basilica next morning, under guard but still wearing my toga, the streets were lined with residents – many of them no doubt roused from bed and co-opted for the purpose. Yesterday's funereal wreaths and arches had been re-dressed with flowers and ribbons, and were doing double service as festive garlands. As we passed, some of the attendant crowds waved their branches and cheered, as people do at processions for no especial reason but to pass the time.

We had not long to wait. The notes of distant trumpets could be heard, then clarions, drummers and the sound of cheers. A string of infant slaves appeared to strew the way with rose-petals, mounted horsemen followed, and at last Pertinax himself arrived, in a closed imperial carriage with a marching guard.

I had never seen the Governor before, except in statues. He was a little less impressive than his images – a man of middle height, and middle age, with a strong intelligent face, at once severe and just, and an air of dignified authority. In another time and place I would have liked him at once, but as I stood shivering in the courtroom to meet him I was more aware of the stern jaw and the determined stride than of the high forehead and the twinkle in the eyes.

A carpet had been laid out for him, all the way from the top of the steps into the judgement room. He walked sedately along it, though he seemed oblivious of it, to take his seat. It was a kind of gilded chair, almost like a throne, with a footstool before it on which he rested one sandalled foot. With his deep-purple edges and his fine cloak swirled behind him he sat there like a monument to justice, while servants placed a wreath around his brow.

Marcus, who was following, was forced for once to take a lowlier stool. He still wore a mourning band around his toga, and many of the other dignitaries did the same.

I tried to catch his eye, but he refused to look in my direction.

'Set forth the prisoners,' the governor said, and I was led forward. At least a hundred spectators, apart from magistrates and officials, had packed themselves around the walls and doorways, but there was an open space in the middle of the room. I found myself standing in it, with Zetso at my side. His hands, like mine, were bound together at the wrists, but he showed no signs of a flogging.

'What are the charges?' Pertinax's voice was resonant.

I was arraigned first. I had ordered the arrest of the other prisoner, claiming the governor's authority, in defiance of a signed authority which promised him safe conduct as the agent of his master. I had questioned the authenticity of the seals. A clear case of treasonable insult to the Emperor. Was I guilty of these things?

I would be asked the question three times, as required

256

by law, but I could see no help for it. I had no counsel here to plead for me; my only hope was that Marcus would provide one. At the moment, however, he was simply looking excruciatingly uncomfortable, clearly regretting our association, and hoping that I would not try to claim his patronage.

'Guilty,' I said, and felt the court relax. Without a plea in defence, the death sentence was a foregone conclusion, though it must be ratified by the Emperor. Furthermore, a governor was not empowered to impose the most humane of such sentences, *liberum mortis arbitirum* (the freedom to choose the manner of one's dying), whose victims had proved such a willing market for Felix's poisons. When I was sentenced, there would be something to see.

Two more admissions of guilt and I was a dead man. What I did save myself, by making this confession freely, was the necessity of having it extorted under torture.

'Charges against the other prisoner?' Pertinax demanded, and the court turned its attention to Zetso.

The guard reading the indictment cleared his throat. 'I understand, Excellence, there is a counter-accusation. I am not quite clear on the terms. This man was a servant of Perennis Felix, but he disappeared most suspiciously on the evening of the banquet. It appears that there is some evidence of a conspiracy . . . a letter . . .'

'Let it be produced!'

And there was Junio, in a brand-new tunic (which I certainly had not provided), elbowing his way through the crowd to produce the waxed tablet which I had opened. I cringed, mentally. There were penalties for tampering with the mail: Felix had enjoyed imperial protection, and his seal still dangled from the damaged cord.

I glanced at Zetso, expecting to find him gloating and triumphant, but to my surprise he had turned the colour of curdled milk and was visibly sweating.

'I was acting on the orders of my master,' he shouted. 'You should be asking him. I know nothing more about it.'

'Your master is dead,' Pertinax said, grimly. 'I attended his funeral yesterday – that is what brought me to Glevum. He is hardly in a position to answer further questions. I fear that we shall have to rely upon your memory.'

The court, in deference to the governor's rank, rocked with immoderate laughter at this sally.

But Zetso was not laughing. He turned to look at Marcus, and his voice was shaking. 'Dead! So,' he said, 'you have discovered the truth. Well, I regret nothing. The man was a monster and a disgrace to Rome, and he deserved to die. I am only sorry that in the end I had no hand in it. And now my master is dead. You have killed him, and now I suppose you will kill me.'

There was a horrified silence in the court, but Zetso scarcely seemed to notice. He turned to Pertinax. 'Guilty, Mightiness. Guilty. And before you ask me, guilty again. And proud of it. But you will not take me alive.'

He lifted his joined hands and brought them down with all his force upon the neck of his guard, who crumpled and sagged like a snail in salt. Zetso seized the sword in one roped hand and whirled it two-handedly above his head. 'Stop me who dares!' he cried, and springing over the recumbent guard he rushed towards the doorway, still slashing wildly about him.

There was a general panic. Women screamed and drew back at his approach, and a burly guard stepped forward to block his path. Zetso did not pause an instant. He was strong and fit and trained in swordsmanship. One mighty kick in the groin sent the older soldier reeling, someone fell bleeding, and next moment there was almost a riot as men and women trampled each other to avoid his path.

'Stop him!' the governor commanded, but a dozen soldiers had already started after him, unsheathing their swords as they ran.

But Zetso had caught sight of someone in the crowd. He stopped, staring, at a woman in a handsome *stola* who had fled for safety to the official podium. I saw who it was, almost as he did. Julia Delicta, her hood flung back and her lovely hair in disarray, was clinging to her husband for protection.

'No!' Zetso murmured. 'You are dead!' He looked around. The soldiers were forming up about him in a half-circle, backing him against the wall. He whirled the sword again, and they stepped back a pace, almost instinctively. But it was hopeless. He could not – even fully armed – continue to keep them all at bay. With his hands tied, he was doubly doomed.

'I tell you I was acting for my master,' he screamed. 'Even if the Emperor was dead, Felix's seal should have counted for something. Until you murdered him. Great Mars! What have you done to me? I was to have bought my freedom with this service.' The blade went whistling through the air again, but this time as he finished the stroke he flipped the hilt in his hand, ready to turn the weapon on himself.

One of the soldiers caught the action. His sword flashed up and Zetso's blade went spinning to the floor. The cornered man let out a roar of anger and despair, then suddenly charged forward, so deftly that he dodged between their weapons with no more than a bloodied cheek. He made a run for it.

They cut him down before he reached the door.

There was a terrible pause in the courtroom – an embarrassed pause, as if social protocols had been broken. The dignity of the court had been disturbed, and by dying in this way Zetso had cheated both the executioners and the human vultures in the arena. Then Marcus clapped his hands, and the administrative machine lumbered into action.

Officials carried away the corpse for burial in the communal pit. Spectators strained and stared and argued for a view, until the attendant soldiers drove them back at swordpoint. Slaves appeared as if by magic with a tableful of wine and dates for the official party, while other less fortunate menials scurried with mops and buckets to clean the tiles, and take away the splendid woven carpet which was soaked with blood.

They seemed to have forgotten me. For fully half of an hour, while they cleared the courtroom and discussed the situation in hushed whispers, I was left to stand helplessly in my corner – my hands still bound and with a soldier at my side – with nothing to do but think.

I did think. About Zetso and his warrant, and his seals and his letters, and his extraordinary behaviour in the dock. He had appeared to be accusing Marcus of killing his master. For a moment I almost toyed with the idea: Marcus had been oddly uninvolved when Felix died, sitting quietly at the table looking distracted. I had noted it at the time, and put it down to embarrassment. Between Felix's drunken lustfulness, and the Celt's distaste for wine, my patron must have felt completely ill at ease. But now? And why had Zetso seemed to think the Emperor was dead?

And then, and only just in time, I saw.

Pertinax had taken a rod of office from a *lictor* and banged on the floor with it to command attention. 'The incident is over,' he announced. 'We will resume the business of the court. Where is the prisoner?'

I was pushed forward again. Zetso's demise had made no difference to the charges against me. I had defied the Emperor and I could not deny it.

'Are you guilty of the charges?' the governor asked me, for the second time.

'I am,' I said. 'But I claim mitigation.' I found myself

uttering the time-honoured formula which was the only legal grounds for amnesty. 'I acted in the interests of the Emperor, and I have information vital to his safety.'

Chapter Twenty-eight

'So, Felix was plotting against the Emperor!' Marcus rolled over languidly and held out his drinking vessel to be filled. 'Libertus, it seems that you still have the power to surprise me.'

It was the evening after the trial, and instead of dying agonisingly on a tree or being burned alive for the entertainment of the spectators, here I was lying on a comfortable couch in Marcus's villa enjoying a private banquet with the Governor. Gaius and Octavius were also guests, and in defiance of more urban custom Phyllidia and Marcus's wife were eating with us. Admittedly the dish before me was a complicated Roman confection – swan, peacock, duck, chicken, partridge and quail fitted one inside the other, stuffed with aniseed and smothered in fish pickle – instead of the simple roasted sheep which I would have preferred, but in the circumstances I was hardly quibbling. Given that I was also reclining next to the delectable Delicta, if they had served me with fish pickle neat I would have swallowed it with a smile.

I speared up another knife-load of duck. 'Yes,' I said. 'It was all in the wax tablet. "We are too late. The man is dead. Send word to Glevum." I should have seen the force of that at once. Who in Glevum would not have known that Felix was dead? And if Felix was dead, to whom was this "word" to be sent? Zetso knew no one in the city. He had been there even less time than his master, since he spent the day before

263

the feast transporting me to Corinium.'

'So "the man" was the Emperor himself?' Pertinax waited patiently while a slave carved him a single slice through duck, partridge and quail.

'I wondered why Zetso had been so discreet,' I said. 'Avoiding using his master's name, even in a sealed letter. But of course, he meant Commodus – he dared not write that name openly.'

'So that is why Zetso sent to my house?' Gaius put in, in his precise old woman's voice. 'He meant to send to Felix. He did not realise that his master was dead. But surely you must have mentioned that to Zetso? I cannot imagine how he failed to hear it.'

'He told me he had been "out of the public eye", hiding with that ex-centurion in his villa. And I did tell him, or I thought I did. He was boasting of his warrant. Commodus had named him as Felix's agent, so he claimed. I said, "And now that he is dead" and Zetso was amazed. It was genuine surprise – I felt it at the time – but he was applying my words to Commodus. He became very agitated I remember, and asked what he was being accused of. He even asked if we had found the "killers". Plural, you note.'

Junio, standing behind the diners opposite, caught my eye and gave me a most impertinent wink. He had been permitted, as a special treat, to wait on me at Marcus's table and he was enjoying himself hugely.

Pertinax looked grave. 'A man hears what he expects to hear, no doubt. If he was expecting the death of the Emperor, he would jump to such a conclusion.'

'He was astonished when I told him that the death appeared to have been caused by choking on a nut. That was when he wrote his letter and rushed off to "warn the rest". Of course, he sealed it with Felix's seal, which he believed was still legitimate. And when they caught up with him in

Letocetum he kept referring to his "seal". He meant Felix's, of course. I wondered why he never mentioned his warrant, but of course if Commodus were dead that might not have been honoured by the new incumbent.'

'We have sent to Letocetum,' Marcus said, picking at an olive with his pointed spoon. 'We have found the letters. They were in wax. Zetso tried to erase them, but Felix had written so hard that there are marks in the casing. Enough to prove the matter, we believe. We hope to round up the others who were with him.'

'Officers from the northern legions, I believe,' I said, with a sideways look at Pertinax. These were, after all, his soldiers.

The governor sighed. 'Indeed, and I believe that I could name them, too. The same men who tried to persuade me to take the purple, not so long ago. I imagine we can find them – they will have gone back to their legions. They will have learned by now that the Emperor still lives, but they have no special cause for alarm. When Zetso was arrested, the guard was told he was wanted for murdering some unknown Celt.'

'He did that all right,' I said. 'On Felix's orders. Felix took a house and invited Egobarbus to it, with promises that he should be paid what Felix owed him. Then he sent Zetso to say he was delayed, and sent a jug of wine as an apology. Only, of course, Zetso had poisoned it. He told me himself that Egobarbus was "poisoned", though I had never mentioned how he died. We found the phial further down the road. He had not even bothered to disguise it.'

'We have found the Egobarbus party now,' Marcus said, thoughtfully. 'They were discovered yesterday, just where you said they would be, on the road south to Aquae Sulis. A courier brought me word this afternoon. They have been arrested, and are being held awaiting word from me.'

'And was their story as I suggested?'

He picked up his goblet. 'Very largely so. After Zetso called at the hired house they were banished upstairs. Their master was waiting for the Roman, he said, and there was secret business. They heard no more, and when they dared to come downstairs next day they found him dead. But there had been no one there, and they thought they would be blamed. That would have meant instant death for them. They panicked and pushed the body down the well. The senior slave among them appears to have masterminded it. He claims to be a cousin of the Celt, and therefore the heir now Egobarbus is dead. He *was* a barber, by the way. I do not know how you discovered that?'

'I guessed,' I said. 'It is impossible to keep a moustache like that without constant trimming and the application of wax. Egobarbus was vain. He would not travel far without his hairdresser. The man may well be a cousin. All those red-haired men are children of the same father. I imagine he cut off the moustache and fixed it with wax to his own face?'

'He has admitted it. He knew the carriage was arriving and he saw a chance to escape. He dressed himself in Egobarbus's cloak, and assumed his place.' Marcus took a sip of his wine. 'The intention, I think, was merely to come to Glevum and disappear, but there was a confrontation with the carriage-driver. He had been promised extra fare, and the slaves had no money. They had to appeal to Felix.'

I nodded. 'I was extremely stupid there. Of course, that proved that Felix had not met their master. They would hardly have appealed for money to a man who would betray them. Felix must have been appalled – he thought the Celt was dead. But he could hardly say so, and he issued an invitation to the feast. The slaves could scarcely refuse. It must have been a dreadful evening for them – the pretended Egobarbus had poor Latin, hated wine, and his moustache was in constant danger of slipping off. I saw him dab at it a hundred times. He must have lived a night of agony.'

'And then,' Phyllidia said suddenly, 'my father choked and died. The poor slave must have almost done the same. Two deaths at his side in as many days. He would never survive a questioning – so he threw off his disguise and became a slave again?'

'Exactly.' I speared another piece of duck. Unfortunately, it was covered in fish pickle. 'And of course, being a slave, it was easy for him to slip past the guards as part of the funeral procession. He was the one who claimed to be going back to find his father, of course. Meanwhile, the others stayed in the town just long enough to sell Egobarbus's sample trinkets which he had probably hoped to tempt Felix with. Enough to finance their journey home. No doubt some citizens got an unexpected bargain – that was the finest bronze. The slaves could hardly ask the real value, they would have called attention to themselves. They must have been terrified of discovery, and I must have frightened them terribly when I found the piece of discarded moustache. No wonder they attacked me.' I swallowed the pickle with difficulty. 'I thought at first it was Zetso who had joined the funeral, but of course it wasn't. In that fringed military hood he could not have passed for a slave. The keeper of the bawdy-house reminded me of that.'

'Then how did Zetso get past the gates?' Marcus snapped.

'I imagine he just drove through them in that carriage. There was no search afoot at that time, and with that blazon no one would have challenged him. I suspect one soldier noticed him, but he'd been flirting with Zetso earlier, and may have thought to save him trouble. He said nothing.'

'So the death of Egobarbus was nothing to do with the conspiracy?' Gaius said, breaking a piece off his roll. 'Merely an unpleasant accident.'

'I have been thinking about that,' I said, 'and I am not so

sure. Felix had no qualms about exercising power – look
what he did to Marcus's herald. And Egobarbus was not a
citizen, merely a tiresome Celt demanding payment – payment, incidentally, which Felix could easily afford. But even
if he did wish to kill Egobarbus, why the secrecy? One
trumped-up charge, one claim of insolence, and Egobarbus
would have been strung up somewhere for the crows, just as
the herald was.'

I looked around. They were all watching me, spoons and
goblets partway to their mouths. Junio gave me a cheeky
grin. He knew I loved an audience.

'Zetso told me,' I said, savouring every minute, 'that
Egobarbus "barged in" to the house in Letocetum, where
there was a meeting. Think what that means. He cannot have
confronted them, since Felix did not know what he looked
like, but after that he begins to talk of money – serious
money – and Felix takes a house, an entire house mind you,
to meet Egobarbus and pay him. Not a lonely house, or a
house in a town, but a house in a small village where everyone
will see the Celt come, but – clearly – Felix never intends to
be seen. Almost as if he were creating an alibi. Yet up to then,
Felix had ignored Egobarbus – to the extent that the Celt
lost patience and "barged in" to the house.'

'So,' Julia Delicta said, 'you think he overheard something?
And was trying to blackmail Felix?'

'Or Felix thought he was,' I said. 'Which was equally fatal.'

There was a gratifying silence.

'And my slaves?' Delicta said. 'You think that was Zetso's
doing too?'

'Oh, I am sure it was. That was where Zetso went when he
left the banquet. On Felix's orders, of course. He took the
carriage to the ex-centurion's house . . . we know that now?'
I looked enquiringly at Marcus.

He nodded briefly.

'. . . and exchanged it for a horse. We know that it was nothing for Zetso to ride at night, although most men could not do it. He took some "gifts" from Felix's belongings and rode to Corinium. The gatekeeper told me that the rider was drenched: I should have realised that he must have ridden a long way in the rain. I do not know quite what he planned, but when he arrived at the house you were not there, so he looked for you in the town. It was not your slaves he wished to kill, of course, but you. He thought that he had done it too – hence his dismay at seeing you at court. You were either a ghost or a witness against him.'

'Deceived by the hair,' Delicta breathed. Across the room I saw Junio shudder.

'But why,' said Pertinax patiently, 'should Felix wish to kill Delicta?'

'I can answer that,' Phyllidia said. 'He wanted me to marry Marcus. If Julia Delicta was set upon in town, and killed by thieves, then Marcus was free to marry again. It must have been important to his plans.'

No one said anything to that. We were all thinking the same thing. An alliance with Marcus – and hence Pertinax – would be very useful to Felix if Commodus had died. A little false evidence, and the Britannic governor could easily be blamed for planning the murder – after all he had been acclaimed as Emperor once before – with considerable rewards for the accuser. Or if Pertinax rose to the purple after all, his close acquaintance might expect to be a candidate for high office. And, of course, even an Emperor is mortal, especially if there is poison in his cup.

'There is one thing that I do not understand,' Marcus said, at last. 'Who did poison Felix? It was not me, despite what Zetso said.'

'Zetso thought that you had executed Felix for conspiracy,' I said. 'And as for poisoning him, that is the strangest thing.

269

I do not believe that anyone did, at least not deliberately. I think it was a kind of accident.'

'You mean he really choked on the nut?'

'He choked,' I said. 'But that was not what killed him. We have the evidence of the dog for that. Something there *was* poisoned. Not the wine, which everyone was sharing. Not Gaius's potion, though I thought of that. Not Felix's drinking vessel, either. He was drinking from that goblet when he stood up, when he showed not the slightest sign of distress, and he was still holding it when he fell. No, what killed him was what someone gave him later, in an honest attempt to help him when he choked. And there is only one thing that it can have been. Water – the extra water Egobarbus used to dilute the wine he did not like.'

Marcus put down his goblet with a bang. 'Yes, of course, I remember. Felix himself sent for that extra water. He kept on saying that Egobarbus did not drink much wine.'

'It is obvious, when you think of it. Felix had already made one attempt to poison Egobarbus, but it had not worked, or Felix thought it hadn't. And Felix now thought that he knew why. "Egobarbus did not drink much wine." So Felix had Zetso poison the extra water. They expected no trouble – the drains were stinking, and it is easy to blame bad water for a death, as Felix knew already. Zetso hid the bottle in the rubbish-pile as he left. Only, when Felix choked, someone forced the water through his lips. He may even have known it – you saw how he tried to struggle.'

'Poor dog,' Gaius said gloomily. 'It lapped up what was spilt. I always thought it unlikely that a dog would drink spilt wine.'

'So there you are,' Marcus said. 'A judgement of the gods, as Tommonius always said. And speaking of poisons . . .' He summoned a servant to bring him a covered salver from a small table nearby. He lifted the cover and revealed a small blue phial on a cord, which he handed to Phyllidia. 'This is yours, I think?'

She took it with a shudder, and looked at Octavius. 'We shall not need this now, Octavius. The only drink that we shall share is the marriage cup at our wedding. Gaius has given his permission.' She gave the bottle back to Marcus. 'Save this,' she said, 'for some unfortunate criminal. It is the one thing which my father ever did with which I have any sympathy.'

Marcus nodded, and put away the phial. 'If Libertus had been sentenced yesterday, I was going to send it to him. I could not have allowed him to suffer.' He raised his goblet in my direction. 'Libertus is a lucid thinker, Pertinax, although he was once a slave. I do not know what I would do without him.'

Helvius Pertinax rested his elbows on the table and made a triangle with his fingers. 'My father was a freed slave,' he said. 'I have some idea what it means.' He turned to me. 'It seems that the Empire owes you a reward, Libertus. Is there some boon that you would ask of me?'

I hesitated. I could think of a hundred boons, but I knew what politeness required. 'You have commuted my sentence, Mightiness,' I said. 'I already owe you my life.'

I owed him more than that, in fact. The traitor Felix could not be uncremated, but of course there would be no pavement in his honour. As soon as he had learned of this, Pertinax had ordered a small area of pavement in the basilica to commemorate his own visit. I was already amusing myself by designing the border – small ovals representing nuts and a wavy pattern like water.

Pertinax laughed. He had a nice laugh, when he chose to use it, though he was in general a sober man. 'Then I shall have to find my own favours. I have thought of one already. Junio?'

Junio disappeared with a smirk, and reappeared a moment later with a platter, covered with a linen cloth, from which the most delectable smells were arising.

'Oatcakes, master,' Junio announced. 'One of Marcus's kitchen slaves is a Celt and she made them to her old recipe, especially for you.'

I pulled back the linen cover and could not stop myself grinning. I picked up an oatcake and sank my teeth into the delicious warmth. Better than any layered fowl, and not an ounce of fish pickle in sight.

'I had a second idea,' Pertinax said. He nodded at Junio again, and my slave vanished for a second time. This time when he reappeared I did not smile. Instead I felt an expression of foolish surprise dawn on my face.

'A toga!' I exclaimed. 'A new toga.' I glanced down at the pathetic garment I was wearing. 'How did you guess?'

'I saw you in the court,' the governor replied. At that moment he was wearing a *synthesis* himself, a combination tunic and toga that rich men often adopt for social occasions, which saves hours of folding every time the owner dresses for dinner. Nevertheless, I was delighted with my toga.

'And for my last boon,' Pertinax declared, 'I have a proposition to make to you. This Felix business has decided me. When I report this to the Emperor, as I am bound to do, I intend to ask him to release me from this posting – perhaps to send me to Africa as he was suggesting. Britannia is no longer safe for me – there are too many plots and counter-plots. I have already sent my wife and children into exile.'

'Mightiness?' I was disappointed. I was beginning to like this governor.

'However,' Pertinax went on, 'before I leave, I propose to make a tour of all the cities of the province.' He beamed at me. 'And Marcus tells me that you have a burning desire to visit Eboracum. Well, your wish is granted. When I go you may travel with me, in my entourage.'

He was looking at me intently. I glanced around the room. Marcus was sipping at his goblet and pretending not to listen. Gaius and Octavius were discussing dowries for Phyllidia, who in turn was talking wedding plans with Julia Delicta.

I thought of my own wife, and a lurching cart, and a worn, lovely face in the rain. This was so kindly meant. There was a prickling behind my eyes, and I raised my hand to brush them. A passing slave, misinterpreting my gesture, ladled fish pickle onto my oatcakes.

I turned to Pertinax, blinking back the tears. 'Thank you, Mightiness,' I said. 'That would be wonderful.'

After all, the man had saved my life. And it is never wise to argue with a powerful Roman.

The Demon Archer

Paul Doherty

The death of Lord Henry Fitzalan on the feast of St Matthew 1303 is a matter widely reported but little mourned. Infamous for his lecherous tendencies, his midnight trysts with a coven of witches and his boundless self-interest, he was a man of few friends. So when Hugh Corbett is asked to bring his murderer to justice it is not a matter of finding a suspect but of choosing between them.

Immediate suspicion falls on Lord Henry's chief verderer, Robert Verlian. His daughter had been the focus of Lord Henry's roving eye in the weeks before his death and he was not a man to take no for an answer. But the culprit could just as easily be Sir William, the dead man's younger brother. It is no secret that Sir William covets the Fitzalan estate – but would he kill to inherit it? The possibilities are endless, but the truth is more terrible than anyone could have imagined . . .

'The best of its kind since the death of Ellis Peters'
Time Out

'Supremely evocative, scrupulously researched portrait . . . vivid, intricately crafted whodunnit'
Publishers Weekly

'Wholly excellent' *Prima*

0 7472 6074 5

HEADLINE

The Merchant's Partner

Michael Jecks

Fourteenth-century Devon . . .

Midwife and healer Agatha Kyteler is regarded as a witch by superstitious villagers of Wefford, yet she has no shortage of callers, from the humblest villein to the most elegant and wealthy in the area. But when Agatha's body is found frozen and mutilated in a hedge one wintry morning, there seem to be no clues as to who could be responsible. Not until a local youth runs away and a hue and cry is raised.

Sir Baldwin Furnshill, Keeper of the King's Peace, is not convinced of the youth's guilt and soon manages to persuade a close friend, Simon Puttock, bailiff of Lydford Castle, to help him continue with the investigation. As they endeavour to find the true culprit, the darker side of the village, with its undercurrents of suspicion, jealousy and disloyalty, emerges. And what is driving the young foreigner, son of a nobleman, who has visited the normally sleepy area only to disappear down towards the moors?

0 7472 5070 7

HEADLINE

Now you can buy any of these other bestselling
Headline books from your bookshop or
direct from the publisher.

FREE P&P AND UK DELIVERY
(Overseas and Ireland £3.50 per book)

An Evil Spirit Out of the West	Paul Doherty	£6.99
The Outlaws of Ennor	Paul Doherty	£6.99
The Templar's Penance	Michael Jecks	£6.99
Seven Dials	Anne Perry	£6.99
Death of a Stranger	Anne Perry	£6.99
The Legatus Mystery	Rosemary Rowe	£6.99
The Chariots of Calyx	Rosemary Rowe	£6.99
Badger's Moon	Peter Tremayne	£5.99
The Haunted Moon	Peter Tremayne	£6.99

TO ORDER SIMPLY CALL THIS NUMBER

01235 400 414

or visit our website: www.madaboutbooks.com

Prices and availability subject to change without notice.